PLANETARY SPIN CYCLE

TALES OF A FORMER SPACE JANITOR BOOK TWO

JULIA HUNI

IPH MEDIA

First Printing: June 2021
IPH Media

In Memory of

Winnie St John
Friend
Philanthropist
Greyhound lover

ONE

ONE OF THE advantages to having access to everything on the station is I have access to things no one else can see. The new zero-gravity gardens are technically still under construction, but that doesn't stop me from checking them out.

The huge, translucent bubble hangs from an arm extended from deck twenty-four. It looks like a giant, sparkling cake pop sticking out of the side of the station. Or so I imagine. I don't plan on taking any spacewalks to check.

With the flick of my holo-ring, I bypass security on twenty-four, and stroll through the airlock. The transparent tunnel offers a dizzying view of the stars on the two-hundred-meter walk to the garden. Having lived most of my life on station Kelly-Kornienko, also known as SK2, the limitless view doesn't bother me.

The airlock to the bubble stands wide open. Installers and gardeners hurry past me in both directions, none of them giving me a second glance. Once again, my station maintenance coverall renders me invisible. I step over the lip of the internal hatch and pause, dumbstruck.

"Coming through!" someone says behind me.

I jerk my eyes away from the amazing view and step to the side. My magnetic shoes click loudly as they connect with the metallic grid beneath my feet.

"Beneath my feet," is a euphemism. Out here, there is no up or down.

The gardener pushes a pallet carrying bagged soil away from the catwalk. He and his load sail toward the center of the bubble. Around us, tiny green plants grow from clear plastic globes. Shoots twist in all directions.

The entire bubble is filled with a three-dimensional grid of concentric racks. An open tunnel through these racks leads from the hatch to a platform at the center, where the gardener works. He'll slide each bag into a hopper and attach a hose to a smaller sphere. The machine—like a reverse vacuum cleaner—will shoot dirt into the sphere. Later, he'll plant a seedling in each sphere and then suspend them from a rack. In a few months, the bubble will be a riot of green growing in every direction.

A high-pitched giggle brings me around. What the heck?

A small child, somewhere between baby and school-age—I haven't spent much time around kids, so I have no idea— crawls on hands and knees over the airlock lip. With a seemingly practiced kick, the baby launches itself into the air.

"Who do you belong to?" I disengage my magnetic shoes and push off in the baby's wake. "You shouldn't be out here."

The baby giggles as my fingers close around his chubby middle.

The little guy is slippery. I pull him toward me, and he shoots out of my hands, tumbling across the open space. A trail of giggles follows him into the garden.

"Zark!" I look for something to arrest my forward motion, so I can change directions. I've managed to forget the first rule of zero gravity— always look where you're going. When I pushed off to catch the baby, I instinctively followed him and didn't aim for a stopping point. Fortunately, most of the growing racks are already in place. I grab hold of a piece of the scaffolding as I fly by. My shoulder jerks painfully, and my forward motion turns to angular. I swing around the metal bar and activate my magnetic shoes. They touch down on the rack, and I stop.

"Where is that baby?" I mutter, scanning the open space.

From this vantage point, I appear to be lost in a maze of pipes, bars, and grids. I close my eyes and listen. Faint giggles drift over me. Still gripping the scaffolding, I release my feet and twist around.

There. The baby has evidently bounced off something and changed direction. A glistening strand of drool flies out of his mouth as he tumbles, giggling.

I align my body, estimating his direction and speed. Bending my knees, I put my feet against an upright strut and push off. I straighten out, flying through the air like a superhero — hands outstretched, toes pointed. All I need is a cape.

I latch onto another piece of the structure and swing around it. Clicking my shoes together, like a dancer in an *Ancient Tēvē* vid, I activate the magnets and touch down. From the entrance, I must look to be standing upside down and at an angle, but in here, there is no up. I let go of the pipe and snag the baby as he hurtles past.

My fingers curl into his red shirt. His momentum pulls me to full stretch. I feel as if he'll pull me loose, but my magnetic shoes hold.

"Gotcha."

The baby giggles and grabs one of my frizzy red curls with a slimy hand.

"Fair enough," I say. "My hair does look fun to play with. But don't put it in your mouth."

As I pull the baby close, he ignores my command and shoves his fist and my hair into his maw.

I get a firmer grip on him, wrapping my fingers around his chubby leg, and pull my hair away from him. He howls and makes grabby motions.

"Let's get you back to gravity and see if we can figure out who you belong to." I tuck him under one arm and turn to get my bearings.

We've zigzagged to the far side of the garden bubble. The gardeners planted this portion first, so the plants are larger. Wild greenery curls and waves over my head, tendrils drifting in the faint breeze caused by the air handlers. I turn to look toward my feet. The airlock is off to my right.

"We'll have to take the long way," I tell the baby. He ignores me and squirms out of my grip, reaching for my hair again. "Stop that, you little devil."

I pull a zip tie from my belt pouch and fasten it around his wrist. He immediately attempts to shove it into his mouth. While he's distracted, I link two more in a chain and slip the end through his. The spit on the first one makes this slippery work. Finally, I've got us cuffed together. "See if you can get out of that."

Using gentle pushes, I maneuver us through the grids of plant frames toward the center of the garden. From there, it will be a straight shot to the airlock.

"Did you handcuff that baby?" a woman asks. She's standing on a pallet of dirt, looming over my head.

I give a practiced twist, bringing us into alignment. I click my heels onto the pallet, and my shoes stick. "He keeps getting away."

"Why did you bring him in here?" she asks.

"I didn't bring him in here," I say. "I found him here."

"We grow greenery, not babies." The woman plants her hands on her hips, giving me a glare.

"I didn't say you grew him, I said I found him here." I release one shoe, so I can rotate toward the airlock. "He followed me in."

"You should get a babysitter before you go to work," the woman tells me.

"He's *not* my kid." I shake my head. There's no getting through to her. "Come on, Junior, we're out of here." I release my other shoe and push off toward the entrance.

"I should call your supervisor," the gardener calls.

"Good luck with that," I say over my shoulder. "I'm a *former* space janitor."

As I touch down on the catwalk, I hear a yell near the outer wall. "Who broke this? Ew, it's slimy!"

I look at the baby dangling from my wrist. With a flick of my hand, he flips up and over, and I catch him in my arms. "Let's get out of here."

"What are you doing with my daughter?" a woman shrieks. She's wearing a coverall with the InstaGarden logo on the chest. "I'm going to call security! Kidnapper!"

"I didn't kidnap her. I found her." I hold the baby out to her.

She grabs the child and yanks my arm as she pulls him away. "You've tied her to your wrist!"

"He—she was getting away from me. Have you ever chased a baby in zero gravity?"

"Of course I have." She taps the logo on her chest. "I work for InstaGarden. We spend most of our time in space. I've never cuffed her to my arm."

"Well this is my first time, and this little guy is slippery." I pull a utility knife from my pocket and snap open the blade.

"What are you doing?" She shrieks again. "She has a knife!"

"I'm cutting the slip ties," I say. I slide the knife under the plastic around my arm and pop it loose. The woman jerks back, yanking the baby's wrist away. My hand slips, and I cut myself.

"You drew blood." The woman looks around but we're alone in the entryway. Eyes wild, she grips the baby tightly and launches herself toward the center of the garden bubble. "Crazy person!" she cries. "That woman tried to cut my daughter! She's a kidnapper!"

Workers from around the garden converge on the woman like arrows to a target, appearing out of the greenery. Where were they when I needed help catching the little menace?

The woman flings her arms around, her movements sending her spinning. Her friends grab her legs and snap her shoes to the platform. The words tumble out of her mouth so fast I can't understand anything she says. She turns and points at me, losing her grip on the baby. "Someone get her!"

The mob turns as one, arrowing toward me. Unnoticed, the child tumbles into a piece of scaffolding. A loose connector gives way, and a curved section of pipe tips forward. The baby bounces off.

"Watch out!" I wave my hands, gesturing over their heads.

The mob ignores me.

The next piece of scaffolding leans forward. It slows, and I hold my breath. The baby, giggling and blowing spit bubbles, ricochets off another junction. The falling frame hits the tipping point and the whole grid starts to collapse in slow motion.

I shove the closed knife into my pocket and launch myself at the baby. The mob have nothing to push off, and their expressions as I sail over their heads make me snicker.

"Get back here!" the leader cries. How I'm to do that when I'm sailing through zero gravity, he doesn't explain.

"The baby!" I wave my arms again.

They turn as I sail by, eyes widening as they take in the disaster beyond me. I look up as a free-spinning connector bounces off my arm. "Ow!"

Larger pieces swing past me. I yank in my arms and legs, hoping to keep the total number of bruises to a minimum. Two more sections hit my shoulder and butt. Luckily, they're moving slowly, and mass very little. They do change my trajectory—just enough to throw me off course. "Zark!" I'm going to miss the little rug rat by a finger length!

My head swivels, looking for anything that can change my vector. There's nothing. Figures. A whole garden sphere full of disintegrating garden frame, and none of it is close enough to use.

I stretch out to full length, and another piece whacks me. How did I not see that one coming? I twist around, trying to keep the baby in view. I can hear her infectious giggling, and an answering laugh bubbles in my chest. I push it down. Where is she?

There!

She thunks into a globe of dirt. The sphere, pressed between the baby and its rack, explodes, sending dirt everywhere. But the mass is enough to change her direction, and she sails right at me.

"Yes, come to mama! Well, not mama, but me. Come to Triana!"

The baby reaches out, laughing, her sticky fingers grasping. I seize her chubby body and pull her in close. She snuggles against me.

Her tiny mass changes my direction a few degrees. We're moving deeper into the carnage. More pipes and struts tumble around us. I cradle the baby to my chest, trying to create a protective cage around her as I search for safety. She coos and babbles.

I pull up my feet and push off a series of planting globes. Each exploding dirt bomb changes my vector a tiny bit, leaving an environmental disaster in my wake.

"Hold on." I give the baby a quick squeeze, then brush a hank of my hair across her knuckles. She takes the bait, wrapping grasping fingers into the curls.

I let go and stretch out. The tips of my fingers graze the pallet anchored in the center of the garden. Two more swipes, and a finger hooks into a ring set in the corner. I focus my entire being on that finger, pulling against my momentum. I get another finger onto the ring. My body rotates around my hand and slams into the platform.

We start to bounce away, but I manage to get my leg over a cable holding the bags of soil to the platform. With a heave, I roll us against the pile of dirt and slap my magnetic shoes against the frame. I grab the baby again, holding her still until I'm sure she's static. She gives me a sloppy kiss.

As she moves, the end of the slip tie still wrapped around her wrist slices into the bag of topsoil. Pressure of the bag released, the dirt flows out into my hair and across my chest.

I jerk back and sit up, keeping a grip on the child. With my free hand, I brush the dirt off us. The torrent of dirt slows and changes. Something glitters.

I scoop my hand through the dirt, capturing a pile of soft soil and hard, sharp crystals, some of them as big as my pinky nail. I brush away the dirt. "Is that—are those diamonds?"

TWO

"Did they tar and feather you?"

I pause the vid, and Kara's face replaces the hologram of the garden. She wipes tears from her gray eyes and chuckles again.

"They tried to pin it all on me." I poke a finger at my chest. "Luckily, I know how to access the station's vid. After I proved my innocence—no, my heroism—I sent a copy to security." I didn't tell her about the diamonds and cut the vid before that point.

"Ouch. Is destruction by baby considered an act of God?"

I laugh. "They told me the baby was there for team morale."

"Like a mascot?" The vid fizzes, and Kara goes out of focus for a second. Then she's back. "That baby sounds more destructive than an untrained sair-glider."

"It wasn't her fault she was left unsupervised. Babies get into trouble."

"Why, Triana Moore, are you getting soft? I didn't think you liked kids."

"She was cute. But I'd definitely recommend against taking one into an unfinished zero gravity garden."

She runs a loving hand over her baby bulge. "This one is being raised on the dirt." Her image swirls and reforms.

"Where are you calling from? I haven't seen vid that bad since we left the Techno-Inst."

"Our new apartment is on level 7—reception down here is crap." She wrinkles her nose. "It's an old building. But it's cheap. When are you coming to visit?"

My holo-ring vibrates. "I'm not sure. I've got another call coming in—it's Hy-Mi. Can I call you back?"

"Sure. I'm working tomorrow, but I'm home in the evening."

We make kissy faces at each other, and I flick the icon. Kara dissolves, and wrinkled lips appear in her place. I jerk back in surprise and adjust the zoom.

Hy-Mi stands in his office in Mother's penthouse compartment. It's spare and functional—plain walls, understated artwork, a clean desk—a perfect reflection of the man. It's also right downstairs, but Mother insists the staff use electronic means to contact the family. She feels it's less intrusive.

"What's up, Hime?"

His eyelids drop a fraction—the only visible sign of his displeasure. He hates when I shorten his name, but it's a tough habit to break.

"Sorry, Hy-Mi. What can I do for you?"

A twitch of his lips implies a smile. "I am departing for the Ebony Coast to meet the planner. Did you intend to join me?"

"Planner?" I purse my lips. "I thought the next in-person shareholders' meeting wasn't until January?"

He doesn't respond.

"Are you frozen, Hy-Mi? What is up with the vid connections today?"

He blinks. "The planner is for your wedding."

"Oh. That." I bite my lip. It's not that I don't want to get married—I definitely do. But Mother wants to make a big production of it. After the craziness of Lili and Jie's wedding, I'd be happy to sneak away to a Contract Center and sign the papers like Kara and Erco did. But that's not the O'Neill family tradition. And if there's going to be a potentially marketable production, the Ice Dame is going to make it huge.

"Would you like to accompany me?" Hy-Mi lays his right hand on his left wrist. It's as close as he gets to the ancient tapping signal that indicates time is being wasted. Everything Hy-Mi does is understated. "I sent you an invitation yesterday."

"I—sure. Sorry. When do we leave?" My fiancé, Ty O'Neill, is already dirtside on business for the board of directors, so a trip will allow me to see him and hang with Kara. Plus whatever wedding junk Hy-Mi insists on.

"The shuttle is waiting." He bows, as if apologizing for rushing me. Or maybe it's meant to be a gentle condemnation of my lack of courtesy in keeping him waiting.

I glance at the time. "Sorry. Let me grab a few things. Are we taking the executive shuttle?"

"Of course." He bows again. "It will be a pleasure to see you, Sera." The holo snaps off.

Oh, he's cranky. Is it my failure to respond to his invitation or something else? I'll find out on the flight, I'm sure.

I throw some clothes into a duffle bag, including a couple of snazzy tops and a miniskirt in case Kara wants to go out. After sliding into a pair of leggings without holes and a stain-free shirt, I hurry out of my room.

The executive shuttle pad is located on the roof of the station. The board of directors live on Level 83, and a float tube takes passengers from the private lobby to the pad.

I step out of the tube and turn. Windows wrap around the entire room, providing a breathtaking view of the planet on one side and the stars on the other. We're on the night side of Kaku, and tiny lights illuminate the large continent like a ring of fire. The dark center is unpopulated desert, with cities and resorts clinging to the coast. As I stand there, the planet turns beneath me, rotating to the massive, sunlit ocean.

I tear my eyes away from the vast blue orb and look around. The seating area is empty. Hy-Mi stands near a transparent door in the outer wall. An access tube leads from the door to the shuttle parked atop the station.

"Good day, Sera." Hy-Mi bows. "Are you ready to embark?"

"Yes, please." I push the door open and lead the way to the shuttle. As we step into the ship's airlock, the ramp withdraws into the vehicle. "Are we late?"

"Don Putin is scheduled to arrive in a few minutes." Hy-Mi ushers me to one of the plush, wraparound seats. "I didn't think you'd want to encounter him."

Don Putin's son attempted to murder me several times, so he's right. "What's he doing on SK2? Didn't he retire?"

"Yes." Hy-Mi takes a seat and engages the restraint system. "He's here to wrap up some business matters with Don Huatang. And to advise his successor."

"His successor?" Losing a seat on the board was a huge blow to Don Putin's ego as well as a personal financial disaster. The major families control most of this part of the galaxy, and usually a family member will take the vacant seat. But Bobby was Putin's only child, so the seat has been empty for months. "Did they finally name someone?"

"Don LeBlanc will assume Don Putin's position."

"Wasn't LeBlanc involved in some scandal at the Explorer Academy?" I wave off the flight attendant offering a bottle and shove my bag into an overhead compartment.

"His son was. Don LeBlanc is above reproach."

"You could have said the same for Putin," I mutter.

Hy-Mi may be old, but his hearing has remained sharp. "Don Putin bankrolled his son's—" he pauses, searching for the right word "—mischief."

I snort. "Is that what they're calling it in polite circles?"

Hy-Mi looks away, his face set. "You're right, using a euphemism dilutes the severity of his behavior. Regardless, Don Putin was an accomplice. Don LeBlanc was unaware of his son's activities at the academy, so he is blameless."

I count to ten, so I don't snap at Hy-Mi. It's not his fault wealthy parents indulge their children to the point of criminal behavior. He certainly made sure I never crossed that line. Or any other line, for that matter.

"I don't know anything about the LeBlanc case, so I won't weigh in. If Mother thinks he'll be a good addition to the board, I'll trust her judgement."

My audio implant pings, followed by a pleasant voice. "Welcome to the SK'Corp shuttle. We are ready to depart SK2. Please enjoy the ride."

The invisible seat restraints press gently against my lap. I lean back as the shuttle lifts smoothly from the station. The tiniest jerk indicates the transition from the station's artificial gravity to the ship's system. The blank wall that hides the cockpit glows and resolves into a view of the stars as we wheel away from the station. It's as if we're sitting in the cockpit ourselves. I've flown the commercial shuttle that docks on Level 40, and this beats it by a light-year.

The ship rotates and arcs away from the station, angling across the curve of the planet. We circle the globe, sliding through the atmosphere like a hot knife through soft butter. The landscape rotates beneath us, and we cruise above the dark continent. The maneuvering engines fire, and the ship makes a few gentle corrections to hover over the private shuttle pad at the end of the peninsula named the Ebony Coast. Then we settle to the tarmac.

The restraints fade, and I stand to retrieve my bag. "You didn't bring any luggage?"

Hy-Mi shakes his head. "Mine went into the cargo."

I pat my bag. "I don't need very much."

"You do, but I took care of that," he says with an uncharacteristic grin.

A cold ball of dread forms in my stomach. "What do I need?"

He waves a hand. "I took care of it."

I follow him out of the shuttle, down an enclosed ramp, and into a private bubble. Like all of Mother's transportation, this is top of the line. The comfortable seats conform to the passenger, cradling a body weary from the long twenty-minute descent. I bite back a snort.

"Are you mad at me for some reason?" I drop my bag beside my seat. Automated straps wrap around it, securing it for the arduous journey home.

"No, Sera." Hy-Mi flicks the "go home" icon. The bubble lifts a few centimeters off the ground and slides down the lighted path leading to the public road. The thick jungle closes in around us.

"You seem put out."

He shakes his head. "I thought you'd be more interested in this event. It's your wedding, after all."

THREE

THE BUBBLE PULLS to a stop in front of a locked gate. Hy-Mi flicks his credentials and the gate slides away. The bubble moves forward. Much easier than the last time I visited Mother's Ebony Coast estate.

"Is it really my wedding?" I stare out the window, barely noticing the exotic plants as we glide past. "It seems more like Mother's wedding. A big, SK'Corp production designed to impress and amaze the stockholders. You know she's invited hundreds of people. I had to sneak my friends onto the list!"

"I have your list—no sneaking required." Hy-Mi taps his holo-ring and brings up the caretaker's dashboard. He checks the temperature, lights, and supplies. He undoubtedly reviewed all of this before we left SK2, and ordered any additional food or sundries we needed, but Hy-Mi never leaves anything to chance. Triple Check should be his middle name.

The bubble stops before the front door, its movement so smooth we don't feel a thing. It settles to the ground and the door opens. The tangy sea air rushes into the cabin, pushing out the carefully sanitized environment. I take a deep breath.

And choke. "What is that smell?"

Hy-Mi sniffs and his face wrinkles. "Fish? I will find out and have it eliminated." It wouldn't do to have SK'Corp visitors smelling fish by the sea.

From here, the house isn't unbearably extravagant. It appears to be a single story. Tall windows with adjustable opacity form the long walls on each side of the broad entry. The helocraft pad on the roof is invisible from the front drive. We hurry up the shallow front steps to the wide entrance.

The estate, formally known as Sierra Hotel, occupies an enormous chunk of the most expensive real estate on the planet Kaku. The house is nestled into the top of a high cliff overlooking Diamond Beach. Except for the tiny public access park—Sparkling Strand— at the far end of the peninsula, the black sand beach is owned by huge corporations and ultra-wealthy individuals.

Sierra Hotel sits between the Starfire Estate, owned by Maximillion Corp, and the private retreat of the Premier of Lewei. The Starfire is used primarily for high-end corporate retreats. A tall stone wall separates it from Sierra Hotel, but a big arched, wooden gate connects the two properties. The key is kept on our side of the wall, to keep the riffraff out. As a kid, I frequently used their carved stone steps to reach the beach a hundred meters below.

The Leweian property, on the other hand, is considered a sovereign nation and bristles with armed guards twenty-five-seven. I've never been inside.

Lights burn in the windows of Sierra Hotel, welcoming us home. The double-wide front door swings open, and we step into the enormous entry hall. The formal gathering hall, with thick carpets, wide windows, and rows of stuffy portraits between fluted columns stands to our left. An equally impersonal dining room—large enough to seat fifty—occupies the right. A wide staircase in the center leads to the lower levels.

Most of the house is out of sight from the front lawn. Guest areas fill the top two floors, with the family spaces nearer the bottom. The kitchen, supply storage, and apartments for the household staff are burrowed into the hillside behind the main house, accessed by a separate set of stairs— those areas don't need windows. The whole house could be operated automatically, but having human staff who are barely seen implies a level of wealth few can aspire to.

A man dressed in a long robe greets us with a jaunty salute. He's wearing a pink turban over long brown dreadlocks. As we get closer, the detail embroidered into his white-on-white robe becomes visible—strange flowers, birds, and animals.

"Is that a *whifflepuff?*" I point at what appears to be a character from a children's game.

The man smirks. "Hy-Mi said I could get whatever I wanted on my robe, so I got *Sachmos*. There's a *griblygor* here." He raises his arm and points to the wide sleeve.

Hy-Mi's lips press together. Is he showing disdain or hiding a smile? It's often hard to tell. "Sera Morgan, this is Leonidas. He's the new caretaker and responsible for the household staff."

"Nice to meet you, Leonidas." I hold out a fist to bump. "Call me Triana."

"Not when Dame Morgan is here," Hy-Mi says.

The caretaker bumps my fist. "You got it, Triana. I'm Leo. Welcome home."

I turn to look around the hall. The last time I was here, Vanti had just taken down a pair of thugs in the gathering room. "It's nice to be back."

"Your luggage has been delivered, and the staff are unpacking." Leo turns to lead us down the steps.

"My luggage?" I narrow my eyes at Hy-Mi and pat the bag tucked under my arm. "I brought my luggage."

"There are a couple of events that will require your attendance." Hy-Mi proceeds down the steps as if a coronation awaits us at the bottom.

"What events?" I hurry after him, stumbling when we reach the landing before I expect it.

"What is the source of the unappealing smell outside?" Hy-Mi asks.

Unappealing? That's a phenomenal understatement.

"You noticed that, huh?" Leo bounces down the steps like a little kid.

"How could we not?" Hy-Mi raises an eyebrow at me as we pause on the next floor—officially the fourth.

A wide parlor stretches to the floor-to-ceiling windows that overlook Ebony Beach. The lights of Paradise Alley sparkle in the distance. Dark hallways extend to either side, leading to the many guest suites.

"Something going on next door." Leo shrugs. "It started about a week ago. The air filters keep it clean in here, so I kind of forgot about it. I don't get outside much. Too much to do in here! Oh, that reminds me." He pauses on the third-floor landing. "Your delivery arrived. I put it in your suite."

The library, with real books, fills the space beneath the parlor. Halls parallel to those on the floor above lead to more guest rooms, a game room, Mother's public office, and another parlor for guests.

Hy-Mi bows and continues downward. On the second-floor landing, a single door stands in the blank wall. Leo waves his holo-ring at the access panel, and the door pops.

Lemons and jasmine waft out. The lights grow from a glow to full brightness. The thick carpet underfoot cushions our feet as we step into the family room.

The full-length windows are opaqued, reflecting dim versions of ourselves. Big, comfortable couches and chairs cluster around a fireplace. A cheerful fire burns, even though it's summertime. I look closely—this is a real fire, not a digital reproduction like Mother has in her office on SK2. The faint imperfections are the tell—nothing real is as perfect as a faux version.

I turn at the door leading to the family bedrooms. Mother and I have suites on this side, and two more are reserved for my half-siblings who rarely visit. Hy-Mi has a small apartment on the other side of the family room, near Mother's private office. There's also a pair of "family guest" rooms, a dining room, and a small kitchen near the back of this floor.

"What's the schedule?" I ask.

"We have a meeting with the nuptial architect at ten." Hy-Mi waves to dismiss Leo.

Leo bites his lip as he retreats, but the smile peeks out.

"Nuptial architect?" I repeat. "Sounds fun."

"You'll find appropriate attire in your closet, Sera. Have a pleasant evening." Hy-Mi bows and retreats.

I hike my bag up on my shoulder and wave my holo-ring at the door. It opens, and I step into a long corridor. The doors on the left lead to the family suites. The first one is Mother's. I can access that room if necessary—the entrance to our safe room is concealed beneath her bed. Last time I visited, we used the small apartment—and left it in a bit of a mess. I'm sure it's been cleaned, but I hope I don't have to hide in there again.

My room is the next one. I press my hand against the access panel and rub my fingertip against a finely scored file. The device collects a sample of my skin cells to check my DNA. This room is accessible to staff when I'm not in residence but activating the DNA check locks out everyone but me.

I step inside and survey my domain.

It has changed since I was last here as a teen. The canopied bed has been replaced by a huge, tailored model with reclining back rests and integrated lights. The other furniture has been changed to match. Modern artwork hangs in place of the fairytale masterpieces.

I stride across the room and pull open the heavy curtains. This wall of windows is set to transparent, which I prefer. The lights of Paradise Alley wink at me. "The weekend is coming," I tell them. "Kara will come, and we'll visit."

THE NEXT MORNING, the sunrise over Paradise Alley stabs into my room, waking me at five AM.

I whimper and flick my holo-ring to dim the glass. The room returns to black. I pull the covers up to my neck but can't get back to sleep. With a sigh, I sit up.

My stomach growls, reminding me station time is off from the Ebony Coast. I pull a long sweatshirt over my tank top and shorts and stumble to the family room.

I could use the AutoKich'n in my room to create any breakfast I want, but I'm curious what else has changed in the house. Kara and I visited here about a year ago, but the terrorists occupying the place kept us from exploring much. We'd spent most of our visit in the safe room.

Clattering draws me to the kitchen at the rear of the family room. The unmistakable smell of bacon increases my speed. I stop on the threshold, gaping.

FOUR

DRAPED IN A MASSIVE FLOWERED APRON, Leo stands by the stove, a checkered hat covering his dreadlocks. The pan in front of him sizzles and pops as he picks up strips of meat and places them on an absorbent towel. When it is empty, he dumps a bowl of small, white cubes into the pan and arranges them with his tongs.

"Fried potatoes?" My stomach rumbles in response to the delicious aroma.

Leo looks up, his eyes wide. "I didn't hear you come in. Good morning, Triana. Do you like *Merican Breakfast?*"

"Who doesn't?" I cross the room to dig in a cupboard for a mug. "Do you have coffee?"

"Silly question." He points to a carafe on the counter, then turns to crack some eggs into a bowl. "One egg or two?"

"Two, please." I add cream and sugar to my mug and pour the coffee in. I suck in a deep breath of morning goodness and hitch myself up onto the counter. "Do you cook *Merican Breakfast* every day?"

"Usually only if I've gone surfing." He lifts the pan and flicks his wrist, sending the potatoes into the air. Every piece lands in the pan. "But Hy-Mi said you'd like it, so I made an exception."

"He knows me." I sip my coffee. "You surf?"

"It's why I took this job," he says. "Surfing the Turquoise Ocean was the dream when I was a kid. Don't get me wrong—there are some great waves on S'Ride. But Kaku has monsters. Living here, I can get to Windlaw Beach in a few minutes on the HyperLoop. I spend most of my days off there. And usually catch a wave or two down here most mornings before work." He points toward the family room and its full-length windows overlooking Ebony Beach.

"How'd you know I'd be up so early?" I slurp down the last of my coffee and fix another cup without getting off the counter.

"Your mother's been down for a few visits since I started here. The time change always gets her, too." He tosses the potatoes onto a plate, flips the bacon beside them, and slides the whole thing into the warmer. Then he pours the eggs into the pan. "I'm kind of surprised the station isn't set to the same time zone we are. Surely that's one of the perks of being chair?"

I slide off the counter and dig through the drawers until I find utensils. I set two places at the tall counter and grab a glass. "She travels enough that matching only one of her homes to SK2 time is pointless. Now, if she could match them all…Juice?"

"I'll take sweezenberry."

"Excellent choice, ser." In response to my commands, the AutoKich'n fills the one glass with red and the other with orange. "You'll find this vintage exhibits a tart sweezenberry bouquet."

"With fruity sweezenberry overtones?" Leo slides the eggs onto two plates and deposits them on the counter. He grabs the bacon and potatoes, whips off his apron, and sits beside me. "Looks like an excellent year. Oh! The bagels." He's off his stool, extracting two toasted bagels and a small pot of cream cheese from the AutoKich'n before I can respond.

We eat in silence, enjoying the good food. I soak up the last of the egg yolk on the final piece of my bagel and sit back. "That was outstanding. Where'd you learn to cook like that?"

"I attended the Child-Hooper Institute of Culinary Programming."

"Does Dav know that?" I sip my coffee. Dav is my mother's pastry chef. He makes every pastry by hand and has a deep distrust of those who program AutoKich'ns.

"He knows." Leo slides off his seat and picks up the plates. "We have a relationship based on mutual distrust."

I chuckle. "He's always threatened to cut me off from his chocolate chip cookies if he ever discovers them in an AutoKich'n map."

"I would never sell his recipes—or his food." Leo puts his hand over his heart. "Stealing another chef's creative property goes against the Child-Hooper oath."

"There's a culinary school oath?"

"No. We steal other people's food all the time. But I wouldn't do it to a coworker. And I would never sell it to one of the big food mappers. That's my personal moral code."

"But all bets are off if you quit?" I hand him my mug.

His lips press together. "That would be living the letter of the law. No. I won't steal Dav's food."

"I believe you. I don't know if Dav will." I hop off my stool. "Thanks for breakfast. I have a long day ahead of me."

He looks up from loading the dirty dishes into the AutoKich'n. "You don't sound like the happy bride."

"I'm a very happy bride," I say. "I'm not thrilled about the Ice Dame turning my wedding into a marketing opportunity. Everything she does is about the brand."

"Maybe it won't be so bad."

"Have you ever met my mother?"

Hy–Mi and I meet the wedding planner in the front hall. A tall, thin woman surveys the impressive entry, her eyes half closed as if she is too bored to look at it. Spiky, fluorescent green hair runs in a strip from her brow to her nape, with long waves of orange springing from the sides. A pair of torn green pants hang from her bony hips, and a short orange shirt with wide neckline drips off one shoulder. The shirt bears an abstract logo on the left breast, and a large Lether bag hangs from her elbow. My holo-ring vibrates, and her contact information pops up: Lilia, Nuptial Architect.

"We'll redo it in shades of mauve and puce." She waves a languid hand at the walls. "Then we'll drape the windows with olive gauze."

Hy–Mi clears his throat. "That won't be necessary. Your area of responsibility is restricted to the ceremony venue. That will be—" he turns and steps into the gathering room.

"It will be on the back lawn," I say. "This way."

Hy-Mi steps between me and the stairs. "Dame Morgan wishes the event to take place in the gathering room."

"Dame Morgan isn't the bride." I flash a blinding smile at the little man and push past him. At the first landing, I turn. The others regard me from the top of the steps. "Come on."

Hy-Mi shakes his head, his face impassive. Lilia stares through me, her foot tapping on the marble floor.

I cross my arms. "Seriously?"

"I only take instruction from my employer." Lilia turns and strides into the gathering room. Hy–Mi follows her.

I stomp up the steps, slapping my feet against the marble stairs as loudly as possible. "I should elope."

Lilia drones on about hideous colors and bizarre decor. I let the words wash over me and pretend it's someone else's wedding. I've attended Mother's events my whole life, and it's easier to just let it happen.

When she starts talking about processions, I pull away from the wall I've been slouching against and move closer.

"The bride will enter from there." Lilia waves a languid hand toward the door at the back of the room.

"That's the service hall," I say. "I don't think the Ice Dame wants her daughter entering her wedding from the bot ducts."

Lilia jerks as if she's forgotten I existed. She surveys me from the top of my barely tamed red curls down my rumpled sweatshirt and faded leggings to my bare feet. "No one will know that."

"You think total strangers are attending this shindig? Lots of these people have seen the servers bring canapes from that door. None of them have been through it, so they know it leads to the kitchens." I shrug. "I don't care, but Mother won't like it."

She stares down her nose at me—which is a feat, considering she's half a head shorter. "Where do you suggest you enter from?" Her tone makes it clear she's humoring me by asking.

"I suggest you open this." I wave at the wall separating the formal gathering space from the spacious parlor behind. "The view from there is killer. Then I can come up the main stairs and in through the entry hall."

She turns to Hy-Mi. "This wall opens?"

Hy-Mi bows and flicks his holo-ring. The panels bearing the family portraits contract and turn, leaving three-meter gaps between the fluted columns. The wall panels fold around the columns, displaying the portraits on each side.

"It's a shame those beautiful columns are hidden," Lilia says, as if she sees transforming rooms every day. Maybe she does.

"We can remove the panels, but Dame Morgan would prefer to keep the portraits on display."

"This is much better." The angular woman strides into the next room, her head swiveling left and right. "I was concerned by the paltry size of that gathering hall."

The paltry room she's just maligned can comfortably hold over a hundred people. I glare at Hy-Mi. "How many people have been invited?"

Hy-Mi ignores me.

I step closer and tap his shoulder. "Hy-Mi, how many people has Mother invited to *my* wedding?"

Leo chooses that moment to bound into the room. "What did I miss?" His hair is damp, and he's wearing the white robe from yesterday.

I squint as he comes closer. Actually, it's a different robe—the white embroidery is hearts and flowers on this one.

"We were just discussing how many guests would be attending my wedding." I fold my arms over my chest and give Hy-Mi the stink-eye.

Hy-Mi clears his throat. "The current list stands at three hundred and forty."

"Three hundred?"

"And forty," Hy-Mi confirms. "Plus the groom's family and friends."

My eye starts to twitch. "That doesn't count O'Neill's side?"

"And any personal friends you've included, of course."

I close my eyes and take a deep breath. It's not Hy-Mi's fault—I can't take my anger out on him. "Send it to me."

Hy-Mi goes even more still than usual.

I thrust out my hand and make a gimme gesture. "Send me the list. Now."

Hy-Mi flicks his holo-ring and swipes a file to me.

My ring vibrates. I pop open the list and scroll through the names. The board of directors and their families. Major stock-holders and their plus-ones. The next block of names I don't recognize. I click on the first one and bring up the affiliations. "Mother's sorority? She hasn't spoken to any of these women in my lifetime!"

"Apparently, they had a pact," Hy-Mi says.

My eye starts to twitch. "A pact? That they'd invite each other if they ever had a kid get married?"

"I'm not conversant with the details, but Dame Morgan mentioned a pact."

I close the pop-up and scroll farther. "Who are all these people on list two b?"

"Those are your siblings' guests."

I rub my forehead. "My siblings are bringing guests? I wasn't sure they'd even bother coming. Why are their guests on the main list, but mine aren't?"

Lilia smiles a brilliant white smile. "This will be the event of the century. Anyone who can possibly wrangle an invitation will be here."

"Yay. Who is Ser Smith?"

Hy-Mi looks away.

I advance on him, pulling the holo bigger so the name stretches the length of my arm. "Hy-Mi, who is Ser Smith?"

"He's an important guest who prefers to keep his name anonymous." A sheen of sweat appears on Hy-Mi's upper lip. His unflappable exterior is appearing undeniably flapped.

"This is a private list of guests to my wedding." I can hear my mother's hard tones in my voice. "Who is Ser Smith?"

Hy-Mi looks at Leo and Lilia, then his eyes dart to the door. Lilia sniffs and lifts her chin.

Smith is obviously a pseudonym. It's the second most common name in the galaxy after Zhang. I glare at Hy-Mi. "I'll find out eventually."

"Ser Smith's privacy and security needs are extraordinarily tight. No one can know he's attending until he's actually here. And then, if word gets out, he'll be at risk. I can't tell you who he is without jeopardizing his agreement to come."

"Since I don't have a clue who he is, I don't give a crap if he can't come." I fling the list away into the ether. "The only people I care about are on my and Ty's list, which I provided to you weeks ago."

"They're here." Hy-Mi scrolls through his copy of the file, down, down, down. "Here they are. List twenty-five c."

I thrust a hand through his holo and scroll back up. "What's this red line?"

"That's the emergency cut off," Lilia says, as if she can't stop herself from jumping back in. "People we can include if some of the people above the line decline."

"My friends and O'Neill's entire family are on the extras list?" I stare at them in outrage.

Hy-Mi opens his mouth, but I fling up a hand. "No, don't even try. I'm done." I swing around on my heel and stalk from the room.

FIVE

"I CAN'T BELIEVE Hy-Mi would do that to you!" Kara leans forward to pour more *Champaignia* into my orange juice.

"It wasn't him; it was the Ice Dame." I spit the words between gritted teeth.

"But he could have stood up for you." Kara refills her own glass.

"Hey, you can't drink that." I pull the bottle from her hand. "You're preggo."

She waves my concern away. "It's non-alcoholic."

"What? Then why am *I* drinking this?" I peer at the bottle label. Sure enough, it says it's a sparkling non-alcoholic wine in the style of the *Champaignia* region of Frince. "Where the heck is Frince, anyway?" Absently, I pour the rest of the bottle into my glass.

Kara shrugs. "I think it's a manufacturing city on the west coast. They aren't known for their grapes."

We're sitting in the lounge of Kara's two-bedroom apartment. She's warmed up the brown industrial flooring with a few throw rugs and covered the walls with cheap prints and family pictures.

A small kitchen and eating space take up one corner of the open floor plan, and the doors to two bedrooms and the bathroom are hidden behind curtains she's hung across non-existent windows at the back of the room.

Kara has opened a new salon here in Pacifica City, and every credit she can spare goes into the business. Erco still works for the local SK'Corp office, but I've seen the numbers—low-level security agents don't earn much.

I set down the bottle and sip my virgin mimosa. "Ugh! This is terrible. Next time, I'm buying the wine."

Kara sips hers. "It reminds me of the Shuttle Port."

"That is a terrible bar, so I'm not surprised. I don't think I ever tried a mimosa there."

"I didn't either." Kara hands me a plate. "But this stuff smells like the air freshener in their bathrooms."

I pick up a crepe and take a bite. "These are good," I mumble through my food.

She grins and puts three on her plate. "Thanks to you. I'm not sure I'd survive this place without the food maps you put on my AutoKich'n. You've spoiled me for real life."

Once Kara and I had cleared the air about my past, I'd upgraded our appliances. Even a cheap AutoKich'n could create masterpieces with the right—that is, expensive—food maps. "Which reminds me. Leo, the new caretaker at Sierra Hotel, is a Child-Hooper graduate. I'll bet he gets a discount on new food maps."

"Now that you're the Ice Dame's intern, you don't really need bargains. Or are you thinking about running again? This wedding thing is really over the top."

I shake my head. "I'm done running—no matter how attractive it might be. When I said yes to Ty, I promised myself I wouldn't interfere with his career. If I take off, my mother *will* fire him. Besides, I'd want him to come with me...see, it's all so much more complicated than it was when we were students."

She pats my arm with one hand and shoves another crepe into her mouth with the other. "That's what happens when you grow up."

"What am I going to do about this stupid wedding?"

"You could elope."

"That's what Leo said. But I can't—"

"She wouldn't fire Ty if you eloped, would she?"

"I don't know. But as the official heir to the Morgan family, I have to do what's right for the corporation and the brand, not just myself. If only weddings weren't such an unusual occurrence—but it's so unique, everyone wants to come. Even Ser Smith."

"I thought it was Zhang." She polishes off the last of the crepes and starts on the scones.

"Zhang, Smith, whatever. Are you going to eat *all* of those?"

She laughs and hands me the plate. "Sorry, the little one is hungry today." With a pat to her bulge, she picks up a bowl of strawberry mousse. "What have you heard about the diamonds?"

I almost spit out a mouthful of mimosa. I choke and cough. Kara pounds my back and hands me a napkin.

"What diamonds?" I pat my lips, hiding behind the napkin.

"The diamonds you didn't tell me about in the dirt bags." Kara points her spoon at me. "Why didn't you tell me?"

I shrug. "Security wanted it locked down. Remember what we were just talking about—the good of the company? How did you hear about it? Please tell me it was Erco."

She lifts her nose. "Erco doesn't tell me secrets about work." She frowns a little and shovels in another scoop of mousse. "He doesn't tell me anything about work."

"It's safer that way—hard to spill a secret if you don't talk about anything. But where'd you hear it?"

"On *CelebVid*. Didn't you know they'd gotten the recording?" She sets down the bowl and taps her holo-ring. With a swipe, a vid flips from her ring to hover over the table. It's the same security vid I showed her the night it happened.

"How'd they get that?" I stare at the bright pink and orange logo in the bottom of the holo, then turn to her. "This is the vid I showed you."

"I know." She giggles as the baby spurts out of my hands. "I've watched it sixteen times. It's hilarious."

"But I sent that vid to you—no one else has it."

"It's a security vid. Someone on the station probably leaked it." She pauses the recording on a frame of me with my mouth wide open and eyes rolled back in my head.

"This vid is spliced together from multiple cams. I made it, sent it to you, then deleted it. You're the only one who got it."

"Maybe someone else used the feeds and create a similar vid."

"No, Kara, this is my work." I stretch the vid and show her the markers below the logo. "I set my system to automatically add a tag to every vid I create. How did they get this?"

"I didn't give it to them!" Kara cries.

"Did you send it to anyone else?" I didn't tell her it was secret, so she might have.

"Just my mom. She loves your adventures. But she wouldn't send it to *CelebVid*—those people are vultures, and she likes you."

"I know, but I need to ask her." I flick my call program and put a message through to Kara's mom, Larin.

"Triana! So good to see you!" Larin looks just like Kara—except for the hair, eye, and skin color, which Kara changes on a weekly basis. But they have the same heart-shaped face, the same straight nose, the same bright smile. "Or should I call you Annabelle, now?"

"No. Triana is good. Did you happen to send that vid of me to anyone?"

Larin's eyebrows draw down, then smooth. "The exploding garden one? No. That was hilarious, but I would never damage your brand."

"Damage her brand?" Kara hoots with laughter. "Where'd you learn that?"

"I've been taking some marketing classes," Larin replies. "Annabelle Morgan is a huge brand. She needs to protect it."

"I know that. I'm just surprised you know it." Kara wrinkles her nose. "If you didn't send it to *CelebVid*, I wonder who did?"

"*CelebVid*? I would never!"

Kara cuts her off. "I know, I know! We're just trying to figure out how they got it."

Larin shrugs. "Triana sent it to you, you sent it to me. That's two transfers that could be intercepted. Maybe they're trapping your comms."

Trapping my comms? Who is this woman? "You've been taking more than just a few marketing classes. But my comms are heavily secured."

"I'm working on a new degree." Her face falls. "My comms aren't secure. They probably stole it between me and Kara. They must know we know you."

"Probably. I'll send you some loops to secure your connection." I turn to Kara. "That doesn't explain how they know about stones. I didn't mention those in the vid."

"Stones?" Larin asks, then waves her hands. "Nope, don't want to know. If I don't know, I can't compromise you."

"If you watch the *CelebVid*, you'll know, but I can neither confirm nor deny the truth of their statements."

Larin's eyes sparkle, and she signs off.

"Tell me about the diamonds!" Kara grabs another bowl of mousse and digs in.

SIX

I LEAVE Kara snoozing on the couch and meet my security detail outside her apartment. I can't travel anywhere on Kaku without at least two agents shadowing me. This is one of the many reasons I ran away seven years ago.

"Can't you just put a drone on me?" I ask the uniformed woman as I exit the apartment. Her nametag says Yellin. "You're so visible."

"That's part of the deterrent." She mutters something under her breath—probably to a team-mate waiting above.

Kara's apartment is on the seventh level of an older apartment stack in Pacifica City. Unlike Réalta, the charming neighborhood she grew up in, this part of town is full of below-ground dwellings. They all have a central atrium with the apartments around the sides. The first few floors from the top aren't bad, but anything below level three gets no real sunlight, and unless the building owner has sprung for expensive net connections, communications are spotty.

"Roger." Yellin turns to me. "We're scheduled to swap out the team. They can meet us at your next destination. If you'd tell us where that is." She manages to hide a sigh and still make it obvious.

I smirk and head for the float tube. "SK'Corp headquarters. That'll make your swap easy."

We exit the float tube on the ground floor and another agent—Thompson—closes in behind me. Three more appear from outside, forming a cordon between the door and the street. A bubble with the SK'Corp logo waits by the sidewalk.

"Were you expecting the press?" I climb into the bubble. My original two agents pile in behind me, but the other three move to a second logo-emblazoned bubble.

"Yes. Have you seen the *CelebVid*?"

I wave that away. "They're always posting crap about people. No one pays any attention. I mean, look around. No one."

On the sidewalk, a young woman points as we slide by, yanking on her friend's arm.

"Okay, almost no one. And they just happened on us—they weren't stalking me."

"We've received credible threats, so we've ramped up security. You're not to travel on foot at all." The bubble merges into a stream of traffic, then turns right.

We zigzag through the city, then slide down a ramp and into a parking garage. The bubble stops by an unmarked blue door. The agents jump out of the bubble behind us and form up again. When they're in place, the steps fold down. One of my agents precedes me out of the bubble, and the other follows.

As we go through the blue door, the bubble floats away down the maintenance tunnel. The plush lobby has thick carpeting, fresh flowers, and a golden mirrored door. It opens, and the agent closest does a quick sweep inside the old-fashioned elevator.

It's not really old-fashioned—it's just made to look that way. The car is armored and has an independent air system in case of biological attack. I've heard it can also blast out of the shaft like a rocket in case of emergency, but since that destroys a large portion of the building, use of that feature is generally frowned upon.

"Has anyone ever launched this thing?" I ask as the door closes. No one answers, but one of the agents shifts uncomfortably. It's a huge tell in a team this highly trained. I make a note to dig into the story later.

I place my hand against the access panel, and the car drops, fast enough to send my stomach into my throat. I flex my knees as we stop almost as quickly, bouncing a little at the bottom. The doors slide open, and one of the agents pushes past me to check for threats. I roll my eyes as obviously as I can and follow him out.

We're in a large, white foyer. A tall desk stands near a metal gate. The uniformed man behind the desk registers me, using my holo-ring to confirm my identity. The gate opens. "You can go in, Sera Morgan. Do you know where you're going?"

He hands badges to the agents around me. Theirs are white with their names and a holo-image of the person. Yellin's looks well-used, as if she's worked here a long time.

"Don't I need an ID thingy?" Last time I came here, they gave me a green badge.

"No, ma'am." He shuffles through his holo-screens and slides one up where I can see it. It has a picture of me and the words "Morgan Heir" flashing under it. "Your holo-ring is sufficient identification. But if you tell me who you're here to see, I can get you a guide slip."

"Is that safe?" I ask Yellin. When she doesn't answer, I tell the guard, "I'm here to see Agent O'Neill."

He flicks his holo, and my picture disappears, to be replaced by a roster. He scrolls down to O. "Aretha O'Neill or Tiberius O'Neill?"

"Aretha O'Neill?" What's he talking about? Is Ty's sister an agent? "Is she new?"

"No, according to this—"

Yellin cuts him off. "I'll take her to Agent O'Neill. This way, Sera."

I follow Yellin through the gate. It pings loudly, but the agent watching the readout waves me through. I wonder what set it off—probably the tranq ring I've been wearing since I landed. I hate all of this guarding stuff, but I'm not stupid enough to go into Kara's neighborhood unprotected.

"Who is Aretha O'Neill?" I hurry to catch up to Yellin.

She ignores me, her feet clattering loudly in the wide corridor. As we continue, the hallways get more crowded—agents doing paperwork and remote surveillance, I suppose. We twist and turn through the enormous underground facility, then stop at a door labeled "Board Security."

"Agent O'Neill is inside."

"Which Agent O'Neill?" I grab Yellin's arm.

"Your fiancé." Yellin pulls away. "That kid at the desk is an idiot."

"But there's another O'Neill here."

Yellin steps back, her hands up. "I don't know anything about that. You'll have to ask him." She points to the door then hurries away.

"I will."

People walking by look away as they pass, as if they're afraid to make eye contact with me. When a woman meets my eyes, her face blanches, and she stops to bow. My mother's reputation precedes me, I see. I nod at her and swing around to confront the door.

A wave of my holo-ring opens it, and I step inside a plush outer office. Thick carpet covers the floor and comfortable wing chairs stand on either side of a projection table. A woman behind a desk leaps to her feet and hurries to me.

"Sera Morgan, so nice to see you. May I show you to Ser O'Neill?" She doesn't wait for a reply but turns and hurries through another door, standing by the jamb to hold it open for me.

The short hallway is a continuation of the fancy outer office, with the simulated wood paneling and lemon-scented air. A door to the left leads to large room with a heavy wood table surrounded by a dozen well-upholstered chairs. The logo for a high-end projection system hovers over the table, spinning lazily.

The woman leads me past the conference area to a corner screened by live plants. A small couch and two chairs sit on a colorful rug. Behind it, a top-of-the-line AutoKich'n peeks out from a half-closed cupboard. "Have a seat. He'll be right in. Can I get you a beverage or something to eat?"

"No, I'm good, thanks." I sit on the couch.

While I wait, I wonder about Aretha. Could there be another Aretha O'Neill? It's not a common name. Why would Aretha—a lawyer on Grissom—be employed by SK'Corp?

Before I can concoct any outrageous back stories, O'Neill arrives. I jump up to greet him.

As always, he takes my breath away. Something about his beautiful chocolate brown eyes, his curling dark hair, and those broad shoulders gives me a thrill every time I see him. How lucky am I to be engaged to this beautiful man?

He pulls me into his arms. I lean close, breathing in his understated cologne. Our lips touch in a spine-tingling kiss. My heart goes into overdrive, and fireworks flash behind my closed eyelids. I am lost—and found.

Ages later, he pulls back and smiles. "I've missed you." He nudges me to the couch, and we sit.

"I've missed you, too." It's only been two days since we were together, but what can I say? He's so shiny. I scooch closer for another kiss.

Eventually, he pulls back again. "I shouldn't take advantage of dating the boss. I'm supposed to be working. Did you come all this way just to see me, or was there something?"

My foggy brain snaps back to the present. "There are a couple of some-things. But first, who is Agent Aretha O'Neill?"

His brow furrows. "I don't know what you're talking about."

I tell him about the kid at the entry desk. "And I saw the roster myself, so don't try to tell me he was mistaken."

He shakes his head. "I wouldn't. But I truly don't know." He pulls up the organization's roster and scrolls down. "There she is."

I cross my arms. "You're surprised?"

"Not that you're right. But that this person exists…" He flicks the name, and the identification pops up. A woman with dark hair and his smile stares back at us. "That's my sister."

"You didn't know she joined the company? How long has she been here?"

He flicks the picture and pulls up the record. "It's locked."

"I thought you had access to everything."

"So did I." He flips the file to me. "You should be able to open it."

I catch the file and flick the lock icon. It flashes red once and remains locked. I flick it again. "What the frappe?"

O'Neill chuckles. "New curse word?"

"I got tired of fork and I like frozen coffee." I flick the file again, but nothing happens.

He puts his hand over mine. "I'll find out what's going on. It's probably not my Aretha—just a mistake. But if it's a super-sensitive need-to-know kind of thing, we'd both be locked out of the files."

"If it's super sensitive, why would they list her on the company roster?"

"So she qualifies for health care?" He runs a hand through his hair, which falls magically into place. "Not to change the subject, but do you know how *CelebVid* found out about the diamonds?"

"That's the other reason I came to see you." I jump up and stride across the seating area to the AutoKich'n and back. "That vid they're pimping—

that's mine. I cut it together and sent it to Kara. She sent it to her mother. No one else."

"Are you sure her mother didn't send it on?"

"She says she didn't, and I trust her." I pace across the room again. "Besides, the vid cuts out before the diamonds. I know not to spill that kind of stuff, even to Kara. *CelebVid* doesn't show the diamonds—they just talk about them."

He stands and catches my shoulders on my next pass. "I'll have someone check their comm IDs. Personal communications are supposed to be private on Kaku."

He slides his arm around my shoulders, turning me toward the door. "But since they didn't know about the diamonds, I'm guessing there's a data breach on SK2. That's the only way they'd get both the vid and the info about the rocks. The team is already looking into that."

I stop before we reach the end of the conference table, turning to face him. "Can we elope?"

"Run away to get married?" He laughs, his eyes softening. "Is Hy-Mi getting crazy?"

"Not him—it's the Ice Dame." I tell him about the nuptial architect and the guest list. "Your family and our friends aren't even on the primary list! Let's go to Grissom and do it there."

He smiles, and my heart stops. Then he gives me a little shake. "I will do whatever you want, as long as we get married. My family would love to have it at home, like Lili's wedding. And with Bobby gone, there's no reason to worry about poisoned cakes."

I smile at his joke, then let out a sigh. "If we do that, Mother might just poison the cake herself. This whole thing is a big marketing extravaganza to her." I poke his chest. "But I won't let them make your family second class guests. That list is getting a makeover. Hey, that reminds me…"

"What?"

"Do you know a Ser Zhang? No, wait, it was Smith."

"What are you talking about? There are billions of Zhangs in the galaxy. And billions of Smith."

"This Ser Smith has security so tight even *I* can't know his name. But you should be able to find out. Since my security is your job."

He smiles and pulls me close. "I'll see what I can do."

SEVEN

I RETURN to Sierra Hotel with Agents al-Karendi and Limberghetti. They demand identification from Leo when he answers the door, then turn me over to him as if I am a package ordered from Nile Online Everystore.

I turn my back on the agents and pace past Leo. "At least the fish smell is gone."

"I took care of it." Leo shuts the door and turns to survey me. "The caterers just left. You missed the tasting."

"I thought that was on the schedule for tomorrow?" I stomp my foot. It's childish, but I can't help it. Everything about this wedding is going wrong. "I was really looking forward to the cake."

"You didn't miss the cake—that is tomorrow. Just the dinner. And appetizers. And the—"

I fling up a hand. "Stop." I can pull an Ice Dame and demand they bring the caterers back for a second round. But after this morning, I'm not sure anyone would take me seriously. I clearly haven't mastered her death glare yet. "I'm going to my room. Or maybe I'll go for a swim."

"Excellent idea. Do you surf? You could come with me tomorrow morning." Leo drifts down the wide steps, and I follow him.

"I've never done it. Could you teach me?" I think about al-Karendi and Limberghetti. They would have a fit if they knew I was heading to the beach with only Leo. A grin tickles the corners of my mouth. "What time?"

"The best waves are early. I leave at five."

"Five?" I gulp. "Fine. I'll meet you in the kitchen at five."

He waves open the door on the second floor landing. "I'll have a protein shake waiting for you."

"Ooh. Yum." I smirk at Leo and head for my room. "See you at dinner."

I change into a swimming suit and head for the pool. A wide teakalike deck surrounds three sides of the huge pool. The grassy yard stretches away on either side. The pool has a transparent aluminum wall on the side facing the cliff, and from the deck it appears to pour over the hillside and into the ocean below.

I dive into the water and swim to the bottom. Holding my breath, I let the water silence my simmering anger.

Sunlight sparkles through the transparent wall. The wavey green grass and cliff edge are visible as a watery impressionistic painting. Someone walks past, visible as a dark ghost.

I burst out of the water and grab the edge of the pool. A boy stands on the grass, staring up at me. He's got strawberry blond hair, brown eyes, and a thin build. He doesn't look old enough to be a threat, so I relax.

"Who are you?" I ask.

"Who are you?" he says at the same time. His low voice cracks on the word you, jumping an octave higher. He flushes.

"I'm Triana, and this is my house. How did you get in here?"

"I came over the wall." He gestures toward the west. "I'm Cas."

"You came over the wall? From the Lewei house?" I look across the wide lawn. The wall is out of view, behind several hundred meters of carefully manicured trees and a wide grassy perimeter. "That wall has security features baked into it. How did you get over?"

"You mean the lasers?" He shrugs. "I turned them off."

"You shouldn't be able to get into our net and turn off our security." I shake water off my fingers and flick my ring to pull up the household system. "And there aren't actual lasers."

"Whatever." He points at the invisible property again. "They didn't want me to leave, but I was getting tired of being alone."

"They're keeping children locked in the estate?"

Cas grins and shakes his head. "Not children, just me. I'm twelve."

"Ah, an adult, then. Who are you that you're important enough to be locked in the Lewei premier's personal estate?"

"His son." Cas crosses his arms and stares at me in challenge.

"You're the son of the premier of Lewei?" I repeat stupidly. "And they don't know you're here?"

"Nope. Can I swim with you? I wore my suit." He sticks his thumbs into the waistband of his stretchy pants.

I gaze toward the other house again. From here, the top of the roof is visible behind the screen of trees. "If they have a cam up there, they're going to see you. But if you don't care, I don't."

"The cam is currently turned the other direction." In a flash, his clothes are in a pile on the deck, and he cannonballs into the pool. Water sloshes over me, then he breaks the surface.

"Don't you have a pool over there?"

"Sure, but there's no one to play with. Come on, I'll race you to the other end."

EIGHT

WE PLAY in the water for an hour or so. Noting how pale Cas's skin is, I adjust the solar screen to full coverage. No tan for me today. He beats me in every race, and finally I climb out to lie on a chaise lounge on the deck.

"How about some water *poli*?" He surges across the deck and grabs a ball from the teakalike storage along the wall.

"Let's save that for tomorrow. I'm exhausted."

"Getting old does that." He nods wisely.

"I'm not old, you little turkey! I'm only twenty-six."

"That's not too old. So, why are you so tired, then?"

"I had a busy day." I tell him about the wedding planner, spinning the story into a crazy adventure. He laughs, but it sounds rusty, as if he doesn't get to do that often. "What about you? What have you been doing? Is your father with you?"

His eyes narrow and his spine straightens.

I hold up both hands. "Sorry—none of my business. I was just wondering if you're alone over there."

"The staff are there, of course."

"No other kids?"

He glares. "I'm not a kid."

"Right, I forgot. In our culture, twelve is not an adult." I half bow from my seated position. "I'm sorry if I offended you."

He nods regally. "I will forgive you this time."

"Wow. So magnanimous. If you want to play in my pool, you'd darn well better forgive me."

His head cocks to one side. "I just said I did. Do you not believe me?"

"I think we're experiencing some cultural confusion. Are there any young men of your age to hang out with?"

His head shakes, water drops spraying from his sopping curls.

"Ew! I just got dry!" I yank a towel over me. My holo-ring buzzes. "I gotta get ready for dinner. Hy-Mi'd have kittens if I showed up like this."

"If he has kittens, I would like one," Cas says.

I stand. "It's just an expression. It means he'd be mad. And that I gotta go inside."

He puts a hand to his heart and bows. "Thank you for your hospitality. I hope we can do this again. Maybe tomorrow?"

"I've got a crazy schedule, so I'm not sure when I'll have time to swim. But next time I'm out here, you're welcome to join me. Can I send you a message?"

He flicks a contact code to my holo-ring.

"Got it. Don't come over here if I'm not home. If they catch you, there'll be heck to pay."

"They won't catch me." His eyes twinkle when I glare at him. "But I will respect your hospitality and wait for your invitation."

"Thanks." I can't tell if he hears the irony in my voice. "It was a pleasure to meet you, Cas."

"Likewise, Triana." He scoops up his clothing and sprints across the lawn. In moments, he's disappeared into the trees.

I flick open our surveillance system but don't catch him climbing over the wall. All of our cams and triggers are active. After dinner, I need to do some sleuthing and figure out how he got in without tripping any alerts.

THE SECOND-FLOOR LANDING DOOR OPENS. "Honey, I'm home!" O'Neill's voice rings through the room.

I jump up from the couch and fling myself at him. He catches me and wraps me in his magic embrace. Blood sings in my ears and my skin tingles. He kisses me, and the rest of the world ceases to exist.

A soft throat clearing breaks us apart. Hy-Mi stands in an opening in the full-length windows. Behind him, a table set with dishes sits in the early evening sun. "Welcome to Sierra Hotel, Ser O'Neill. Will you join us for dinner?"

"I already told Leo." I pull O'Neill's hand, leading him toward the balcony.

"Coming through!" Leo pushes a float tray loaded with covered dishes. O'Neill and I step back to give him access to the table. He lays out the food, removing the covers with a flourish. After setting drinks by each place, he removes his apron and tosses it across the float. A flick of his wrist sends it back to the kitchen. He pulls out a chair next to Hy-Mi and sits. "Let's eat!

"Ty, this is Leo." I flap my napkin at the house manager. "He studies at the Child-Hooper, so you know dinner will be good."

O'Neill bumps fists with Leo. "I saw your resume when we did the security check. Very impressive." He holds my chair, then sits next to me.

Leo winces. "I was kind of amazed I passed that."

O'Neill's head pops up. "Really?"

"Just kidding!" Leo laughs, a little too loudly. "Nothing to see here! I got in a bit of trouble as a kid. And I haven't lived a very constrained life." He holds his hands parallel, palms facing each other, as if pressing against an invisible box.

"We definitely had our work cut out for us. Tracking down your references was a challenge." O'Neill sips his beverage, then raises it. "But worth it for this alone. I haven't had a decent Virgilton Sunset anywhere but Grissom."

"The secret is sourcing the limons from Grissom. Everything else can be local, but Grissom limons have a special flavor." He winks at me. "I ordered them for the wedding, but today we're testing the menu items."

"The wedding menu is not part of your responsibilities," Hy-Mi says gravely.

"No, but the menu for house guests is." Leo lifts his nose and does a credible imitation of Lilia. "I'm sure Dame Morgan would want only the best for her guests."

After dinner, Ty and I wander down to the back yard. We stand by the invisible barrier at the top of the cliff overlooking the bay.

"I wanted to do the ceremony here, but I've been overruled." I glare over my shoulder at the massive, blocky house. "Although, then we'd have to look at that thing."

Ty turns to gaze at the angular structure. "It's not that bad. I bet the glare off those windows gets intense in the middle of the day, though."

"Don't be silly. They have anti-glare technology built in."

"Really?" His lips twitch.

"No. Mother doesn't care what some random boater sees. But the solar shield over the pool extends to the edge of the cliff, so it's not bad from here." I turn back to the view. "I would have had the minister here, and we could stand here—does your family have a personal chaplain or rabbi or something? Should we have asked the woman who married Lili and Jie to do the ceremony?"

"I don't know anyone who has a personal chaplain. That sounds like an Ancient Earth royalty thing."

"Who do you think you're talking to?" I lift my chin and channel my inner Ice Dame. "Top-levs are royalty." I sigh and grimace. "Hey, speaking of royalty…" I cut myself off. If I tell Ty about Cas, then he'll spend the rest of the night beefing up security. Which might tip off the Lewei staff that something is amiss. Or lead to an interplanetary incident if they take it as a signal of aggression.

"Yes, your highness?" He bows, forehead to knees.

I slap his shoulder. "Nothing. Can we elope?"

He straightens and slides an arm around me. "As you wish."

"If only it were that easy." I rest my head on his shoulder. "What's the latest on the diamonds?"

"We believe the garden company was the unwitting transport for a smuggler. The stones have been traced to a mine in Lovell."

Diamonds are easy to fabricate, but the manufactured ones are perfect. Or perfect copies of existing stones. The tiny flaws that exist in naturally mined diamonds make them more valuable to collectors but also make them easy to trace.

"Are they investigating the gardeners?" I think of that baby, and a little fuzzy glow warms my heart. What is happening to me?

"Of course, but they employ a fair number of people under the table. Paying cash and probably including room and board as part of the compensation. That's a lot harder to track."

"Any hunches? You must have a theory on who hid them and what they're for." I lean against him and wrap my arms around his strong torso.

"Do you really want to talk about diamonds?" he asks in a low voice, his breath tickling my ear.

"Maybe not right now." I half-turn and urge him back to the house.

NINE

THE ROOM IS cool and dark. The glow from Paradise Alley has faded which means it's very late—or really early. A figure sits on the arm of a chair, silhouetted against the open window.

"Who's there?" I sit up, pulling the covers with me. Ty left last night—he had an early meeting in Pacifica City this morning. No one should be able to enter my room when I'm here—that's how I set the security. I try to remember if there's anything within reach that I can use for a weapon.

The figure turns and a holo-ring glows, lighting her face and copper hair from below.

"Vanti? What are you doing here?" I glance at the door. "How'd you get in?"

"Grav belt to the balcony." She crosses the room to the bed, moving like a dancer, sure-footed in the darkness. She stares down at me, and the holo-ring goes out. "I thought we were surfing this morning."

I rub my eyes and flick my holo-ring. It's a quarter to five. "We? I—how did you know? And how did you get through the security protocol on the window screen?"

Vanti laughs. "Board security, remember? I have access to everything."

A glow starts around the edges of the room, slowly increasing to a useful level—my preprogrammed wake-up call. I swing my feet out of bed.

"Does that include audio from my home?" I stumble to the bathroom, stopping to pick up my new suit on the way. "Does the Ice Dame know you have access to her private conversations?"

"The kitchen in the family apartment isn't strictly private," Vanti says. Through the open door, I see her drop into a different chair, legs draped over the arm. "At least, not private from us. Although I can see why you might think it is."

I shut the door as I mull that over.

"What *is* considered private? Is someone listening to this?" I step out of the bathroom with the surf suit halfway up my stomach. My swimsuit is bunched up above the tight fabric and giving me a serious wedgie.

"You're putting that on backwards." She stalks across the room, eyeing my struggles with the blue and green material. She's wearing a flat black body-hugging suit that covers her from mid-thigh to neck and looks fantastic, as usual.

I wriggle out of the thin fabric and turn it around. I pause, one leg on, ready to push my other foot through the opening. "Am I supposed to wear this swimsuit underneath?"

"It's up to you. I do—you never know when you might need to shuck the outer suit. Running naked through the streets is frowned on here." She says it as if it's perfectly acceptable everywhere else.

"Thanks for the tip." The suit goes on much easier this direction. I pull it up to my waist.

Vanti holds up a hand. "If you're going to eat anything, you might want to wait to put that the rest of the way on."

"It's not that tight," I protest as I follow her out of the room.

"In case you need to use the facilities again." She puts her hand against the door panel, and it lights up purple. "To answer your previous question, this suite is private. See?"

I peer at the screen. A small green icon blinks in one corner. She flicks the icon, and it turns red. "Now house security can listen while you're away. In case anyone else knows how to get through the window."

"Yeah, about that." I hurry into the living room behind her. "I added some very sophisticated loops to that window. You shouldn't have been able to get in. How'd you do it?"

She smiles slyly but doesn't respond.

Leo steps out of the kitchen holding two tall glasses. He hands me the one full of green slush and—thankfully—keeps the blue goo for himself. He raises an eyebrow. "I didn't know you were bringing a friend."

"I didn't know I was bringing a friend." I sip the green stuff. It's cold, thick, and tastes like sweezenberry. "That's not bad."

"Every chef's dream review." He grins and extends the blue glass to Vanti. "I can make another of these."

She doesn't move. She's standing near the couch, staring at Leo, her face blank.

"Vanti?" I wave in front of her face.

She starts. "Sorry, I was on a call."

Doubtful. Lots of people freeze when they take an incoming call via audio implant, but Vanti is not one of them. She is an expert at carrying multiple conversations simultaneously and undetectably.

"This is Vanti," I tell Leo.

"I'm here to provide security on your surfing adventure." Vanti waves off the blue drink. "I already ate."

"Cool." Leo slurps the goo.

It looks—and sounds—like gelatinous glop. I suppress a shiver.

After a quick stop in the loo—Vanti was right, as usual—we head out. The edge of the sun peeks over the top of the hills beyond Paradise Alley, sending brilliant pink and orange streaks across the sky. The grass by the pool is covered in dew, leaving my feet damp and cold by the time we reach the cliff edge.

A slim figure stands beside the locked float tube entrance in the corner near the wall separating Sierra Hotel from Starfire.

"Hi, Cas. What are you doing here?" I lift my left hand and point at my holo-ring.

He ignores the hint. "I heard you were going surfing, and I wanted to come."

I glance at Vanti. She's surveying the yard, her head swiveling in robot-like efficiency. A half-dozen holo-screens are already arrayed round her, and I'm sure she's listening to our conversation, too.

"How'd you hear that?" I jerk my head to the side, urging him away from the float tube. Leo steps past and unlocks the system.

"She was talking about it this morning." He nods at Vanti.

"She was inside my room. How did you hear her?" I really should have taken the time last night to go through security again, but Ty was here. Besides, that's what Mother pays Vanti to do.

"Your window was open."

"My window is covered by a state-of-the-art security shield. Sound travels in but not out, unless I choose to change it."

Vanti swipes a couple of holos closed and points at Cas. "Who is this?"

"This is Cas. He lives next door. We met by the pool yesterday." I don't mention his family connections—I know too well the unfair burden of famous parentage.

"Starfire or Lewei?" Vanti asks. "Never mind, I can see his footprints on the heat map. What's your role over there?"

"Do you want to surf, or stand here and chat?" Leo taps his wrist. "I'm heading down, if you want to join." He steps into the float tube and drops from view.

"I'm going with him." Cas follows Leo.

"Me, too."

Vanti puts a hand on my arm. "I don't like this."

"He's twelve. Not exactly a threat."

She shakes her head. "Maybe here. But on Lewei, twelve is an adult. He's probably been in training since he was eight. He could be an assassin or spy."

"If he was an assassin, I'd already be dead—assuming I'm the target. And I don't know why the Lewei government would care about my wedding, so I doubt he's a spy."

"It could be industrial espionage. Get in good with you, then he can ferret out information on SK'Corp." She purses her lips. "I'm not sure we should go down with him."

I roll my eyes. "I'm going. You'll keep me safe. I promise not to talk about any trade secrets." Especially since I don't know any. I pull my arm free from her grip and step into the float tube.

TEN

WHEN I REACH THE BEACH, Leo and Cas have already pulled surf boards from the storage unit hidden in a man-made cleft in the cliff face. It's hidden for aesthetic reasons—the beach is protected by security shields, so we're not worried about theft. Our holo-rings will allow us to swim beyond the shield and surf back but keep unwanted visitors out.

The wind has picked up with sunrise, whipping white foam across the sea. The waves crash against the black sand, rougher than usual for Azure Bay.

Leo takes a deep breath and yodels. The notes warble up and down, echoing against the cliff face and out to sea. Birds startle and launch into the sky.

"What the frappe?"

He grins. "I love the beach. Let's do this!" He shows us how to tether the boards to our holo-rings so they won't float away or hit us on the head if we fall off. "*When* you fall off. You're both beginners, right?"

Cas and I nod.

"How'd you know she isn't?" I point at Vanti.

Leo looks Vanti over and shrugs. "Just a feeling."

Vanti smiles, a tiny quirk of her lips.

After a brief lesson, we paddle into the waves. About fifty meters out, a faint tingle runs over my body—the edge of the secured zone. I glance at

Vanti. She's watching a hologram floating over the tip of her board—a map of the area with tiny arrows. Probably tracking us and everyone else along the bay.

Leo waves us to a stop, and we sit on our boards, watching the waves. He explains what we're looking for and what to do. "The best way to learn is to just try it. Here comes a good wave." He shoves my board perpendicular to the beach.

I paddle furiously, trying to keep my board going the right direction. The waves catch me, and I move faster. The back of the board lifts. I glance over my shoulder, ignoring Leo and Cas's yells.

"Here we go," I mutter.

A bigger wave swells beneath me, and I push off the board. It drops away, and a scream catches in my throat. My feet land unevenly.

"No! Wait! Wah!" The board bucks, and I tip sideways, arms windmilling. I hit the water with a loud splash, and the wave swamps me.

When I surface, my board bobs nearby, held in place by the tethering app. I snort out salty water and suck in a deep breath.

The water is shallow here, so I put my feet down when I reach the board. The waves lift me off the sandy floor and drop me again. I struggle onto my board and paddle back to the others.

As I head out, Cas flashes by me. He's standing on the board, his arms out, hair flying, a huge grin on his face. He whoops, and Leo yodels in response.

Splat!

Cas flies up, tumbling backward. His board zips away, then turns to circle back to him. The boy splashes into the water and comes up spluttering.

I bite back a giggle. "Are you okay?"

"I hit a wall." He rolls onto his board and paddles toward me.

"It sure looked like it."

"No, really. I hit a wall." Balancing on his elbows, he slaps one hand into the other.

I push my hands into the water and paddle toward Leo and Vanti. "There aren't any walls out here."

"There's a virtual wall," Vanti says in my ear. "The security system. He's not an authorized guest of the estate, so it keeps him out."

"Have you been listening to me all this time?"

"How else am I going to protect you? It's standard protocol. The ocean isn't private."

"Apparently my head isn't either."

"I can't hear anything inside your head." She grins as we reach them. "I can only hear what you say."

"Give Cas a guest link so he can surf." I turn to the boy. "Vanti says you hit our security wall. How'd you get over the wall if you can't get past the security?"

Cas smirks. "That's my secret."

"It's going to be my secret, or you get no guest access." Vanti crosses her arms.

"Maybe I'll go surf at Sparkling Strand." Cas crosses his arms, too.

"You do that," Vanti says.

"Never mind." Leo flicks his holo-ring. "It's done."

"That is not your place." Vanti turns on Leo. "Security is my responsibility, and I don't trust him."

"Then turn it off when we go back to the house. We're missing all the good waves." Leo swings his board around and heads for shore.

He's amazing to watch. He pops up as if pulled by strings, then swings his board across the waves. From here, they don't look nearly as big as they felt, but Leo makes riding them look like a five-star sporting competition. He swivels and crouches, yodeling as he goes.

Before we can move, Cas follows him. The boy is a natural—when he isn't smacking into virtual walls.

After swallowing sea water a few more times, I paddle myself back to shore. The surfboard goes back into storage, and I pull out a chair so I can watch the others.

Vanti is as good at surfing as she is at everything. She glides across the water, catches the wave, and pops to her feet like a pro. I shade my eyes against the sun glaring on the water and turn to survey the beach.

This would be a perfect location for a wedding. The glittering black sand, the sparkling waves, the white and blue buildings of Paradise Alley in the background. And the fat angry man yelling at me.

I rise and walk across the damp sand. "Good morning. May I help you?"

The man stands on the beach about a hundred meters away. I can see that he's irate, but the crash of the waves covers his voice. He pounds a fist on the invisible wall at the boundary of the estate and gestures wildly. His thin ginger hair blows across his red scalp.

I move closer until I can hear his words.

"Where's my son?" Spit flies from his mouth and sizzles against the barrier.

I stop. "Are you Cas's dad?" The premier of Lewei, who isn't supposed to be here?

The man stops pounding. "Who are you?"

"I'm Tri—Annabelle Morgan. This is my family's house. Who are you?"

"I am—" He breaks off as if he's realized he shouldn't advertise his name. He waves at the cliff. "A guest of this estate. And you have my son."

"I don't *have* anyone. If it's Cas you're looking for, he's out there, surfing." I point across the water.

Cas has just popped up on his board and is flying along a low breaker. He yodels like Leo did, the joyous sound carrying over the crashing waves.

The man's eyes go wide. "He can't take that kind of risk! He—"

"He's doing great and having a lot of fun. Lots of kids surf. He's using a smart surfer, so he won't get hit by the board, and Leo will make sure he doesn't go under. Why can't he take that minor risk?"

"He must be kept safe!"

I watch the surfers. Vanti's head turns, and she zeroes in on me. She leaps to her feet. Her board spins and lifts out of the water, skimming across the waves toward us, propelled by some unseen force. She races along, crouched low over her ride. The board hits the sand, and the front end bounces up. Vanti flies into the air, tucking into a somersault. She lands on her feet mid-stride and reaches us in seconds. She steps between me and the stranger.

"Who are you?" A stunner has appeared from somewhere, and she points it at the man.

"Where did you get that?" I step to the side so I can see her face. "And how did you make your board go so fast?"

She ignores me.

"I am a guest of this estate," the man says. "You've taken my son surfing without my permission."

Vanti's eyes flicker over the man, then out to Cas. "He said he's twelve. Isn't that the age of consent on your planet?"

"We aren't on my planet." The spit is flying again. "He's not to be put at risk. Tell him to return to me at once!"

"Not my call." Vanti crosses her arms. The stunner has disappeared again. Where is she keeping it?

They both look at me.

"Don't look at me. He just showed up and asked if he could come." I flick my holo-ring and connect to the contact Cas gave me. "Unknown contact. That little frappe."

"What did you call my son?" The man leans forward, and blue sparks flare against his nose. He jumps back.

"Frappe. It's a coffee drink." I smile pleasantly. "I'll call Leo."

This time, the ring connects. "You dropping out, Triana?" Leo asks.

"Could you tell Cas his father is here? And yeah, I think I'm ready to head back up."

"His father?" There's silence for a moment. "The good waves are gone anyway. Cas!" His yell cuts off as he disconnects.

The two of them yodel as they surf toward shore.

"Would you like to come in? Or shall I send him home when he gets here?" I ask.

"No." Vanti holds out an arm. "We don't invite threatening, unidentified visitors onto the property."

"He's not unidentified—" I start.

The man cuts me off. "I do not wish to enter your property. I wish to take my son home. And I wish you to not invite him onto your property again!"

"Technically, I didn't." I glance over my shoulder.

Cas and Leo are on the beach, laughing about something, when Cas looks up. His eyes land on his father, and his face goes blank. He straightens his back, and the bounce goes out of his steps. He drops his surfboard on the dry sand and stalks toward us. Leo picks up the boards and takes them back to the storage unit.

Cas shoots me a venomous glare. "Did you call him?"

"Of course not. Why would I do that?"

He shrugs one shoulder. "I dunno. To get rid of me."

I shake my head. "If I wanted to get rid of you, I'd call my security team. You're always welcome here. Well, you should call first."

A grin crosses his face and disappears.

"No, you are not welcome there." Cas's father's face has turned red. "You are welcome here. Studying. Working. Being a good citizen of Lewei! Come. Now." The man strides away, the dry sand giving his steps a weird bird-like gait.

Cas watches his father for a second, then bows to each of us. "Thank you for your hospitality. I will not intrude again." His lips twitch. "Not without calling first." He hurries across the black sand.

"Wait!" I step forward and smash into the invisible barrier. I jump back on one foot, shaking my stubbed toes. "Ow."

"I'm recalling the visitor pass you gave him." Vanti flicks through holo-screens at eye-watering speed.

"I said he can come back."

She glares. "He can call first. And I'm doing a full walkthrough on the estate's security. He shouldn't have gotten through the first time. Did he tell you how he did it?"

"Nope." *And I wouldn't tell you if I knew.*

ELEVEN

AFTER SHOWERS AND A FULL BREAKFAST, I feel ready to face the day. Or take a nap. I could go either way.

Vanti stalks through the house, flicking holo-screens and muttering to herself.

"Do you want some help?" I ask as she passes my chair for the third time. "Maybe you should eat something."

She looks at the remains of my breakfast and pauses. "Is that bacon?"

"You couldn't smell it?" I pick up another piece and breathe in. Delicious. If I weren't stuffed to the gills, I'd eat it. Oh, who am I kidding? I take another bite.

Vanti flicks something away and swipes an icon. "Maybe just one piece." A crispy strip disappears from the plate faster than the eye can track. She nibbles the end, then plops into a chair. "This is good."

"Leo is the master of the *Merican Breakfast*." I shovel some eggs onto a plate and stack more bacon on top. "Toast?"

"Definitely not."

"It's homemade bread. With cinnamon. And fresh honey butter." I point my knife at the ramekin.

She shakes her head, her mouth full. I guess that's how she stays so fit. Sad.

"Did you find it yet?" I ask a few minutes later as I sip my highly sweetened, cream-heavy coffee.

She swallows. "Nothing. There's no way he should have been able to get in."

"You did."

"I have access. He doesn't. I can't find any traces of him in the system. A twelve-year-old can't be that good at covering his tracks."

"I thought you said twelve-year-olds were adults on Lewei." I contemplate another piece of toast, since Vanti isn't going to eat it.

"Exactly." She points her fork at me. "He has inside help. They probably have a whole team of security specialists helping him break in. I need to check." She drops her fork, her meal only half-eaten, and shoves her chair back from the table.

"Where are you going? Can I come?" I hurry after her.

"I'm going to the control center to work on this." She waves her ring at a seemingly blank stretch of wall, and a door slides open. A hall leads to the service areas behind the main house.

"Ooh, I haven't been back there in ages."

Hy-Mi steps between me and the doorway. "We have work to do today, Sera."

"More tastings?" Although I'm full to bursting, the thought of cake makes my mouth water.

"This afternoon. This morning, it's music." Hy-Mi turns and stares at Vanti.

"I guess I'll see you later, then." She disappears down the hall, and the door slides shut.

I heave a sigh and follow Hy-Mi to Mother's private office. This is a showpiece, of course, but unlike the public office on the upper floor, she actually uses it for more than meetings. The huge desktop is made of stone quarried nearby. Normally, Mother isn't very interested in buying local, but Kahwenska marble meets all her other requirements: expensive, beautiful, and scarce.

The chairs are imported from somewhere. I used to have the entire tour memorized. That's right, there's a tour of the house on *CelebVid*, complete with a carefully scripted voiceover. The only parts of the house not on it are my bedroom and Mother's. And the security center, of course. It's been on the net for ages, and as a kid, I used to watch it when I was feeling homesick.

I drop into one of the aforementioned imported chairs and lean back, appreciating the thick Joister upholstery. "Hit me with the music, Hy-Mi."

Hi-Mi's lips turn down, and his eyelids close a fraction—I've just been reprimanded.

I sit up and fold my hands in my lap. "Please, proceed."

We spend the morning listening to Mother's preferred musical selections. They're all fusty, ancient stuff, with outdated singers who continue to make the cruise ship and resort circuits years after they should have retired.

Two hours later, I'm exhausted all over again. And disappointed. "Can't we have someone a bit more modern?"

Hy-Mi's eyes soften. "This is what Dame Morgan wants." He taps a stylus against his lip, staring through me. "How about this? We can have an after party. You select the venue, the food, music, everything. It can be your private reception, without all the A-list guests—unless you want them, of course."

"Do you think Mother will go for that?" It seems highly unlikely to me. The possibility that my private event could eclipse her magnificent production in any way would be unacceptable.

Hy-Mi nods decisively, as if he's come to a significant conclusion. "Perhaps we won't mention it."

My spirits soar, then crash. "Do you really think that will work? She knows everything."

"She'll know. But she'll pretend she doesn't. Isn't that good enough?"

***

Vanti wanders out of the service corridor, her face pale, eyes bloodshot, and her hair sticking out. I've never seen her look anything less than perfect.

"Are you sick?" I take her arm and guide her to a chair.

"How is he doing it?" she mutters.

"Are you still trying to figure out how Cas got in?" I pour some water and hand her the glass.

She sips. "He shouldn't be able to get through. The protocols are all in place. We have virtual trip wires that will tell us if anyone has subverted the routines…"

"Do you even know what you're talking about? That's all nonsense." Her head pops up and I hold up a hand. "I'm kind of an expert at this, remember?"

Her eyes light up. "You are. Come with me." She grabs my hand and pulls me toward the service corridor.

I look around, but no one is here to stop me tonight. Hy-Mi retired early to deal with some estate business. Leo is off for the night, and O'Neill had to stay in the city. "Are you the only one on duty?"

"No. The rest of the team is operating from the caretaker's house. Since Leo isn't living there, we decided it would be less intrusive."

The narrow hallway cuts between the kitchen and Hy-Mi's office, burrowing into the hillside behind the house. We turn a corner, and the hall widens.

I've been back here before—most recently when Kara and I infiltrated the house after it was taken over by terrorists. This time, I don't have to sneak through the halls. Leo is the only staff member living here, although someone has come in to clean and do laundry every day.

Vanti stops by the heavy door at the far end of the hall. She places her hand on the access panel and the door pops ajar. On a whim, I put my palm on the panel, and it flashes red.

"Hey, how come I can't get in here? I'm supposed to have access to everything."

Vanti smirks. "Everything else. This area belongs to board security." She pulls the door wide and steps through.

Inside, the lighting is dim. Three workstations sit idle, a fourth one is on but inactive. Vanti steps onto a circle on the floor. A red glow surrounds her, and a pleasant voice says, "Fioravanti, Lindsay. Identity confirmed. Guest recognized: Annabelle Morgan. Approved. Opening security program."

"Wow, fancy." I step onto the circle by the next workstation. The red glow comes on, and some kind of forcefield wraps around me, providing better support than a chair. In fact, it grabs my shoulders and pulls them back, putting me into correct alignment for optimum efficiency. Either that, or it's a torture device.

"Annabelle Morgan. Identity confirmed. Access denied."

"What?" I wave a hand. "Tell this thing I have access. This is my *frapping* house! No, frappe is not going to work for that. It's my *forking* house."

Vanti snickers. "I told you, board security." She swipes something, and my screens light up.

"Holo-share initiated."

"Thanks, you *forking* robot," I mutter. Lines of code appear around me.

"That's the current security protocol." Vanti scrolls the text. "You can see it's standard stuff. Here are the extra systems that our net guys installed last week." Another wall of data appears. "Most of that makes sense to me, but maybe you'll see something I don't."

"Where are the vids from the west wall?" I scan the code, but it all looks good. In fact, that one little bit there is genius. I copy that section and save it to my holo-ring. I'm always in the market for some novel programming.

She sends me some links. "I've checked them all. There aren't any gaps or loops."

"I have a few tricks up my sleeve." I download one of my favorite vid checkers and run the files through it. "You're right—there are no gaps in these vids. If he slid in some spoofed vid, this would spot it."

We spend hours working our way through every vid on the property. There's nothing to indicate where he might have snuck in.

"There must be dead spots." I swipe all the files away and set the work-station to idle. "I need a bathroom break. And a snack. And maybe a drink."

"The system was set years ago to eliminate all the dead spots, and none of the cams have been moved." Vanti shuts her station down, too, and follows me out of the room. "We do a complete review before the Ice Dame arrives. We've got one scheduled for just before the wedding, but we could do a perimeter walk now."

"That sounds so exhausting." I say it because she seems to expect it, but I'm wide awake and ready to go snooping. "I suppose I'll manage."

She snickers. "There's the nosy Triana I've been looking for. I was afraid it had all been rinsed out of you by domestic bliss."

"I've been suppressing it. Trying to be a good heir for Mother's sake."

She takes me down a flight of steps to the industrial kitchen. "There are some protein bars down here somewhere."

"Ew. There's tonnes of real food in the family kitchen. Why eat that stuff?"

"I don't want to upset Leo by messing with his stuff." She rummages in a cupboard and pulls out a couple of bars. She offers me one, but I wave it away. There's bound to be an AutoKich'n here somewhere. She peels the wrapping away and nibbles on a corner.

"You don't usually care what anyone thinks." I open and close random cupboards but only find equipment.

"This kitchen won't be stocked until closer to the big event." Vanti holds out the protein bar again. "Let's go on a walk-about."

TWELVE

I TAKE the protein bar with a sigh, unwrap the end, and sniff. Chocolate with a hint of peanut butter, and is that cinnamon? I try a bite—it's actually tasty instead of the preformed blandness I expected. A bit rubbery in texture, but all protein bars are. I take a bigger bite and follow Vanti out the service entrance.

A tunnel leads from the kitchen to a huge, underground garage. Three SK'Corp branded cargo bubbles hang from the ceiling, shiny and clean as if they've just been delivered. We skirt past them to the vehicle exit.

The long tunnel slopes upward. At the end, Vanti lays her hand on the access panel, and the huge door slides away. I put my hand on the panel, and the "access denied" icon flashes. The door stops and reverses direction.

"Get out here." Vanti makes hurry up motions at me.

I sprint forward, sliding through the door with a meter or more to spare. It clangs shut behind me. "Why don't I have access to this door? I should have access to everything! I do on SK2."

"You still have maintenance privileges on SK2. You never had that here."

"But when Kara and I snuck in last year, I was able to get into everything."

"We've tightened security since then." She points into the darkness, and we trudge across the long driveway toward a thick hedge.

The night is silent. Very little natural wildlife remains in this part of

Kaku—anything dangerous or even unsightly was eliminated when the wealthy took over this stretch of land. New flora and fauna were imported, and the property owners' association employs a staff of biologists and botanists to maintain the pristine environment. Heavy duty security barriers at the entrance to the peninsula keep out any native wildlife.

As a result, there are no creaking insects, like on Grissom, no dangerous snakes, and no unattractive scat left behind. Vira bats live in the caves below the cliff. They're omnivorous scavengers, so they take care of dead plants and any animals that get through the screens.

The faint scent of fish reaches us, but it isn't as overpowering as it was the first day. It kind of complements the salty tang of the ocean and overcomes the sterile nature of the place. In the distance, waves wash quietly on the sand below the cliff.

"You've tightened security by locking out the owners?" I flick my holoring and turn up the brightness. The glow lights my feet and a few meters around me.

"We locked you out. The Ice Dame still has access because we know she won't abuse it. I can't keep you safe if you're constantly messing with the security system." She pushes her hand into the hedge, and a section hinges toward us.

"Is that a door?" In the darkness, I can't see how it's built, but it swings soundlessly.

"Yup." She waves me through, then closes it behind us.

The trees close around us. This section is forested but carefully maintained to allow guests to wander at their leisure without encountering any sharp thorns or dangerous splinters. The ground is covered in a dense carpet of tiny leaves that give a little bounce to our feet. The trees stand exactly two meters apart, their uniform trunks carefully pruned to provide optimum shade in the daytime. Tonight, it's dark, with the moons not yet visible above the horizon.

"Is that why you were able to get past my security loops?" I point a finger at her. "You trapped me inside a fake system! I was beefing up security for a faux house."

A little quirk of her lips is the only response. She heads off into the trees. I hurry behind, already plotting how I'll get around her. She might be *good* at security, but I'm mage level.

A few meters on, a small shed stands against the hedge. Vanti opens the door and pulls out two hoverboards. "Have you ridden one of these before?"

I take one and pair my ring. Then I set it to ten centimeters and toss it down. The board hovers a hand's breadth above the ground. It sinks a fraction as I step on, then compensates.

Vanti looks me over and tosses her board down. "Let's go." She steps on and glides into the trees.

I lean forward, and my board slides after her. I haven't used one since I was a kid, but muscle memory kicks in. Leaning left or right turns the board. Setting my weight back slows it down. Like the old cliché says: "As easy as falling off a hoverboard."

I pull up behind Vanti and initiate a call rather than speaking aloud—to show her I'm a good partner. "You never explained how you know Leo."

"What makes you think I know him?" Her voice is even but doesn't match the startled look she throws over her shoulder.

Ha! I've never succeeded in rattling Vanti before. "You obviously recognized him this morning."

Her shoulders twitch. "Of course I recognized him. I reviewed the staff files before I arrived."

She's lying. I'm not sure why I'm so certain, but I am.

"There's the wall." She points ahead, as if I can't see it.

A two-meter-high wall surrounds the estate. Inside, a two-meter-wide strip of grass separates the wall from the trees—a security zone with clear lines of sight. Dim lights shine from the top of the wall, just enough to illuminate the security zone, but they can be turned up with a simple command. Cams sit between the lights, monitoring.

We turn left, using the security zone as a road to the sea. Vanti slows our pace, and I pull up next to her. As we move, her eyes flick over the wall, the ground, and the cam footage in her palm.

"What are you looking for that we couldn't find inside?" I flick my own ring to bring up the closest cam.

"Blank places in the vid feed and physical entry points. The system should have alerted us if anyone tunneled under or broke through, but Lewei may have devised a way to spoof our system."

"If this is really an attack by the Lewei government, shouldn't we call the Kaku Intelligence Agency?" I shine my holo-light on a section of the stone wall, looking for secret doorways or evidence of alien portals. Lewei is an alien planet, even though the inhabitants are humans. I snicker. "Maybe we should just knock on the door and ask them to take us to their leader."

Vanti ignores me. It wasn't that funny.

The land slopes gently toward the cliff at the southern edge of the property, and we pick up speed. I set my board to a constant velocity and focus on the cam feeds. "You watch the wall; I'll watch for dead spots."

Vanti grunts and swipes away some extra holo-feeds.

We stop several times so Vanti can examine the stone wall. She slides her hands over the rock, pressing and prying, but no secret passageways open under her fingers.

What feels like hours later, we finally reach the end of the wall. I step off my hoverboard and rotate my tight shoulders. "You don't think anyone could get around the end, do you?"

"No." Vanti pokes her holos, then looks at the wall again. "Why? What do you see?"

The wall doesn't physically keep anyone out. If someone wanted to get over, they could use a hoverboard set to three meters or a grav belt. It's the electronics that keep the place secure—like the invisible barrier Cas ran into when surfing. The system queries an individual's holo-ring for clearance and only lets them in if they're on the list. Since it's a positive check, if they aren't wearing one at all, they can't get in.

"What if someone put a hole in the security at the end of the wall? Slide out there on your board. I want to see if you're visible."

Vanti looks over the edge of the cliff. A meter-high invisible force shield will keep the unwary from falling off but won't stop a determined jumper or a hoverboard set high enough.

"You want a grav belt? In case you fall off the board?" There's nothing to keep her from falling to her death if she missteps.

"I already have one." She taps the narrow belt around her waist. It must be one of the newest models because it's very sleek and unnoticeable. She rises off the board and glides out over nothing. Even though I understand the mechanics of hoverboards and grav belts, my chest tightens as she hangs over thin air.

She puts one hand on the wall and rotates around the end.

"Don't go all the way around," I whisper. "I've heard the Lewei security guards are dangerous."

"I shouldn't be able to go all the way around." Her voice comes clearly through my audio implant. "Their security should stop me."

"Should?"

She reappears at the end of the wall and grins. "It didn't. I think we found our access."

"Just because you can get in there doesn't mean they could get in here. Besides," I flick the hologram in my palm, "the cams would—oh frappe."

"There's a dead spot, isn't there?" She raises an eyebrow. "This is how Cas got in."

THIRTEEN

"He didn't have a hoverboard," I protest. "Or a grav belt."

"There are hand and foot holds in the end of the wall." She drops so her head is level with the top of the cliff and runs a finger on the wall stub protruding from the stone. "Perfect for a little boy to climb on."

"Don't let him hear you call him little." I flick a few more commands. "That doesn't explain how he got through the Sierra Hotel force shield. There must be a hole. Come back over here, and we'll plug it."

"In a minute." Vanti disappears again. "I want to see what kind of physical security they have on this side."

"Vanti, come back here! That's Lewei soil—a foreign planet. Have you checked Kaku-Lewei relations lately? I don't think we're allies. You don't want to start an interstellar incident."

"Relations are good right now. Come over. There's no one here."

"Come over there? I don't have a grav belt."

"Use the hoverboard. If you go slowly, it's perfectly safe."

I consider declining, but I've never been over there, and now I really want to see it. I step onto my board and set the height to one-point-two meters. "Has anyone ever told you that you're a terrible security agent? You're supposed to *stop* me from doing stupid things."

"Bring my board with you. We might want to make a fast escape, and my belt doesn't move as quick."

I tether her board to mine, and it obediently bobs up behind me. With one hand on the wall, I inch forward. The moons are still low in the sky, leaving a dark abyss below my feet. The waves crash softly onto the sand, but instead of comforting, it's now menacing. They'll wash over my bones if I fall here.

A narrow band of metal sticks out of the end of the wall. I grab it, the well-worn material smooth against my fingers. Keeping my feet firmly planted on the board, I lean to the right. The board tips—probably only a few degrees, but it feels like I'm going to slide right off. My hand clamps onto the metal bar.

There's another one. I stretch out my left hand, and my fingers brush against it. They slide off, and the board skews back. I lunge to the bar, catching it this time.

Now I'm stuck at an angle, with my feet way too far from the wall for comfort. I pull my feet toward the wall, my arms and abs straining. My lungs constrict, and my heart goes into overdrive. Sweat pours down my face.

"If I make it out of this alive, I will start core training," I whisper to the Big Guy.

My feet creep closer to the wall. My arms seize, and I press my face against the rough stone. *Breathe.*

"What are you screwing around for?" Vanti grabs my arm and yanks me away from my new best friend, the wall. I tumble off the board, landing on a grassy bank.

"You almost killed me!" My voice is hoarse in an attempt to keep the volume down but still express my outrage.

"There is zero possibility you will fall to your death." She picks up a rock and holds it up. Then she tosses it over the edge. It drops.

I don't hear it hit the ground, but we're way too high for that.

"Go look." She points at the cliff.

I roll to my hands and knees and crawl forward.

The rock is suspended in the air two meters below the edge of the cliff. "We don't trust top-levs to be careful. There's a catch trough all along this cliff. Maintenance has to come out here and clean up empty dishes and junk after every party."

"Did you test it before you came around? What if it's offline over the gap?"

"I'm not going to risk your life." She points to the end of the wall. A trail of small puddles lay in the invisible trough. "Water will dry before morning and not leave a trace."

"We're currently on Lewei soil," I remind her. "You're still risking my life."

"We can talk our way out of that if we need to."

"So, talk," a deep voice says.

We freeze. My heart, which had finally slowed close to normal, stops, then goes into triple-time. I look up.

And up and up. This guy is huge.

The bald man towering over us holds an evil looking gun, which is currently pointed at Vanti. Clearly, he's discerning enough to pick out the greater threat. He jerks it up a little. "Get up."

I push back onto my heels and stand slowly, taking stock. Our hover-boards are still hanging over the abyss by the end of the wall. Vanti undoubtedly has a weapon of some kind stashed in her skin-tight outfit, but I don't know where she's keeping it. I didn't bother putting on the tranq ring she gave me, so my only weapon is my wits, which is not encouraging.

From a standing position, the guy is still huge. He's wearing faded jeans and a tight T-shirt that barely covers his bulging muscles. A dark tattoo of a dragon or maybe a snake curls out of his collar and around his neck. His belt has multiple bulges—like the utility belts Vanti sometimes wears. Probably has cuffs, stunner, maybe a knife, and poison.

"Who are you?" Vanti asks.

"Who are you?" the giant replies.

"I'm Triana." I hold out a fist to bump. "Nice to meet you."

They both turn to stare at me. My hand drops.

"I am Loki."

"Like the god of mischief or the superhero story?" I ask.

His brow furrows. "Like my father and his father before him. It's a family name."

"Cool. That's Vanti. We live over there." I jut a thumb over my shoulder. "My friend Cas said we could come visit."

"You know Cas?"

I glance at Vanti. Should I have outed him? His father already knew he'd been to Sierra Hotel—surely the security staff had been briefed?

"Yes. He went surfing with us." Vanti points to the water, taking a half-step toward the cliff as she does.

"Don't move." Loki waggles the gun. "I will check with Master Caspian." He flicks his holo-ring and mutters something. Another flick and the ring goes dark. "We must wait. It's late. He might be asleep."

"Oh. Hey, is that his dad?" Vanti points over Loki's shoulder.

He turns. Vanti grabs my hand and drags me toward the cliff. She leaps off the edge, pulling me with her.

I scream as my feet windmill against nothing. I fall and clamp my eyes shut. My knee slams into the invisible trough. A sharp pain spikes into my knee. Water seeps into my leggings.

"Hey!" Loki yells. "Where are you going? Stop!"

"Come on!" Vanti yanks my arm out of the socket. I scramble to my feet. Keeping my eyes focused on the cliff, rather than the terrifying *nothingness* beneath me, I duck around the end of the wall and under the hoverboards, still hanging in the air.

Vanti drops beside me and wraps an arm around my waist. "Hold on."

"To what?" I screech as she yanks me up. The grav belt flings us upward two or three meters. She pushes me over the invisible wall. My feet catch on the edge, and I collapse on the grass, flat on my face.

Loki yells. My head snaps around. He stands on the invisible barrier, his head canted forward at an odd angle. As we watch, he twists and moves as if he's trying push through an opening too small for his massive frame.

Vanti chuckles.

Loki stops struggling and maneuvers his weapon up to point at us. "Come back here."

"Not likely." Vanti pushes me closer to the wall, out of range of his gun. She stalks forward and shoves the barrel down. "This is the soil of Kaku. You have no business being here."

"You had no business being here!" Loki stomps a foot on nothing.

"He's got you there, Vanti."

"Shut up, Triana," she says without turning. "Go home, Loki."

"I thought you wanted to see Cas." The big guy ducks and pulls back, extracting his head from the hole in the force shield.

"Yeah, but you were pointing a gun at us."

The gun disappears around the wall. "I won't point it anymore. See?" He sticks both hands through the gap. "We can be friends."

"Nice try. I don't think so." Vanti makes shooing motions. "And don't try to come through here again—I'm plugging that hole."

"But Cas is lonely. You should come visit him."

"I think we'll use the road next time." Vanti turns away.

"No! His father doesn't allow visitors."

I sit up, brushing grass from my legs. My hand hits something hard, and it pokes my sore knee. While Vanti and Loki argue, I flick on my holo-ring and take a look.

My leggings are wet and torn. A little blood leaks from a puncture on my knee. And caught in the ripped fabric is a huge, square diamond.

FOURTEEN

"It must be four carats." I hold up the stone.

O'Neill's eyes crinkle and he chuckles. "Trust a top-lev girl to know the value of a diamond."

I roll my eyes. "One of my many underrated top-lev skills." I pull up an app and wave my hand over the diamond. "The 4-C app says it's 3.89. And exceptional clarity and color."

"Not underrated, just rarely useful." He winks and my heart melts.

He's still in Pacifica City, so I called him from the secure comm system in my room. "Does Vanti know about the diamonds? I didn't tell her about this one."

"She's aware but not involved in that investigation. I'll come get it in the morning and bring it back to be analyzed. If the Premier of Lewei is the source of those diamonds you found on SK2, we need to know."

"I'm coming to visit Kara again tomorrow—I can bring it to you." I drop the stone into a small wooden box and slide the lid shut.

He considers for a moment, then agrees. "I'll meet you at Kara's tomorrow afternoon. After we drop the stone at headquarters, I can come back to Sierra Hotel for the weekend."

"Oh, good. You can meet Kara's mom. The two of them are coming out for the weekend, too." I should probably warn Hy-Mi and Leo. I make a mental note to send them a message after I'm done talking with O'Neill.

"Sounds like girls' night. You sure you want me there, too?"

"I will always want you here."

———

VANTI and I take the HyperLoop to Kara's apartment. Despite her somewhat erratic methods, O'Neill trusts her to protect me. Of course, I didn't tell him about our foray into foreign lands last night—I implied I found the diamond while we were investigating the gap in the security system. Which is technically true.

If he knew we'd gone onto the Lewei property, we'd both be in trouble.

Agents al-Karendi and Limberghetti meet us at the HyperLoop station. Vanti briefs them on their duties as we ride to Kara's, then to the seventh level. "They'll watch the place while you're inside."

"Is this really necessary? I lived on Kaku for four years with no security at all."

Vanti's eyes narrow. "I was here the whole time, remember?"

Kara sits on a mat on the floor, her pregnant body twisted into a pretzel. The hologram of a woman dressed in black leggings and a fitted, pink tank top is frozen in the same pose. "Did you follow Triana to our house that first Christmas?"

Vanti's eyes flicker. Maybe she doesn't know I climbed out of the dorms through the laundry chute that year. I make a mental note in case I need to sneak away. This apartment might have a similar delivery system.

"Why don't you make Triana do some of that yoga with you?" Vanti grins. "I heard her making a deal with the Almighty last night, and it's time to pay up. I wish I could stay to watch."

My face warms. I did promise to work on my core. I didn't realize Vanti heard me.

Kara points across the room. "Grab a mat—I've got a spare over there. You can stay and join us, Vanti."

"Wish I could. Got a meeting." She makes a face. "And some research to do. I'll see you at headquarters." She points at me. "Don't leave the building without your detail."

"Why are you being so cautious? Is there some kind of threat I don't know about?" I grab the mat and unroll it next to Kara. "I don't need a full security detail."

Vanti snorts. "Two agents do not a full detail make. If there was a threat, you'd be locked in Sierra Hotel." She gets to the door and turns back. "You've gotten a lot of publicity lately—that vid went viral. That always brings out the crazies. Please, don't make our job harder than it has to be."

"Fine." I plop down on the mat. "I won't go anywhere. Today."

Vanti smirks and slips out the door.

"Do you have a laundry room?"

Kara rolls her eyes. "Yes, but I'm not showing you." She flicks her holo-ring, and the instructor starts breathing again. She still doesn't move.

"I am not doing that."

"You couldn't do that. I'll find an easier routine." She swipes the woman away and flicks through some options. "Here's a beginner's class."

Six women appear around us, all wearing stretchy clothing and sitting cross-legged on mats. Every one of them has a huge belly.

"They're all pregnant."

"It's prenatal yoga." Kara gestures to her own bulging abdomen.

"But I'm supposed to be strengthening my core, not stretching it out." I lean back and push out my stomach.

Kara snickers. "The baby does the pushing out. Yoga keeps me from getting saggy afterwards. This should be easy without a baby." She smiles and hits the start button.

We start out on our hands and knees, arching and dropping our backs in a way that makes me laugh. I feel a little twinge in the knee I banged last night. I can't complain, though—I'm doing this with a woman who's eight months pregnant.

"Move into pointer dog." The instructor lifts one leg and the other arm, freezing, fully extended. Kara copies her. I stretch out. This isn't so hard. Vanti can—I tip over.

"You're supposed to use the opposite arm." Kara points at her thigh then stretches out again.

"Oops." I copy her pose.

The women in the holo straighten, reach up, then arch back, resting their hands on their ankles.

"That is not possible." I point at the hologram.

"What isn't possible?" Kara folds her body back and grabs her feet. Her stomach sticks out like a beachball.

"That." I lean back. My knees creak. My arms wave in the air, coming nowhere near my ankles.

"That's a good start," Kara says.

I growl.

We stand and touch our toes, then straighten and do it again. Easy!

Kara swings her arms back, and they jut out from her shoulders at a completely unnatural angle.

Show off.

We stand.

"And into tree." The instructor slides one foot up the other leg, her knee poking out to the side.

Kara lifts her foot and tucks it against her crotch, her hands overhead. I lift my left leg and get it to my knee before getting stuck. No matter—I'm a beginner. I stretch upward. My right ankle wiggles, but I steady it.

I breathe deeply, following the instructor's count. I am a yoga queen! This could be my new go-to exercise. I might even learn to teach this stuff.

My ankle wiggles again. My arms flail. I grab blindly, trying to find something to hold onto. My foot slips, then my toes catch in my pants fabric. "Wah!" My arms pass through one of the yoga women, and I land on my side.

Kara barks out a laugh, then claps a hand over her mouth. "Sorry, it's not funny."

"It's pretty funny." I roll to my back and rub my arm. "I'm going to just lie here for a minute."

"The corpse pose. That's perfect for you."

FIFTEEN

THE DOOR PINGS.

"Will you get that?" Kara calls over her shoulder as she pulls another dish out of the AutoKich'n.

As far as I can see, the best thing about pregnant yoga is you get to eat afterwards. Four other dishes sit on the counter, and we've set the table for three.

I open the door. Kara's mom is having a spirited debate with al-Karendi. O'Neill watches, bemused.

"—trust me. I've lived in Réalta for twenty-five years. That place has the best ants' egg soup. They use the tiny ants, not the gigantic ones from Armstrong."

"I'm from Armstrong." Al-Karendi's arms are crossed over her chest, and her chin juts out. "Those tiny Kakuvian ants are flavorless."

"Larin!" I fling my arms around the older woman. I used to think aesthetic mods to hide aging were the norm, but apparently that's only among the upper-levs of the galaxy. Larin has dark hair with fine strands of silver. The laugh lines around her eyes give character to her face. But aside from those two features, she could be Kara's older sister.

I release Larin and give O'Neill a warm kiss. "Ty, did you meet Larin, Kara's mom?"

O'Neill's eyebrows draw down. *"Larin?"*

"Triana, honey, maybe you should start calling me Elodie." She links her arm through mine and steers me through the door. As we cross the threshold, she turns back and points at al-Karendi. "Just try the soup. You won't be sorry."

"Are you hawking the ants' egg soup again?" Kara gives her mom a quick hug and returns to the AutoKich'n.

"Why would I call you Elodie?" I hand her a glass.

"Because it's my name." She sips and kisses her fingers at Kara. "Delicious."

"Your name is Larin. That's what I've always called you."

She chuckles. "*Larin* is a nickname. It means 'Mom' in Réalta. If you thought that was my name, didn't you think it was weird that Kara used it?"

I stare from one to the other. "I didn't think about it. She told me to call you that."

"It's okay, you can still call me that. But when you introduce me, you should probably use my actual name." She winks at Ty.

He grins and raises his glass. "Nice to meet you, Elodie."

———

"Why don't we have Vanti meet us at the HyperLoop station instead of going to SK'Corp?" I ask. "It would save some time."

"I have to drop off your little discovery, remember?" He raises an eyebrow.

"I gave it to Vanti. You should have had it hours ago." I pick up Kara's bag. "What are you carrying in here, gold?"

"Vanti has it? I thought—she didn't give it to me when I saw her." He flicks his holo-ring and steps outside.

"What's that all about?" Kara asks.

"I found something last night that he needs to—something he needs to research. I told Vanti to give it to him."

Kara wrinkles her nose. She's not Vanti's biggest fan. "I know you like her, but I wouldn't trust her around my man."

"You know she works with Erco, right?" I sling the bag over my shoulder. The weight throws me off balance, and I almost end up on the floor again. "Seriously, what's in here?"

"It's my weighted blanket. I can't sleep without it these days." She stretches out a hand. "And I'm not worried about Erco. He's crazy about me."

"You think I shouldn't trust Ty?" I unzip the bag. "You don't need this—we have PerfectSleep blankets at the house."

She pulls the blanket out of the bag. "No, I'm sure you can trust *him*. But they have a history."

I chuckle. "That's why I'm not worried. *Larin*, are you ready?"

"DID YOU FIND THE... STONE?" I ask O'Neill as we settle into our seats on the HyperLoop. Kara and Elodie sit across the aisle. Vanti is farther back in the pod, near the door. She didn't acknowledge us when we reached the station, so I ignore her back.

"Yeah, she dropped it at the labs." O'Neill frowns. "I wish she'd told me. I was going to—" He breaks off.

"What?"

"Nothing. We—Vanti and I—should speak with Cas while we're there."

"Why? Was that diamond from the same planet?" I fasten my harness.

The pod pings softly, and an androgynous voice warns we will depart in thirty seconds.

"Not just the same planet—same mine."

We're pressed back in our seats as the pod launches. Once we reach full speed, the pressure releases. The HyperLoop takes us the seven hundred miles to the Ebony Coast in about thirty minutes, using a dedicated underground tunnel. No one lives in the desert center of the continent, so there are no stops between Pacifica City and Paradise Alley.

When we arrive, the estate bubble awaits. As we climb in, Elodie and Kara ooh and aah over the plush seats and fabulous sound system.

"Is Vanti riding with us?" I pause by the door and look for the redhead.

"No, she'll meet us at the house. She's going to do a fly-by of the Lewei estate."

"Fly by?" I stow Kara's bag in the cargo compartment and sit. "She's not flying *over*, is she?"

"That would cause an interstellar incident, so I hope not," O'Neill mutters, giving a warning jerk of his head toward Kara and her mom.

"Interstellar incident?" Kara repeats. "I wanna hear about that!"

"It's nothing—" O'Neill starts.

"We live next door to the Premier of Lewei," I tell them. "You know how Leweians are—just looking at them wrong can set off a furor."

"I met a Leweian man a few years ago," Elodie says. "He never took offense to anything I said."

"That's because he was hot for you," Kara says. "And he wasn't Leweian. He was from Legaeria."

Elodie chuckles. "I always get those two messed up. I'd like to visit there some day."

"Where? Lagaeria or Lewei?" O'Neill asks.

"Either. Both. I want to travel the galaxy. I've never been off Kaku."

My jaw drops. "Not even to SK2?" I thought everyone on Kaku had been there.

"We move in very different circles." She pats Kara's hand. "Even when Kara was living up there, I couldn't afford the shuttle fees."

When we arrive at Sierra Hotel, Leo and Hy-Mi meet us in the family room.

"I've given your guests rooms on this floor and added their credentials to the access panel," Leo says. "Do you want to give them the grand tour or shall I?"

Kara drops onto a couch, rubbing her belly. "I've already seen it. *All* of it." She gives me a conspiratorial grin. "But you should go, *Larin*."

"Go for it." I wave at the door. "Kara about killed me with yoga today, so I need a nap."

WHILE LEO GIVES Elodie the full tour, Kara and I snooze on the couch. I hear snatches of conversation between Vanti and O'Neill, but none of it sinks in. I wake with a vague feeling of irritation and the idea that I need to prove myself.

Leo creates another masterpiece—this time cooking in a huge, flat pan over a grill on the balcony. "It's an Ancient Earth dish called Pie Ava. I don't know why—there's no crust involved." He uses an enormous wooden spoon to stir the rice, sausage, chicken, and shrimp.

"We have this on Grissom." Ty leans over the pan and breathes in deeply. "But I think it's spicier. We call it jambolia."

After stuffing ourselves with Pie Ava, I'd rather take another nap, but Kara's ready to go out. "I can't drink, but I can still have fun." She drags me to my suite and pulls clothing out of my closet with wild abandon.

"Who's been shopping for you?" She holds up a short gold dress with matching sandals. "If I weren't the size of a house, I'd borrow this."

"It must have been Hy-Mi." I flick my holo-ring. "I'd better check his app and make sure I'm not supposed to save that for some specific event."

I pull up the Dress-Success app. Twenty-odd events are listed, starting two weeks before the wedding. "What is all of this? Ugh, meet and greet with board members, art gallery opening, cigar shop? Charity *poli* tournament. Mother is getting her money's worth out of this wedding."

Kara peers over my shoulder and sighs. "All that luxury is wasted on you."

"You are more than welcome to come with—or better yet, go instead."

She scrolls through the listings. "Hy-Mi would never allow that. By the way, where is the old sweetie? I want to say hi."

"The old sweetie? I thought you said he hit on you?"

Her face goes pink. "He's a serious flirt, but he's not creepy."

"Hy-Mi—my Hy-Mi—is a flirt? I have not seen that side of him."

She shrugs. "Probably not."

"He's visiting grandchildren. Or great-grandchildren. He'll be back Monday, if you want to hang around that long."

"We'll see. Put this on. We need to get going because I turn into a pumpkin really early these days."

"In this gold dress, I'm going to look like a pumpkin." I take the dress and slide it on.

"No, I'm the pumpkin shape. You look fantastic. Let's get your hair done and go."

When we arrive in the living room, Leo, Ty, and Elodie applaud. I'm not sure if it's because we look so good—we do—or because we finally got here.

"Is this girls' night?" Leo asks. "Because if it is, I still want to come."

"Everyone is welcome." Kara waves her arms widely. "The Ice Dame is buying."

I smirk. "Where's Vanti?"

"She's checking the perimeter. She'll meet us in the garage." O'Neill gestures toward the hall.

SIXTEEN

PAST MOTHER'S PRIVATE OFFICE, Hy-Mi's apartment, and the guest suites, a door leads to the garage. The same bubble that picked us up at the Hyper-Loop waits, humming quietly. Vanti sits in the controller's seat, dressed in a short, tight black dress. Her hair is up, and she's wearing chunky ten-centimeter heels.

"Are you providing security in those?" I point at the glamorous shoes, then hold up a hand. "Never mind. I know you're more than capable."

Her lips quirk. "Yes, I am capable. But I'm not on duty tonight. Everyone in. I see we've got the whole gang. Did you bring enough BuzzKill, Griz?"

Griz is Vanti's nickname for O'Neill. Neither of them has ever explained why. I grind my teeth a little.

"There's a bottle in here." He flips open a compartment and holds it up. "But I'm not drinking tonight. There's no way I could keep up with these three if I did." He points at Elodie, Kara, and me.

"Great, I'm ready for shots." Vanti swipes a hand through the control panel, and the door folds shut. "Here we go."

The bubble shoots up the ramp and onto the drive. We pass through the jungle enfolding the estate and pause briefly at the gate. Then we're on the highway and heading around the bay to Paradise Alley.

If I'd been controlling, we would have shot off the cliff and bounced across the water—it's safer and more fun than it sounds. That way is faster but apparently not approved by SK'Corp security.

We arrive in town as the sun is dropping behind the ocean. A golden trail of light shimmers the length of the bay at the base of the cliffs.

Vanti stops us at one of the float tubes and flicks the return to base icon. "What time do we want to be picked up?"

"Give everyone a recall code slip, so we can leave when we want." I raise my eyebrows at Kara. "Some of us will want to go home earlier than others."

"Who're you looking at? I'm ready to party all night!" Kara yawns.

"I actually meant me, but you won't be far behind." My holo-ring vibrates as the code slip arrives. "Where to first?"

We take the float tube to the top of the cliff and hit the first bar on the list. From there, things go downhill—literally.

Thank you, sers and seras, I'll be here all night.

I lose track of how many bars we visit and how many drinks we sample. There are sweet Neptune Iced Teas, slushy Teresh-tinis, tangy Klimuk Kargaritas served with a side of oxygen, Grissom Ale, and another round of Teresh-tinis. Maybe three rounds. At some point, O'Neill offers to escort Kara to the bubble.

"Ha! I win!" I crow.

Kara pats her belly. "The only time, ever!"

O'Neill points at me but speaks to Vanti. "Keep an eye on her. On all of them."

Vanti heaves a sigh, then pulls something from her pocket and pops it into her mouth. "Sober as a judge, ser."

O'Neill nods and guides Kara out the door.

Leo and Elodie are huddled in a corner of the booth, arguing about an ingredient in the appetizer in those loud whispers drunks employ.

"I'm serious, the Feg-Fet-Fergeni Chives from Cernan are much superior in this dish." Leo stabs a finger at the plate. It hits the rim, flipping the plate into the air. The last two fried orgo skins go flying, sprinkling bacon and inferior local chives over his skinny jeans and T-shirt.

Elodie giggles. "You've got Fergeni Chives in your lap."

"No, these aren't Fergenis!"

Vanti leans closer to me. "Do you know that man?" Her face is blank, but her voice is low and intense, without a hint of inebriation.

Or maybe she just sounds sober in my fuzzy mind.

"What man?" I sit up and look around.

She yanks me back against the backrest. "At three o'clock."

I blink at her, then point straight ahead. "Twelve." My finger moves a tick to the left. "One."

She grabs my hand and pushes it into my lap. "You're counting the wrong direction. Three o'clock is that way." Holding her hand below the edge of the table, she points to the right.

I stare at her hand, then follow the line of her finger with my eyes.

A short, broad man sits on a barstool, staring at us. His thick hair is dyed orange, and a snake encircles his neck. I blink, and the snake stops moving.

I giggle. "He looks like a troll. And the tattoo looks like Loki's."

Vanti snaps her fingers and points at me. "Good catch. Why would Lewei be watching us?"

I shrug. "Mebbe Papa is afraid we'll take Cas out drinking? Hey, we shoulda brought Cas with us! Don't look now—the troll's coming over here."

"I should have taken two BuzzKills." Vanti slips another tablet into her mouth as she slides out of the booth. She drops the package onto the bench beside me as she rises to confront the approaching Leweian troll. "May I help you?"

The man is short, but he's as wide as three Vantis. I giggle again at the image of three Vanti clones attacking him with spinning kicks and flips. The real Vanti glares over her shoulder at me, then looks pointedly at the package on the seat.

I hate to kill a good buzz, but both Vantis look angry. And there are only two of her now. She might need my help. I pop a tablet out of the packaging, and it dissolves on my tongue.

The noise in the room increases dramatically as my brain clears. The two Vantis snap into a single tiny woman confronting an angry troll with a dragon tattoo. I twist sideways, so I can half-kneel on the booth seat behind her. Leo and Elodie stop arguing and look up.

"Your friend needs to come with me." The short man reaches out to push Vanti aside.

She stands firm as if she's rooted into the ground. "I don't think so."

The man looks at Vanti's ten-centimeter heels and at his hand. He pushes her aside, harder.

Vanti doesn't budge—not even a tremor. She shakes her head. "No."

My audio implant vibrates—incoming call from Vanti. "Get out. Climb under the table and go out the front door."

"What about Leo and Elodie?" I whisper.

"They aren't my responsibility. You are. Get out. I'm recalling Griz."

I slide the BuzzKill packet across the table. I have to tap it against Leo's hand before he takes his eyes off Vanti and the troll. His brows come down, and he stares at the package.

"Take one!" I hiss as I slide under the table.

It's disgusting under here. There are lumps of something on the underside of the table, and the floor sticks to my sandal soles when I duck-walk past Elodie's feet, trying to keep from touching the ground.

Leo's knees slide forward and knock into my head. I shuffle sideways as he slides under the table, too.

"What are you doing?" Elodie lays down on the bench to peer under the table. "Looks like fun!"

"Did you give her the BuzzKill?" I hiss.

"Give her what?" Leo asks.

I close my eyes and count to five. I don't have time for ten. I tap Elodie's leg. "*Larin*, let's go."

"This is stupid," Leo says. He surges to his feet, his rounded back slamming into the bottom of the table. With a loud shriek of tearing plastek, the top rips from the central pedestal and hinges over my head.

I duck back, my shoulders slamming into the edge of the seat. My right hand lands in a puddle with a sticky splash. Ew.

Leo roars and shoves past me. His pant leg catches on the jagged top of the pedestal, but it doesn't slow him at all. Fabric tears. Vanti leaps out of the way as Leo and the tabletop plow into the troll.

Elodie's eyes are the size of dinner plates. "Awesome!" She jumps to her feet, narrowly missing my fingers with her clunky platform shoes. She lurches, then turns to hold out a hand. "Come with me if you want to live!"

I take her hand and pull myself up. Except Elodie is still very drunk, and instead of levering me to my feet, she lurches forward. I yank my hand away and fling myself backwards, getting my shoulders and elbows onto the booth seat.

Elodie keeps coming, and her platform shoe smashes down on my toes.

"Gah!" I launch myself up, pushing Elodie upright as I go.

That yoga must have been much more effective than I realized.

I grab Elodie's shoulders and twist her around. Leo has the troll and two innocent patrons pinned between the bar and the tabletop. Vanti grabs my arm and shoves me toward the door. "Go!"

We stumble across the room, my toes throbbing with each step. Elodie stops suddenly, and I plow into her.

"Go!" I yell.

The people in the next booth look up. They stare at us with blank eyes, then lose interest.

"My purse!" Elodie cries.

"You didn't have a purse." I push her ahead of me.

We lurch between the tables, ping-ponging into buzzed patrons. "Sorry! My fault!"

A man stands, blocking our escape. He's huge—bigger than Loki—with a blond buzz-cut and the same neck tattoo. Someone screams.

It might have been me.

Elodie freezes and whimpers. I flick my holo-ring then swipe and fling a code slip away. "The next round's on me!"

Silence falls. Every head turns, every eye in the place focuses on me.

The bartender starts, then looks at his bar screen. "Payment confirmed. Open bar!"

With a roar, the entire room erupts. A deluge of thirsty patrons plows into the giant blocking our escape, carrying him toward the bar with the inexorable flow of a tsunami.

"Leo!" Vanti snaps.

I look over my shoulder. Leo is still pressing the troll against the bar with the table, as he's shouting an order at the bartender. At Vanti's harsh bark, his head snaps around. His eyes focus on her, then on the flood of people being pushed toward him.

He puts a foot on the broken stub sticking out of the bottom of the tabletop. His muscles bunch and he flies into the air. His other foot pushes off the top edge of the table, sending the tabletop spinning into the crowd.

With an impossible flip, Leo flings himself over the wave of shouting drunks and lands beside me. He shoves through the crowd, and the tiny Vanti sweeps us out the door.

SEVENTEEN

"WHERE'S GRIZ?" Vanti herds us up the street toward the closest float tube. "He should have been back by now."

"You said you recalled him," I gasp between breaths as we jog along. "What's that mean?"

"Ooh, look at that!" Elodie grabs Leo's arm and points at a store window.

"No! No looking. Keep moving!" I push Elodie away from the upscale kitchenware store.

She resists. "But they have brushed Koa soup ladles!"

"Koa ladles?" Leo stumbles to a stop. "Are they certified?"

"Those are just for show. No one who shops in Paradise Alley actually cooks." I push them away from the window.

Leo nods wisely. "She's right. Real chefs shop at Terrine's Tourines in Frobisher Cove."

"Chefs shop, chefs shop," Elodie chants.

"Where are we going?" I ask Vanti. "And what did that troll want with me?"

She shrugs. "I've recalled the bubble, so we're headed to the drop off."

"Unless you overrode the protocol, it'll drop Kara first, then come back for us. It could be a while. We might need to hide." I look over my shoulder. People stream past us, headed for the bar we just left. News of an open tab travels fast, even in ultra-wealthy Paradise Alley.

Or maybe especially here. Some of those people got wealthy by being ultra-cheap.

"Just get them into the float tube. The sooner we're off this street, the better." Vanti points across the street.

A narrow walkway leads to the float tube that stretches from the beach to the top of Paradise Alley. It angles up the steep hillside, with fragile-looking bridges to each level of shops.

I take Elodie's hand and push Leo ahead of us. "Time to go down. All the way to the bottom."

"What's down there?" Leo stops to peer over the side of the bridge at the lights below.

"Another bar. They have Ferengi Chives on the fried orgo skins." I push him along.

Elodie giggles. "That's Fergeni Chives. Chefs shop."

A shout echoes down the street.

"Move!" Vanti hisses through my audio implant.

I shove Elodie into the float tube and Leo after her. Vanti barrels across the bridge, slamming us both into the float tube as Leo's head disappears. We bounce off the back wall and drop.

"Get down!" Vanti grabs my arm and pulls me to a crouch. With both of us in the float tube at the same time, it's a tight fit. As we drop below floor level, I see someone pause at the end of the bridge.

"I think they spotted us."

Vanti is staring between her knees. "That idiot! Leo got out at the next level."

"Is Elodie still going down?"

She shakes her head. "We should just leave them—decoys."

"You wouldn't." I meet her eyes. She would. I point up. "It doesn't matter —we need to get out before they get in."

"They'll know where we got out—we wouldn't have time to get to the next level down."

I duck under the top of the opening as we drop and dive out before we reach ground level. My years of childhood martial arts training kick in, and I do a shoulder-roll as I hit the floor. Probably not as graceful as I might like, but I make it to my feet. I should probably start training again. Someday.

We hurry across the metal and transparent aluminum bridge, dodging between sightseers.

Above us, someone shouts.

"I think they spotted us!" Vanti grabs my arm and hustles me into the street.

She's shorter than I remember. "Where are your shoes?"

One swings from the end of her finger. "The other is wreaking havoc."

Whomp.

"Short range EMP. I just took out the float tube. They'll have to go around to the next one."

"Or down the stairs." I point up the hill at the steps snaking between the buildings.

"Or that." She breaks into a jog, her grip still tight around my wrist.

"Hey, I know you." Leo stops in the middle of the street when we hurry by. "Where ya' goin'?"

I grab at his arm but miss. "Come on. Elodie's getting away."

"What?" Leo sprints past us and tackles Elodie against a wall. "I got her!"

"Leggo me, you big thug!" Elodie punches Leo in the chest.

"Oof." He releases her and rubs his pec.

"Leave them." Vanti increases her speed.

"No." I pull away and grab Elodie's arm. "Come on!"

Elodie points at Vanti. "Good idea." In a flash, she's kicked off her shoes, leaving them laying in the road.

Behind us, a woman calls, "You forgot your shoes."

As we run, Vanti's head almost spins, identifying targets and potential havens. At least I think that's what she's doing. "We need to hide."

I point at a large store, bustling with customers. "Let's go inside."

"Around the corner, first." She darts into the cramped passage between two buildings.

High walls on either side loom over us. A single door stands in each blank wall. I rattle the handle on the first one. "Locked."

"We'll have to go up." Vanti points at the steep steps climbing from the end of the narrow alley. It's a long climb.

"No, I have a better idea." I flick my holo-ring and connect to the net. Using a pair of slightly—scratch that, highly—illegal apps, I unlock the closest door. "In here."

"How did you do that?" Elodie asks.

I push her into the darkness. "I'll show you later." I won't, of course. But she probably won't remember asking. I shove Leo after her, then follow them in.

Vanti brings up the rear. "Lock it."

I stare at her, the blue glow of my holo-ring lighting our faces. "I don't know how to do that."

"You just unlocked it—reverse that."

"That's not how it works. This app is for opening doors, not closing them." I swipe through the interfaces, shaking my head. "I got nothing."

"I got this." Elodie pushes past me, a broom in her hand. She shoves the broom through the door handle, then tucks the end behind the sturdy shelves beside the door.

Vanti nods. "That's pretty good. Let's find another exit."

Using our holo-rings for light, we weave through the crowded storage space. Row after row of shelves holds boxes whose labels are illegible in this light. I could scan them with one of my many apps, but I don't really care what's in them.

A door opens and light spills in, illuminating Vanti. "This way."

I pause on the threshold, staring at the lighted store. "Are you sure we want to go in there?"

"Mingle with the customers. Hide in plain sight." Vanti pushes me through.

I glance back. The door is marked "staff only" in discreet silver letters. We're standing in a short hallway leading to another kitchen store.

Leo peers over my shoulder. "I'm in nirvana!"

"Wait!" I thrust out an arm to stop him. "BuzzKill first, then shopping."

He makes a face but holds out a hand.

"Give him some BuzzKill, Vanti," I say.

"I gave you a whole packet. How much did they drink?" She slides her hand into her pocket and produces another flat package.

I pop two tablets into Leo' palm, then give a pair to Elodie. She wrinkles her nose but finally tosses them into her mouth.

"Are we being chased?" Elodie asks, her voice clear.

"Yes, and we need to hide." Vanti nudges her toward a display of knives. "Pretend you want to buy those but can't afford them."

Leo picks one up. His eyes widen, and he sets it carefully on the shelf. "No need to pretend. That is crazy over-priced." He holds out an elbow and Elodie puts her hand on it. They meander away through the well-dressed crowd.

"We'll go this way." Vanti's voice is coming through my audio implant again. "Exit the store in about five minutes. Cross the street and go into the next one, then take the stairs down to the lowest floor. We'll meet you there." She takes my arm and steers me away.

We browse through a selection of spice racks, then move on to defrosting trays. When we reach the front of the store, Vanti buys a pair of branded CooksCucina caps and crams one onto my head. We stroll across the street without a care in the world. No one stops us—none of the tattooed goons puts in an appearance.

The store across the street specializes in baking.

"Why are there so many kitchen stores here?" Vanti asks. "Nobody who can afford to shop here actually cooks, do they?"

I shrug. "Dame Buffett likes to bake, but she's not very good."

"Probably because she buys stuff like this." Vanti taps an electronic device that claims to steam dumplings. "Why would you need this? An AutoKich'n can do it faster and easier."

"So you can pretend to be a chef?" I nod toward the back corner of the store. "The stairs are over there."

EIGHTEEN

I HAND the CooksCucina caps to a couple of tourists standing near the top of the stairs. "They're having a sale. If you show them the cap, you get a discount."

The man says something in reply, but his Armstrong accent is almost impossible to understand. The smile and wink are easy to translate.

We hurry down two flights of steps into the restaurant supply level. It's dark here, and a chained gate blocks the wide opening.

"They're only open during the day." Leo rattles the gate. "Not that I would ever shop here. Their customer service is impossible."

"Can you open it, Triana?" Vanti's question comes out more like a command.

"I appreciate your confidence in my abilities, but I'm not sure." I pull a hair-thin wire from the purse belted around my waist and plug it into the lock mechanism. The other end attaches to my holo-ring. "This one isn't as high-tech as the last one, which means I have to physically connect." I work my way through the loops.

"Why are these guys after you?" Elodie asks. "Who are they?"

"We think they're Leweian." Vanti is busy on her own ring but answers the question. "I don't know why they're after her. I don't care at this point. My job is to get her back to the estate. Griz, where are you?" She looks up and nods.

She must have reached O'Neill. I keep working on the lock, and it finally pops.

"Everybody in." Vanti holds up a finger and swirls it around, then points into the dark store. We shuffle past her, and she locks the gate behind us. "I hope there's no alarm."

"I disabled it, of course. Where are we going to meet Ty?"

"It looks like there's a service exit over there." She pushes me to the right. "Far corner. It goes under the next two buildings and exits on Sprint Street."

I unlock another gate, and we jog up a huge sloping tunnel. Lights flare at the end, and Vanti slams me against the wall, her arm like a steel band across my stomach. After five breathless seconds, she relaxes. "That's Griz. Go."

Leo stumbles and falls to his knees. I slow, but Vanti pushes me past. He waves me on. "I'll catch up."

I reach the mouth of the tunnel, out of breath and sweating. The Sierra Hotel bubble sits patiently waiting. As we approach, the door opens, and Ty jumps out, a weapon in his hand. "Get inside!"

Vanti pushes me up the last few steps and into the bubble. Ty follows me in and dives into the control seat. Elodie and Vanti come in behind.

"Where's Leo?" Elodie asks.

"There he is!" a voice yells.

Vanti yanks the door shut. Through the clear bubble, we can see Leo limping out of the end of the tunnel. His eyes go wide. Two men rush past us and grab each of his arms.

"Why are they taking Leo?" Elodie asks.

"Go help him!" I shake Vanti's arm.

"No! Griz, get us out of here!"

"Stop!" I swing around and slap a hand on Ty's arm. "We have to help him!"

"Vanti, I've got this. Help him." Ty swipes a control, and the door opens.

I whip back around to watch, but Leo is nowhere to be seen. The two goons chasing him are also gone. "Where did they go?"

Vanti heaves a sigh and jumps out of the bubble. "I'll find him. You take the Runner home."

"I wish you wouldn't call me that," I mutter, but she's gone. The door folds shut, and the bubble moves down the street.

"I CAN'T BELIEVE you left him there alone! He's like family." I stand in the family room at Sierra Hotel, glaring at O'Neill. Elodie has gone to check on Kara. We haven't heard anything from Vanti.

"You are my primary responsibility!" Ty crosses his arms. "Your safety is the top priority. If you want to change that, you'll need to talk to your mother." He steps forward, his arms outstretched. "You know Vanti will find him."

I glare for a few more seconds to make sure he knows I'm mad, then close the distance and let him fold me into his arms. "I know. But it feels so wrong to leave him behind."

"Sometimes the mission requires difficult things." He strokes my back. "But we aren't leaving him out there. I already have someone looking into his background to find out who those men were."

"They were from Lewei. They all had the same tattoo." I draw a finger across my neck, then shiver.

"You're sure they're the same guys who were chasing you?"

I nod against his shoulder. "I recognized the troll. They weren't after me at all."

His holo-ring vibrates against my back. He releases me and swipes the interface, throwing Vanti's hologram onto the coffee table, so I can see and hear.

"They had grav belts." She's standing against a blank wall, probably in an alley. Her hair falls smoothly to her shoulders, and she looks like she just stepped out of a salon—cool, professional, unmussed.

I glance down at my wrinkled gold dress and scuffed sandals. I don't want to think about how my hair must look.

"They hustled him back into that service tunnel, knocked him out, and lifted him out—right over my head!" I've never heard Vanti sound so disgusted with herself. "I can't believe I let them do that."

"How would you have stopped them?" I ask. "You didn't wear a grav belt, did you?"

Her lips compress. "I should have."

"You weren't even on the clock tonight, Vanti," Ty says. "Limberghetti and al-Karendi were."

"They were?" I stare from one to the other. "I didn't see them at all."

"You weren't supposed to." Her smirk changes to a scowl. "They didn't do a very good job, though. They should have stopped those guys."

"I think the mayhem in the bar might have thrown a few wrenches into their plan." O'Neill drops onto the couch. "And the fact that your troll—" he raises an eyebrow at me "—had more help than you originally saw."

Vanti flashes her feral grin. "I've pulled the surveillance feed—there were at least six of them. We did a pretty good job of avoiding them. If we'd realized who they were after…" Her voice trails off.

"You would have abandoned Leo in the float tube!" I thrust an accusing finger right through holo-Vanti's chest.

"You're right, I would have. My job is to protect you, not the chef."

"You weren't even on duty tonight!" I can't think with her being all logical like that. I stomp into the kitchen and fire up the AutoKich'n. A cup of cocoa and some chocolate chip cookies are required, right now.

I pull a mug from the cupboard. A note is curled inside. "Homemade chocolate syrup and milk in the fridge. Much better than the AutoKich'n. Heat one minute. L."

My eyes sting, and I sniff as I pour the milk and syrup into the mug. I make two mugs, then relent and make a third. Vanti will be home soon, and while I hate that we abandoned Leo, she was doing her job. Plus, she stayed behind to help him. I wipe away a tear and carry the mugs into the family room.

Elodie returns as I'm handing a cup to O'Neill. I give her the extra and make one more.

"We need to go to the security center." O'Neill stands when I reappear. "Vanti will meet us there."

We troop down the hall and through the heavy door. O'Neill steps onto one of the red circles. The system lights up, and holograms of the three of us appear. "O'Neill, Tiberius. Identity confirmed. Guest recognized: Annabelle Morgan. Approved. Guest recognized: Elodie Ortega Okilo. Confirm approval."

O'Neill swipes an icon, and the red light above Elodie's hologram switches to green.

"Opening security program."

I step onto another circle. The forcefield wraps around me, and the system denies me access again.

"You need to fix this." I glare at O'Neill.

His lips twitch as he swipes a few more commands. My screens glow green. "Temporary access granted."

"Temporary?" I hold up a hand before he can change his mind. "We can discuss that later." I flick the security program and add a few lines to my profile that should prevent them from locking me out again. Then I bring up the west wall of the estate.

When Vanti arrives, I'm deep in the weeds. I've found the hole Cas exploited to visit us and reopened it. The first drone I attempt to send through is fried immediately. The second one, too.

"We need to go in person." Vanti perches on a stool next to Elodie, sipping her cocoa.

"We?" O'Neill raises an eyebrow. "I hope you mean you and I."

"Triana's pretty good in an undercover sit." She ducks behind her Keep-Warm mug.

O'Neill doesn't say anything, just stares her down.

Elodie raises her hand. "I can go undercover. They don't know me."

"They saw you with us tonight," I protest.

"Yeah, but they didn't get a DNA sample. And Kara can change my looks. I'll just go knock on the door and ask for Cas. What are they going to do?"

"First of all, you won't get anywhere near the door—these houses all have gates. Secondly, they'll want to know how you know Cas." I flick through another file, looking for weaknesses.

"I can ask for work. I'm a pretty good chef. I'll tell them I heard the premier is looking for someone to compete with the guy at Sierra Hotel." She grins. "You can make up a fake background for me, in case they check my credentials."

"That's not a bad idea," Vanti says. "But I'll do it. No way I'm putting civilians in the front lines."

"You just said Triana is good at undercover, and she's a civilian." Elodie pouts.

"That's adorable." Vanti points at Elodie's face. "But it won't work on me. I also said I wasn't taking her."

"You better hope they don't want a sample of your cooking." O'Neill gives a dramatic shiver. "No one will believe you're a chef."

"So, I'll do some other domestic thing." She turns to me. "What other jobs do the super rich give humans that should be done by bots?"

I bite my lip to hide a grin. "You can always be a housemaid."

O'Neill's system pings. "Got the report." He swipes a file, and it populates a screen on every station. A vid of Leo appears, without his dreadlocks and beard.

"He looks different," I say. "But familiar. Like I've seen him this way before."

Vanti snaps her fingers. "I knew I knew him!" She pokes the closest file and flicks her fingers to stretch the data. "Look."

A vid from an old news report pops up. It shows the fat old man we met on the beach and a teen who looks a lot like Cas but older. A crowd of security stand in a semi-circle behind them. The two bow to someone, then turn to enter a bubble. I flick the unmute button, and the voice-over starts. "—the premier of Lewei and his son. Personal details of the son—including his age and even his first name—have been kept completely under wraps by the Leweian government. He's estimated to be between fifteen and twenty-four years old."

As the voice goes on, the computer compares the face of the young man and the vid of Leo. "Certainty of match: ninety-seven percent."

"Holy saffron!" Elodie's face has gone white. "I was drinking shots with the heir of Lewei!"

"He also made us dinner," I remind her.

She leans over and puts her head between her knees. Vanti pats her shoulder.

"What about those goons who grabbed him?" I ask. "Are they—"

"*Spiitznatz.*" O'Neill swipes another file open, and pictures of men and women bearing the dragon tattoo appear.

"*Sprzężaj?* Poelish mafia?" I ask.

"No. The *Spiitznatz* are the Lewei secret police. They may have been related to the *Sprzężaj* a couple of centuries ago, but they're an official government organization now." Vanti flips through the files and swipes one to my screen. "A special unit that provides protection for the premier."

Pictures of the troll, Loki, and a tough-looking woman appear on my screen. "What's this?" I poke at a flashing red icon. The symbol grows and requests a password.

"This is where it gets interesting." O'Neill flicks a few commands, and the file opens. "These three *Spiitznatz* have been disavowed by the Leweian government."

"Let me get this straight." Elodie sits up. Her voice is strangled, and her eyes look haunted. "Your house manager—our friend—is the secret son of the premier of Lewei, and he's just been kidnapped by a trio of renegade security agents."

"That pretty much sums it up," Vanti says. "Now what do we do?"

NINETEEN

"WE HAVE TO RESCUE HIM." I jump out of my workstation. Or at least, I try to, but the wrap around force field keeps me firmly in place. I slap at the control screen and the pressure falls away.

"How do we do that? I didn't get a chance to put a tracker on him." Vanti turns to O'Neill. "Did you?"

"Why would I track the chef? That's an invasion of employee privacy. As I've said three hundred times tonight, his security wasn't our mission. If I'd known who he was—why didn't our employment team catch this?"

"We only got it today because of the *Spiitznatz* connection. Those tattoos are a stupid giveaway. Those three should have gotten them removed." Vanti rubs her neck as if she's trying to wipe one off.

"Maybe they're trying to prove their loyalty to the crown by bringing back the heir," Elodie suggests.

"That's possible, but technically there isn't a crown. Or an heir." Vanti smirks. "Lewei claims to be a democratic republic."

Elodie flicks her holo-ring and flips a vid to the screens. "According to the rest of the world, that's not true."

A vid pops up with a pair of *CelebVid* talking heads debating the succession in Lewei. "The crown prince is believed to be living in Lewei City, but the media has no images other than—" The same vid we saw earlier runs.

"Just because they call him that—" Vanti starts.

"It doesn't matter what they call him." I hold up both hands. "He's our friend, and he's been kidnapped by rogue agents. We need to get him back."

O'Neill exchanges a look with Vanti, then turns to me. "We'll look into it." He rotates his hand so his thumb points at him and Vanti, excluding me and Elodie. "You need to stay out of it. We can't find him if we're busy protecting you. For Leo's sake, let us do our jobs."

He's right—I know he is. But the idea of just sitting here while they look for Leo makes me want to scream. "I want to help."

"I know you do." O'Neill crosses the room and wraps his arms around me. "But this is our job. Vanti is an expert at this kind of investigation and extraction. Let her do it. We'll keep you in the loop, I promise." He runs a finger down the side of my face.

A delicious shiver runs through me. I kiss him.

"Get a room," Vanti says.

"I have a room." I pull away reluctantly. "Elodie, let's get out of the way and let them find Leo."

Elodie wrinkles her nose. "I'm not a security risk. Maybe I can work with you."

Vanti shakes her head without looking at us. Her hands fly through files and icons, sweeping and flicking. "This is a job for the pros. You two should go to bed. We'll be here all night. And tomorrow, I'm applying for a job at the Lewei compound."

O'Neill gives me one last kiss and returns to his workstation. I heave a sigh, then grab Elodie's arm and drag her from the room.

"We aren't going to bed, are we?" she asks hopefully as the thick door shuts behind us.

"Don't be silly." I lead the way to the family room and plop down in one of the couches. With a flick, I throw a file onto the coffee table projector.

"Isn't that classified or something?" Elodie asks as the picture of the three rogue agents appears.

"I guess, but as the Ice Dame's daughter and intern, I'm authorized to view any data. If I know it exists. That's how they 'keep me safe'—by hiding stuff from me."

"They seemed okay with showing you all this." She waves a hand through the holo.

"Only because they couldn't keep me out." I flick through the files. "Hey, this is weird." I poke my finger into the holo of Loki.

"I don't remember seeing him out there." Elodie flicks the woman's holo. "I didn't see her, either."

"I didn't either, but that's not what I'm talking about. These three agents have been disavowed by the Lewei government. But Loki was there. Protecting Cas." I point across the room in the direction of the Lewei estate. "Why would a disavowed agent be guarding the son of the premier?"

"We have to tell Vanti and Ty." Elodie launches out of her chair.

"They know." I pat the seat beside me. "Vanti was with me when we met Loki."

She drops to the couch. "Is Loki with those other two rogue agents?"

"Brunhilda and the Troll?"

She laughs. "Those are good nicknames."

"Actually," I stretch the holo larger, "Her name really is Brunhilda."

"That says 'Fitri Brunhill.'"

"Brunhilda is funnier." I flick through the three rogue agents' files. "She's fifty-four and a weapons expert. The Troll, aka Enrique Mos, is also a weapons guy. Not as many awards as Brunhilda. Loki's expertise is in hand-to-hand combat and childcare."

She chuckles. "Great combination. I guess that's why he's watching Cas."

"Don't call Cas a child," I warn. "I wish I had a way to contact him."

"Did you say he gave you a contact number?" She covers a yawn with her hand.

"It was the number to the local frozen yogurt shop. They deliver, by the way."

"Why'd he do that?" She yawns again.

"I asked for a number, and he didn't want to say no?" A yawn catches me by surprise. My eyes water. "If we can't go knock on the door and ask for him, maybe we just hang out in the pool tomorrow, and he'll show up? I reopened his secret escape route."

"Do they know that?" She jerks a thumb toward the security center.

I shrug. "If they're any good at their job, they should notice it, but I think I've got it protected, so they can't shut it down. I made it smaller so Loki for sure can't get through."

"If Loki is one of the bad guys, and he's over there," she points toward the Lewei estate, "does that mean Leo might be over there, too? And these other two rogue agents as well?"

"I don't know. But I'd like to find out."

TWENTY

I JERK AWAKE. Bright sunlight streams into the room, and I squinch my eyes shut. A moan nearby pops them open again. Elodie and I are sprawled on the couches in the family room.

Kara stands by the window, flicking her holo-ring. The windows darken. "Sorry, I didn't mean to make it quite so bright. How late did you two stay out?"

I sit up and rub the crust out of my eyes. A smear of mascara stripes my hand. "We weren't out much later than you, but there was…"

"Don't tell me. You met a celebrity and I missed it!" Kara pushes her mother's feet aside and drops onto the sofa.

Elodie rubs her eyes and sits up. She looks like I feel: disheveled, tired, and hungry. "Did you make breakfast?"

"I thought Leo would have something, but I guess he stayed out too late, too." Kara points to the low table in front of the couch. "I whipped up some of his protein shakes."

Three glasses sit on the table, each a different color. They look less revolting than the blue goo Leo drank yesterday morning—was it only yesterday? So much has happened.

"He didn't make it home." I lean forward and take the pink smoothie. A wave of strawberries and cream overwhelms me. "Wow, that is strong."

"It was on the AutoKich'n menu. Probably something Leo drinks, so it must be pretty good." Kara picks up a brown concoction. "This one is mocha. Did he hook up with someone?"

"No." I look around the room, but of course no one is there. "He was kidnapped by rogue *Spiitznatz* agents. We think he's the crown prince of Lewei."

Elodie groans and flails around blindly. Kara grabs her hand and wraps her fingers around the mocha smoothie. "Drink up, Mama. This one has energy enhancers and age rejuvenators. All natural, of course."

"Black coffee would be better." She sips the drink and her eyes pop open. "Maybe not. Although why you think I need age rejuvenators, I don't know."

"Because you're old." Kara ducks away from the hand Elodie swipes at her.

"I'm still young enough to kick your butt, and don't you forget it."

"You wouldn't hurt a pregnant woman!" Kara rubs a hand across her bulging belly. "Your own grandchild!"

"I'm not old enough to be a grandma." Elodie closes her eyes again.

"We are not going to pretend to be sisters. That is so lame."

"Would you two stop?" I put a hand to my head. "BuzzKill might prevent hangovers, but you two are giving me a headache."

They both giggle, sounding like sisters.

"Explain this whole crown prince thing." Kara picks up the green drink and sips.

We tell her about the adventures of the previous night and the intel we uncovered. "Vanti and O'Neill are supposed to be finding him. I wonder if they're still at work in there." I push up from the couch.

"You might want to grab a shower before you check." Kara draws a circle around her face with one finger.

I glance at the mascara smudge on my hand. "He's seen me look worse."

"Go clean up," Elodie says. "Looking like that isn't going to rescue Leo any faster. Besides, I thought our plan was to wait by the pool for Cas to show up? Get your swim gear on."

"Fair enough." I flick my holo-ring and check the house security system. "It looks like Vanti and Ty left an hour ago. He left a message." I listen to it.

"What are you grinning about?" Kara asks.

"Nothing. Just Ty said—never mind. I was right—they're looking into a lead." I finish the smoothie and take the glass to the kitchen. "I'm going to get a shower, then I'm headed out to the wall. I want to see if I can catch Cas's attention. You two coming?"

"I'll wait for Cas by the pool." Kara heaves herself up. "I didn't drop forty credits on a maternity swimsuit for nothing. And I wanna have a nice glow when Erco gets here."

"I'll meet you back here," Elodie says with a conspiratorial wink. "In ten."

———————

TWENTY MINUTES LATER, I return to the family room. My hair is clean but unruly, my face is washed, and my shorts and T-shirt cover my bathing suit.

Something bangs in the kitchen.

"Leo? Are you back?" I poke my head through the door.

Elodie makes a face at me. "Sorry. I didn't think you'd mind if I—" She waves a hand around. Two plates with poached eggs and muffins sit on the counter.

My stomach growls.

Elodie bites her lip, but the corners twitch. "That smoothie woke me up, but I need real food in the morning."

I pick up the plates and take them to the breakfast bar. "It's barely morning anymore."

We eat quickly and put our dishes into the AutoKich'n for cleaning. Elodie grabs a belt from the counter and snaps it around her waist. She loads it with a water bottle, some protein bars in the pouch, and a flashlight.

"You come prepared." I lead the way down the stairs to the indoor pool. "Where's Kara?"

"She's outside already. Ever since she got pregnant, she's become a morning person. It's so weird."

I give an exaggerated shudder as I check the controls for the solar shield. Kara has dialed it down to minimum. I crank it up a few notches, so she won't burn, and we head out onto the deck.

Kara sits in an automated lounge chair under the shade of a huge umbrella. That explains why she turned the solar shield down. The umbrella cuts a lot of the UV rays. The table holds several beverages, lotions, and a selection of reading materials. She's leaning back in the chair, eyes closed.

"You wanna come with us?" I stop by her chair.

"To the corner of the yard? No, I'm good. Holler if anything interesting happens."

"It's sad that your pregnancy has made you such a stick in the mud." I pat her head.

Her eyes open to glare at me.

"She was a stick in the mud before she got prego," Elodie says.

"Nice." Kara's eyes close. "I'm practical. You aren't going to find Leo over by the wall. Ty and Vanti will find him. Me sunbathing doesn't make any difference."

"Maybe," I mutter to Elodie as we tramp across the grass. The sun has already dried out the dew. I suck in a deep breath of sea air. A rank stench catches in my throat, and I choke.

"What is that?" Elodie makes a gagging noise.

"I don't know. We smelled it the first day we got here, but then Hy-Mi spoke to someone—or at least I think he did." I snap my fingers. "We need to find out who Hy-Mi talked to—that could be our in."

"To the estate next door?" Elodie grimaces. "We need a better name for it. A codename." Her eyes sparkle. "Let's call it Leoland."

"That's terrible."

She shrugs. "I know. How about—what's the capital city on Lewei?"

"I think it's called Zijincheng."

"Let's call the estate Zijin. Short and easy." She weaves through the trees, angling toward the southwestern corner of the property. "We need to find out Hy-Mi's contact in Zijin. Where is he, anyway? I was hoping to meet the legendary Hy-Mi."

"He's visiting his own family. He'll be back this afternoon. We have another meeting with the nuptial architect tomorrow." I curl my lip. That woman really rubs me the wrong way. Maybe I'll be too busy searching for Leo to attend said meeting.

"I heard Lilia is doing your wedding!" Elodie gushes. "She's the wedding planner to the stars."

"Nuptial architect," I correct. "She's...opinionated. And since she's the expert, her opinion counts for more than anyone else's. Including the bride's."

We reach the corner. I forgot to bring hoverboards this time, but now that I know the force shield will hold us, it's not a problem. I put a hand against the wall and one foot on top of the low invisible barrier at the top of the cliff.

"What are you doing?" The words burst from Elodie as she grabs my arm.

"It's perfectly safe. This is how Cas gets over here, and Vanti and I tried it." I explain about the force shield, then step up onto the invisible safety wall. "See? And I can step down..." I look at the sand a hundred meters below. Vertigo washes through me, and my fingers clench against the stone wall.

I grab Elodie's shoulder and hold on tight, closing my eyes and taking a couple of deep breaths. "Okay, new plan." I crouch then sit on the invisible wall. My legs dangle over the side. Stretching my right foot, I feel for the solid surface I ran on last time. "Pour some water down there. Vanti spilled some to make sure the shield was active."

Elodie leans over and dribbles some water. The drops splash and coalesce in the air. "Ooh, cool."

I stretch a bit farther, and my toe touches the unseen platform. Sliding forward, I put my weight on the invisible platform while keeping a grip on the equally invisible wall and wishing I had a hoverboard. "It looks like it's holding."

Elodie scrambles onto the wall and flips onto her stomach. She bounces her feet against the force shield. "This is amazing!" She lets go and walks parallel to the cliff, toward the wall.

"Watch your head! The hole is built for a twelve-year-old-boy."

She puts one hand on her hips and flashes a pout over her shoulder. "I may be forty-eight, but I still have the figure of a teenage girl."

"But Cas is short. You might want to duck."

She raises her left arm to face level, the right hand trailing along the end of the stone wall. Her fingers hit something, and she ducks. "I see what you mean." She steps around the barrier.

"Where are you going?" I slide gingerly off the wall and onto the invisible walkway. "That's a foreign government over there. They aren't known for human rights. If you get caught—"

"I'm just looking." Her voice carries easily to me. Which means it probably carries easily to anyone on the other side.

"Shh! Come back here. Their system fried my drones. How am I going to explain to Kara that my neighbors fried her mother's brain?"

"There's no brain frying going—aaarg!"

I lunge around the wall, ignoring the drop beneath my feet. "Elodie—"

She's sitting on the grass, laughing. "You should see your face."

"You should see the goon coming across the grass with a nerve disrupter! Move!" I grab her arm and pull.

Elodie looks over her shoulder, then does a double take. "Crap!"

TWENTY-ONE

LOKI BARRELS TOWARD US. "STOP!" He moves fast for his size and plows into Elodie as she scrambles to her feet.

She launches at me, her hunched over body hitting me square in the chest. "Oof!" I topple backward, seeing my life flash before my eyes as I fall away from the cliff edge.

That's a lie, I don't see my life flash before my eyes. I see Ty with tears in his eyes and Vanti standing behind him shaking her finger at me. And the Ice Dame rolling her eyes, as if she's always known I would end this way.

Then I hit the force shield, slamming the air out of my chest. Elodie lands on top of me like a load of bricks. "Can't breathe," I gasp.

Elodie rolls off me and stares down at the beach a hundred meters below. "At least we aren't plummeting to our doom."

"No thanks to you."

Loki reaches down and grabs my ankle. With one hand he hoists me onto the grass. I land hard, knocking from my lungs the little air I'd managed to suck in. I gaze at the sky, gasping.

Seconds later, Elodie lands beside me. She jumps to her feet and dusts off her rear end. "That is not a polite way to greet visitors."

"Visitors come in through the front gate." Loki points over his shoulder.

She puts her hands on her hips. "We were pretty sure you wouldn't let us in. I'm Elodie. And you are?"

I bite back a grin. She sounds just like the Ice Dame—obviously disappointed in his manners without saying so. It must be a mom-power.

"I'm Loki. My job is to keep people like you out."

Elodie draws herself up to her full height—which isn't particularly impressive against Loki's mass. "Are you implying we're riff-raff? Part of the hoi-polloi? Members of the great unwashed? Do you know who this is?" She points at me.

I hold up both hands. "I don't like to advertise. But yeah, he knows who I am. We've met before." I struggle to my feet and hold out my fist. "Nice to see you, Loki."

Loki ignores my hand, staring at us as if we're insane. Maybe we are.

"We're here to visit Cas." Elodie starts up the lawn as if this were a normal visit to a neighbor.

Loki blocks her with his weapon. "That's not possible at this time."

"Why not? He came to visit us. Twice." She points at the wall. "We're simply providing the opportunity for him to return the hospitality."

"He's not here." Loki looks over his shoulder. "You need to go back before someone sees you. The others won't be as accommodating as I am."

"You call this accommodating?" Elodie waves an arm. "You make us stand out here in the yard instead of inviting us to the house?"

"Elodie, he means his coworkers won't let us leave. We should go." I yank at her arm. "Now."

She shakes me off. "We're here. Let's find out what's going on. Why did your friends take our friend?"

"What are you talking about?" Loki rubs his forehead as if a headache is forming. "What friend?"

"Our friend Leo was kidnapped by a bunch of goons wearing one of those." She stabs a finger at Loki's neck.

His hand goes to the tattoo. "Your friend—you mean Ervin?"

"It's true, then? That our chef Leo is the Lewei heir?" I ask.

Loki's face pales. "I don't know what you're talking about."

"Where's Cas?" I advance on Loki. "Last time we spoke, you were moaning about how lonely he is. If he's so lonely, where is he?"

Loki looks around, whether searching for backup or hoping we remain unnoticed, I don't know. He jerks his head at the wall, urging us closer to the tall, stone structure. "They have him," he whispers.

"Who?" I whisper back.

"The *Spiitznatz*. They'll take him back to Lewei if we don't trade for him." His head whips back and forth between us and the property behind him.

"But you're *Spiitznatz*," Elodie protests.

"Not anymore," I say. "Remember?"

"You know this?" Loki focuses on me, his eyes burning. "Will you help us?"

"I don't have a clue what's going on," I say, taking a step backward. Maybe we can duck around the wall and escape. Elodie gives a tiny nod and shuffles a half-step back.

"Don't move." Loki brings the weapon around to point at us for the first time. "We need help, and you can provide it. Up to the house, now." He jerks the gun again.

Elodie straightens her shoulders and lifts her chin. "About time." She sniffs and strolls past him.

I give Loki a wary look and follow her through the well-maintained copse of trees. She stops several times along the way to look at a plant or point out a view, as if she's trying to prove who's in charge of this little walk.

Behind us, Loki grinds his teeth but doesn't speak.

We step out of the trees. The house looks nothing like the blocky Sierra Hotel—it's a mishmash of steep roofs, low towers, and narrow windows, all decorated with carved wood and brass spires. A formal garden with low hedges, gravel walkways, and flower beds stretches between the house and the cliff. A small gazebo stands in the middle of the garden.

Elodie stops. "This is—wow. So many different parts."

"It's certainly impressive," I agree.

"This house has been the vacation home of the premier of Lewei for two centuries. It has been increased in size many times. Each owner adds his own personal touch." The pride in Loki's voice is obvious. "It is much more welcoming than your home."

"You've seen my home?" I ask.

"A monstrosity. Bare walls and blank windows, staring out into the void." He nudges my shoulder. "Go."

I kind of agree with him about the architecture of Sierra Hotel, but I'm not sure the answer is decorative curlicues and five different colors of paint.

As we approach, a door opens on the covered porch, and two people step out. They each carry a blaster at the ready and are built like—well, like Sierra Hotel. Big and blocky, with blank faces. They don't make eye contact or even acknowledge our existence as Loki urges us up the steps.

We step into a small room. Two more guards stand by the door. Loki points to a bench by the door and a shelf holding a variety of slip-on shoes. "Shoes, off."

"Do you have any with flowers?" Elodie slips off her sandals and points to her shorts. "Something that might coordinate with my outfit."

Loki's jaw tightens, and he looks away.

Elodie winks at me. "Got him on the defensive," she whispers.

"I'm not sure teasing him is a good plan. He has a gun." I pick up a pair of plain clogs that appear to be carved out of wood. "How about these?"

"Those are too big for me." She puts her sandals under the bench, taking a moment to line the heels up against the edge of the rug. Last night, she kicked her shoes off and left them in the middle of the road, so I'm sure she's trying to goad Loki.

While she peruses the shoe offering, I slip on the clogs. They're light weight and comfortable. Elodie finally settles on a pair of fuzzy pink slippers.

The guards open both doors, and we step into a wide, arched passage. "Stop." Loki flicks through some screens on his holo-ring, then nods at a door on the right which pops open. "Continue."

We enter a dark room full of heavy furniture. Dim lamps in a variety of styles glow around the perimeter and on the tables. Two staircases and three open doorways lead out of the room. The spaces beyond are even darker. Layers of small, colorful rugs cushion our feet.

"If I'd known about the carpets, I'd have opted for barefoot," Elodie says.

"Not permitted. Very disrespectful." Loki pushes us toward a grouping of wooden chairs with detailed carving on the backs and arms. They stand around a matching table. The fireplace is empty, and the windows are heavily draped. "Sit."

"And forcing us into your house at gunpoint isn't disrespectful?" Elodie walks around the table, inspecting each place before choosing a chair on the far side.

"Not my house. The premier's house." He stays by the entrance but watches the left stairway. A light flickers on, illuminating purple and orange flowers on the wallpaper. "He comes. Stand."

Elodie and I exchange a glance. "The premier?" Elodie mouths at me. I shrug and stand. She follows my lead.

The man I met on the beach stomps down the steps. The smell of sandalwood and fish fills the room, making my eyes water.

"Where is my son?" He stomps to the table and leans on the back of a chair. "Where have you taken him?'

"That's what we came here to ask," I say. "Your disavowed *Spiitznatz* grabbed him when we were out last night."

The man stares at us. "What was he doing out with you? He's a child!"

"I think we're talking about two different people," Elodie says. "We're talking about Leo. Is Cas missing, too?"

TWENTY-TWO

THE PREMIER'S already pale face goes ashen, and he sways. Loki leaps forward to grasp his elbow, but the older man shakes him off. He pulls out the chair and drops into it, covering his face with his hands.

"What happened?" I ask softly.

He lifts his head with visible effort. His eyes glisten in the light from the overhead lamp. "Cas disappeared. Yesterday. I went out to—deal with some business. I left him here with adequate security. He disappeared from the surveillance cams, so we thought he'd gone to see you again. But my team is unable to penetrate your property. So far. And now this." He pulls a piece of paper from his pocket and tosses it on the table.

"Wow, old school." Elodie takes the note and unfolds it. "We have the boy. You know what we want. Instructions will be forthcoming." She holds it out to me.

I shake my head and put my hands on the edge of the table. "Have you scanned it for DNA?"

"Do you think this is my first ransom note? Yes, we scanned."

I hold up both hands. "Sorry. I didn't know this was a common occurrence where you come from."

"It isn't!" His voice thunders, then cuts off abruptly. He puts his hand over his face again and breathes deeply. After a moment, he looks up. "My team is not as fully conversant with Kakuvian operations as I would like. I require help, so I must—I was deposed, three weeks ago. The boy and I barely escaped with our lives."

"Looks like you're doing okay to me." Elodie gestures to the room. "This is all yours, right?"

"This paltry estate belongs to the office of the premier. We are only safe here because the government of Kaku has granted us sanctuary. Should Lewei send a delegation to claim the property, we would be—how do you say it—out on our ears."

"I would never say it that way," Elodie replies. "But I know what you mean. And now they've taken Cas…"

"Yes, my boy is missing." His eyes glisten again. "The only thing I have left in this galaxy."

"You have us, *lingdao*," Loki says.

The premier waves as if this is nothing. "And now someone else is missing? Why do you think this is related to Cas?"

I stare at him. "Because it was your goons who grabbed him! *Spiitznatz.* Disavowed, according to our information."

The premier looks at Loki. "What do you know about this?"

Loki freezes. His eyes flick to me, then back to the premier. "Their friend is in our custody."

"Why? Do we not have enough trouble? Kidnapping is not approved by the Kakuvian government." He raises his eyebrows at me.

I shake my head.

He points at me. "See—not allowed here. This government has given us sanctuary—we must appear to stay in their good graces. Why did you take this man from his friends?"

A sickly grin crosses Loki's face. "We heard he makes a good *Merican Breakfast,* and we knew you wanted to try it."

Even I don't buy that one. Although if there was ever a meal to kidnap someone over, it would be Leo's *Merican Breakfast.*

"Loki, this is serious business. What were you thinking?"

"We believe we will be able to trade this man for Master Caspian."

The premier slaps the table. "The Kakuvians also do not approve of hostage trading." Another glance at me.

I lift my hand and rock it back and forth. "They don't mind if they initiate it. They definitely frown on foreign powers doing it without their input."

"We are no longer a foreign power, but I take your point. Who is this man that the *Spiitznatz* would be willing to trade Cas for him?"

Loki mutters something under his breath.

I fight down the urge to tell the premier what I know. Our information could be wrong. Or it might be to our advantage to keep that information secret.

"He's your other son," Elodie blurts out.

Silence.

The premier's head turns slowly, and his eyes lock on Elodie. "What did you say?"

The sense of power that radiates from him reminds me this man used to be the leader of the most repressive society in the galaxy.

Elodie's eyes widen, and her warm skin goes gray. It's not a good look.

I sigh. "We believe Leo is your older son, Ervin. Our facial recognition software puts the match at ninety-seven percent." He turns his pale eyes on me, and my stomach drops. "It could be a mod. There was a whole thing on Sally Ride a few years ago. People modding themselves to look like celebrities…"

"She is correct, *lingdao*." Loki pulls his blaster off his shoulder and offers it to the premier with a low bow. "We have Master Ervin."

No one moves for a long time.

Loki's biceps start to shake from holding the gun at arm's length.

The premier pushes the weapon away. "Where is he?"

"In the—" Loki breaks off with a meaningful glance at Elodie and me. "He's downstairs."

"You think we don't know downstairs is code for the dungeon?" Elodie asks in a stage whisper.

"*Larin!*" I hiss.

"What? He's obviously not in the guest suite." She glares at Loki. "Is he?"

The big man ignores her, his eyes pinned to the premier.

"Bring him to me."

"But what about them?" Loki jerks his thumb at us.

"They are not a danger to my family," the premier declares. "Their protectors could be, but these two women are nothing to worry about."

"Hey!" Elodie surges to her feet. "I'll give you something to worry about!"

"Elodie!" I grab her arm and yank her back into her chair. "Shut up!"

She subsides. "I hate it when men discount me just because I'm a woman. I could totally be a threat if I wanted to."

"It's a good thing we don't want to, then, isn't it?" I smile at the premier.

"I know better than to mess with an angry woman," he says with a condescending smile.

"Okay, now you've got me mad, too." I cross my arms. "Lucky for you, we're on Leo's side." I turn to Loki. "You heard the man. Go get him."

Loki bows again, muttering to himself. Or maybe he's talking on his audio implant. As he heads down the closest stairway, the outer door opens again, and one of the guards from the shoe room enters.

The premier shakes his head. The woman with the gun disappears.

"Soooo, what should we call you?" Elodie asks after a few moments of silence. "If you aren't really the premier anymore, should we still—it's kind of an awkward mouthful anyway."

"You may call me Mister Zhang," he says with a regal nod.

"Zhang? That's the most common name in the galaxy." Elodie crosses her arms.

"He's trying to stay incognito," I say. "The Ice Dame has traveled as Sera Zhang on occasion." I turn back to the premier. "That would be *Ser* Zhang here, not *mister*."

He nods. "Thank you. It's the little things that catch you."

More silence.

Ser Zhang lifts a hand, and the door opens again. The guard steps into the room and bows to Zhang.

The old guy holds up three fingers. "Would you like some tea?"

"I—no, thank you, we're good. Right, *Larin*?"

"Absolutely fine, thanks."

Zhang's hand drops, and the guard retreats. The door remains ajar.

"Nice weather we're having," Elodie says.

We both stare at her. Her eyes drop to the table.

Loki returns and whispers in Zhang's ear. He nods curtly, and Loki leaves again.

Why didn't they have that conversation via audio implant? Do Leweians not have them? Loki definitely has one. Maybe high-ranking Leweians don't use them—some archaic form of respect?

Zhang stands. "Come." He makes his way to a shadowed corner and pulls aside a curtain revealing a plain door.

Elodie and I exchange a look, and I gesture for her to go first. Behind us, the outer door clicks shut. Highly trained *Spiitznatz* don't accidentally leave doors open—that guard was eavesdropping.

Maybe that's why Loki didn't use the implant—perhaps forces loyal to the Lewei government have their hooks into the premier's system. Or maybe Zhang just thinks they do.

I follow the others into a well-lit room. There are no windows and only one other door, which is shut. A half dozen plain chairs sit against the walls, with a larger, throne-like one against the far wall. The floor is a soft, bouncy material. The walls are painted a drab beige.

The door shuts behind me with a muffled whomp. This room is sound-proofed and probably lined with ferian-laced paper to stop transmissions. I flick my holo-ring, and it lights but displays a "cannot connect" icon. Zark.

"Why all the secrecy?" I gesture at the walls to let Zhang know I'm on to him.

"There are members of my staff who may not be trustworthy." He sits in the plush chair. "Please, have a seat."

"Why don't you just fire them?" Elodie pulls a chair up next to Zhang and settles in as if she's ready for a cozy chat.

"Keep your enemies close." He says it like a quotation.

I perch on the edge of the chair nearest the door. While Elodie chats with the ex-premier, I flick my holo-ring and try a couple of different apps. I scan the door—it has no electronics. In fact, there are none inside this room, except mine and Elodie's holo-rings and our audio implants. Zhang doesn't appear to have either.

The second door opens, and Loki steps in. His eyes flick around the room, taking in the three of us. Then he moves aside and makes a beckoning gesture through the door.

Another guard pushes a bald man into the room. He bears a striking resemblance to Cas. It takes me a moment to recognize Leo.

Zhang lurches out of his chair. "Ervin!"

TWENTY-THREE

LEO STRAIGHTENS his spine and looks down at his father. He doesn't say anything.

"Leo! Are you okay? What did they do to your dreadlocks? And your beard?" Elodie pushes past Zhang and grab's Leo's arm.

Loki's eyes blaze, but Zhang holds up a hand, stopping his lunge before it begins. The guard snaps against the wall, his face a mask except the watchful eyes.

"Elodie! Triana! What—did they grab you, too?" Leo grips Elodie's hand.

"No, we came to—" She breaks off and looks at me. "Well, we wanted to find you, but I can't believe we did."

"Vanti and O'Neill are looking, too." I let my eyes drift to Loki as I speak. "It won't take long to trace you here."

"We need to move him," Loki says, still standing at attention by the door. "Lady Morgan's goons will find us and take him away."

"Hey, I don't call you a goon," I say. "Not to your face, at least. And my security team doesn't make plans to trade me to the enemy." Although they might have been tempted to once or twice.

"Ah, it's becoming clearer," Leo says in a conversational tone. He fixes a glare on Zhang. "What do you hope to trade me for, *Dad?*" The last word comes out like an insult.

Zhang holds up a hand. "I have no intention of trading you for anything.

I did not know you were here until five minutes ago." He points at the guard. "Speak. What is your plan?"

"We thought we could trade Master Ervin for Master Caspian." The words come out almost too low to hear.

"The *Spiitznatz* have abducted my son, and your plan is to trade my other son to get him back?" Zhang advances on Loki, his voice low, almost friendly. As if they're talking about trading collectibles.

"It was the only thing we could think of, *lingdao*. We didn't think you would mind—you haven't seen Master Ervin in years…" Loki trails off, as if he's just realized this was a bad plan.

Zhang closes his eyes.

"Who's we?" I ask when the silence stretches on too long. "You said 'we didn't think.' Who else is in on this plan?"

Loki appears to shrink into himself as we stare at him.

"Mos and Brunhill," he finally says. "The three of us have served the premier our entire lives. We're loyal to him. And Master Caspian. We would do anything for him."

"There was a time you would have done anything for me," Leo says sadly.

"That was before you left and broke your father's heart."

"Loki!" Zhang says sharply.

"Look, I'm sure you all could use some time to reconnect—and if you need a good family therapist, I can recommend someone." Elodie flicks her holo-ring, then gives up when she sees the "no service" icon. "But right now, we need to help Cas, right?"

All three men glare at her. I bite my lip to keep from smirking. "Elodie is right. We need to rescue Cas. Who has him?"

"Yeah, *Dad*, who has Cas? And why?" Leo throws himself into the throne.

Anger, followed by hurt and confusion, flash over Zhang's face before he wipes his expression. He sits in Elodie's vacant chair. "You must realize by now that there has been a coup on Lewei."

Leo opens his mouth, pauses, and closes it again with a single nod.

"The generals were restless," Zhang says. "Our relations with Gagarin have become strained. Pertaoh rallied the others behind him and attacked. Loki, Mos, and Brunhill remained loyal, and we escaped off-world. The Kakuvian government has agreed to let us stay in this house until the—" He stops and takes a deep breath. "Until the new premier sends a delegation. I am using the time to consolidate my personal funds, so I can finance a new base of operations to launch my return to power." His eyes dart to me. "Don't tell anyone that last part."

I roll mine. "I'm guessing the Kakuvian government can figure that out on their own."

"What about Cas? Where is he?" Leo asks when Zhang doesn't continue.

"The *Spiitznatz* have taken him. I don't know if they really want to ransom him or if they plan to use him as a pawn. Pertaoh is not popular in Lewei. He may think Caspian will give him legitimacy and support."

"You're planning on going back to Lewei?" Elodie asks, her voice incredulous. "Why? Kaku is amazing."

"In Lewei, I am—was the premier. Here, I am no one."

"Being no one has its perks," Leo says. Zhang's chin goes up, but Leo holds up a hand. "We have more important things to discuss. How do we get Cas back?"

"Why do you care?" Zhang demands. "You don't even know the boy! You walked out of his life when he was a baby!"

"He's still my brother," Leo says. "And I surfed with him the other day. He's a cool kid. Besides, I wouldn't leave my worst enemy in *Spiitznatz* hands." He glares over his shoulder at Loki and runs a hand over his bald head. "Do you have any idea where they took him?"

Loki looks at his feet. Zhang shakes his head sadly.

"Maybe we can help." The words pop out of my mouth without checking with my brain. Assisting a deposed dictator is not something I want to do, but Cas is my friend, and I agree with Leo's assessment of the *Spiitznatz*. I hope they don't shave Cas's strawberry blond curls.

Zhang's head pops up, and his eyes lock on me, compelling and pleading at the same time. "Will you?"

I shrug. "I might be able to—let me talk to my security team. I don't want anything to happen to Cas."

"Yes," Zhang says. "Go speak to your team. Leo and Elodie will stay with me."

I jump up from my chair. "Is that a threat? Because if it is, I don't respond well to threats. If you want my help, Leo and Elodie will come with me."

"Or what?" A smirk twitches at the corners of Loki's mouth. "You are completely at our mercy. You have no communications from inside this room. We can move you to the 'basement' and no one will know."

"Oh, please. Do you think this is my first infiltration of a foreign power?" I copy Zhang's bravado from earlier. He doesn't need to know it's only my second, and the first was two days ago with Vanti. "I'm not dumb enough to come over here without a failsafe. If I'm not back at Sierra Hotel by lunch, my security team will launch a full assault on your estate backed by the might of the Kakuvian government. They owe us one for a little terrorism bust last year in Pacifica City. You might have heard of it?" The Kakuvian government was less than enthusiastic about our participation in that bust, but he doesn't need to know that, either.

Zhang holds up both hands. "Please, that was a joke. Loki was trying to… lighten the mood. We value your assistance and trust you have Caspian's welfare at heart. You may return home, of course." He nods at Loki.

The guard bows and opens the door. I gesture for Elodie and Leo to exit ahead of me.

"Not him." Loki puts his hand out, stopping Leo.

"Yes, him," I say. "He's part of my household. He's made it very clear he prefers Sierra Hotel, and after you so kindly put him up *in the basement*, I can see why."

Zhang clears his throat. "I would prefer to have Ervin stay here—it has been many years since we spoke, and we have much to discuss. However, I respect your wishes, Sera Morgan. We need your help, and the goodwill of the Kakuvian government."

"How noble of you, Father," Leo says. "I think I'll stick with Triana for now. Perhaps when we get Cas back, we can have a family pizza night."

Zhang's brows draw down. "What is family pizza night?"

TWENTY-FOUR

"That went better than I expected," I say as I climb over the low force shield and collapse on the Sierra Hotel grass. I roll onto my back and close my eyes, letting the sun warm me. "Next time you want to wander into foreign territory, you're going alone, *Larin*."

She laughs, but it sounds brittle. "Kara must be wondering what happened to us."

I sit up and take the hand Leo extends. He pulls me to my feet, then turns to help Elodie.

"I can't believe they shaved you." I shield my eyes with my hand. "The glare is blinding."

He rolls his eyes. "Dreadlocks and facial hair are frowned on in Leweian society. Maybe Loki felt he was facilitating my reunion with my father."

"He had no intention of letting you see your father." I turn to walk slowly to the house. "He was going to trade you for Cas without mentioning it to Dod."

"Dod?"

"Dear Old Dad. That's how I used to refer to my father—before I met him. Now I call him R'ger." I grin at their blank faces. "It's his name."

"Ah. Yes, I suspect Loki wanted to make sure the *Spiitznatz* recognized me." He shakes his head with a grin, as if he's discussing the antics of a child. "A DNA scan would have been so much easier."

"You don't seem to mind that your former protector was ready to sell you off."

"It wasn't personal. Anyone on Lewei would probably do the same. It's all he knows."

Elodie stops, hands on hips. "And you're okay with that?"

"Obviously not." He points at the ground. "It's one of the many reasons I'm here and not there."

"Oh, yeah." She catches up to us. "Do you really think Vanti and Ty will be able to find Cas?"

"If anyone can, it's them." We step out of the trees, and I nod at the pool where Kara is still lying in her lounger. "How much do you want to tell her?"

"She'd have a fit if she thought we were keeping anything from her," Elodie answers. "But I think we can leave out the threats to hold us captive. That kind of outrage might not be good for the baby."

"Agreed." We step onto the deck, our footsteps loud against the teakalike.

"Where have you been?" Kara raises her hat to peer out from beneath it. "You've been gone forever!"

"Yeah, but look, we found Leo!" Elodie grabs his hand and pulls him forward.

"What did you do to your hair?" Kara examines the scrapes on his scalp. "This doesn't look like the work of a licensed aesthetician!"

I leave them on the deck and hurry inside. The door to the security center opens to my handprint, and I initiate a secure call to O'Neill. "We found him. I mean Leo."

"You 'found' the heir to the Leweian premier?" O'Neill replies. "He was just laying around, waiting to be picked up?"

"He was *visiting* his father."

"Triana, did you sneak into the Leweian compound?" His voice is dangerously quiet. "Where are you?"

"I'm at home. And we're calling it Zijin. That was Elodie's idea."

There's no response.

"They need our help." A good defense is an offensive redirect, or something like that. "Cas is missing, and they've asked if we can help find him."

"First Leo and now Cas? Does the premier always have so much trouble keeping track of his kids?"

"He's going by Ser Zhang since he lost his job. There was a coup on Lewei. We got the whole story. Do you want it now, or wait until you get back here?"

He sighs. "I'll be there in an hour. Don't go to Zijin again."

I grin. He's mad but not furious. "I'll wait right here. Well, in the kitchen. I'm starved."

———

WHILE WE'RE in the kitchen getting lunch, Hy-Mi returns. He steps into the doorway and bows in our general direction.

"Welcome back, Hy-Mi! Are you hungry?" I jump off my stool.

He holds up a hand. "I ate brunch with my grandchildren. Have you had an enjoyable weekend?"

I hide a grin. "It's been interesting. I'd like you to meet Kara's mother, Elodie."

Hy-Mi comes closer and bows again. "Enchanted."

It's so weird to see him around women other than Mother and me—he's a charmer.

Elodie smiles and flutters her eyelashes. "So nice to finally meet the famous Hy-Mi. I've heard so much about you."

Hy-Mi's eyes sparkle. "I hope you didn't believe most of it." His eyes travel around the room. "Nice to see you again, Sera Kara."

"Don't call me that, Hy-Mi. It sounds so silly. Just Kara is fine." She stops loading dishes onto a tray to bump fists with Hy-Mi.

Hy-Mi nods to O'Neill, then freezes when he catches sight of Leo. "That's a new look. Very…Leweian."

Leo runs a hand over his bald head. "It won't be for long. Kara says she can fix it."

"You remind me of someone…" Hy-Mi's voice trails off, and his eyes snap to the western wall of the room. He's obviously made the connection.

"Hy-Mi, I'd like to introduce you to the honorable Ervin Lewei, son of the former premier of Lewei." I watch his face.

Hy-Mi is a master at hiding his feelings. The briefest twitch to his eye is the only indication he's shocked to discover the man who's been feeding us breakfast, lunch, and dinner is a prominent—and formerly missing—political refugee. "Do you prefer Ervin or Leo?"

Leo laughs. "Definitely Leo." He stops stirring and lifts a pan. The rest of us jump to our feet, but he waves us down. "Stop it. I'm still just Leo, your old chef. Let me do my job. I can use the credits." He scoops macaroni and cheese into bowls.

"Is Sera Vanti with us today?" Hy-Mi asks.

"She's in the security center," I say. "We're trying to find Leo's brother."

O'Neill picks up a tray. "And I should get back in there and see if there's anything—"

"She would have called you if there was." I have loops sifting through every surveillance feed on the Ebony Coast. My holo-ring will signal if any of them come up positive or even possible.

"Dig in while it's hot." Leo hands the bowls around. "After we eat, I'm going to take care of these dishes. And then, since I have no skills to help with the search, I'm going to bake something. I need to take my mind off Cas."

"Sounds like an excellent plan," Elodie says. "The baking part, I mean. I'll help."

"Dessert is always good." I follow O'Neill out of the room.

Kara lumbers up behind me. "I want to see what's going on. Besides, I can't work on Leo until he's done with the baking. I know you'd kill me if I interrupted that!"

I smile weakly. "Don't get between me and dessert." It's an old joke, and usually true, but I'm so worried about Cas, I can't even laugh.

"Oh, honey, don't worry. Ty and Vanti will find him."

I don't point out that Elodie and I found Leo, not Ty and Vanti.

"Sit report." O'Neill sets the food on the counter beside Vanti and swipes at an icon.

"We're still sifting the feeds." Vanti flicks something, and a window grows larger. "We caught him on this cam, crossing Sierra Hotel property late last night. He went down to the beach, then walked west. A bubble came across the water, and he climbed in. No indication of force. It's like he wanted to go with them."

"Why didn't you call me when you found this?" I ask.

She shoots me an indecipherable look from under her lashes. "I knew you'd be back soon. The bubble identifier is obscured, and they didn't get close enough to the house for the ID to register on our system."

"How did they get through the barrier?" I grab a bowl of mac and cheese and settle into a chair.

Vanti freezes for a second. Ha! She didn't think of that!

"Probably a Lyfter." Kara sits beside me.

We all turn to stare at her.

"What? Is that stupid?"

"No, it's genius. And you're right—if he was voluntarily meeting them, he could use the guest code I gave him to open the force shield for them." I raise my eyebrows at Vanti. "Unless you revoked his privileges?"

She stares me down. "I did."

"Then I don't—"

"And I gave them back." She looks away. "I felt sorry for the little guy. After we blocked his secret entrance, I set a special guest code that would allow him in. That was before I knew you were going to unblock the secret entrance."

"If you'd told me you gave him the code back, I wouldn't have had—"

"Can we focus on the important thing?" O'Neill steps between us. "Lyfter can tell us who set up that pickup."

"Right." Vanti swipes through a few screens and submits a request for information. While she waits for a reply, she grabs a bowl and takes a bite of the mac and cheese. She stops, the spoon frozen by her lips, and looks at the dish in her hand. "This is amazing."

"That's why they call it comfort food," Kara says. "I can't wait to see what he and *Larin* whip up for dessert."

"I'll have to do a double round at the gym," Vanti mutters around the next bite.

"It's worth it," Kara replies.

Vanti's holo-screen pings and flashes red. "That's not good."

TWENTY-FIVE

MY EMPTY BOWL thunks onto the tray. "What's not good?"

"Cas ordered the Lyfter." Vanti swipes her hand through a screen, and the order confirmation expands, so we can all see it. "Called yesterday—just after we left for Paradise Alley. Origination code is his ring from our network. The little twerp snuck over here to call a cab and run away."

"Where was it going?" I ask.

"Paradise Alley." The address flashes, and a map appears, zooming out from Sierra Hotel then back in to a spot north of the main town. "It's not a good part of town."

"There's a bad part of Paradise Alley?" Kara asks.

Vanti doesn't answer. She's across the room opening a hidden cabinet that contains a small arsenal.

O'Neill joins her. "It's more shady than bad. Kind of high-end disreputable. You won't get mugged if you go there, but you'd better have a good reason to visit. Private security forces watching everyone."

"Oh, so it's for mafia bosses and shell corporations?" Kara leans forward in her chair. Something pokes through her shirt.

"What is that?" I point at her belly.

"Baby didn't like that." She leans back and strokes her stomach. "She's just protesting."

"That was a foot." I'm still staring in horror.

She shrugs. "Or a knee. Or elbow."

"No, I saw toes. That was a foot. It was creepy."

"She's a baby, not an alien. That's what they do."

Movement catches my eye—Vanti and O'Neill easing toward the door. "Are you trying to sneak away without us? That is *not* going to work."

"We're investigating a potentially dangerous part of town. I'm not taking you." O'Neill puts his hands on his hips and stares me down.

"You said it was mafia and shell corporations. That's right up my alley. The Ice Dame is all about shells. And you know I have an in with the Sprzężaj."

"*Kara* said it was shell corporations. I said you'd better have a good reason to visit." He glares at Kara.

She gives him a finger wave.

"What's *your* reason for visiting?" I ask.

Vanti claps a hand over the weapon strapped to her hip. "We're looking for our friend. That's the only reason *we* need."

"Stay here." O'Neill puts a hand on my cheek. "Please?"

How can I say no to that? "I won't follow you. But bring him back, okay?"

"Like we'd do anything else." Vanti gives us a smug grin and flits out the door.

O'Neill kisses me soundly, then follows his partner. I drop into my seat.

Kara picks up the extra bowl of macaroni and cheese and digs in. "We aren't really staying here, are we?"

WHEN WE OPEN THE DOOR, a delicious fog of chocolate, vanilla, and caramel fills the hallway. We follow our noses to the kitchen. Elodie washes dishes while Leo pipes a fancy swirl of chocolate onto a tall white cake.

"What is that heavenly smell?" Kara asks. Her stomach growls.

"How can you be hungry already?" I ask.

She rubs her stomach. "Baby Freya is voracious."

"You've picked a name?" Elodie squeals and drops her scrub brush. She flings the huge flowered gloves onto the counter and runs across the room to hug her daughter.

Kara smiles and shrugs. "I'm just trying it on for size. I haven't told—I mean, discussed it with Erco yet."

"Where *is* Erco?" I stick a finger into the bowl on the counter and swipe a blob of chocolate. When the frosting hits my tongue, my knees go loose. "Leo, this is to die for."

"My man got an extra shift," Kara says. "Gotta suck up that overtime pay now, so we've got a little extra to spend on little Freya."

"If he was here, he could have gone with Ty and Vanti and earned danger pay." I reach for the bowl, but Leo slaps my fingers.

"Danger?" Kara's voice cracks. "No, thank you. I'd much rather have him at headquarters making time-and-a-half shuffling paperwork, thank you very much."

"Is there any news?" Leo pipes another swirl, but it comes out lopsided. He uses a knife to scoop the mess off the cake and holds it out to me.

I swipe the blob off the knife with a clean finger. "I set a drone to follow them." I lick the frosting, then flick my holo-ring with my sticky finger.

"Do they know?" Kara asks.

I grin and pull the hologram big enough for everyone to see. "They should be arriving any second."

Leo drops his knife and leans against the counter to watch. Elodie abandons the dishes again and perches on a stool next to Kara.

The holo shows the backs of O'Neill's and Vanti's heads. They walk down an unremarkable street. Tall, corporate-looking towers line both sides of the street. The occasional bubble coasts past. Discreet signs advertise banks, businesses, and medical facilities. A few pedestrians dressed in boring corporate style hurry past.

If I didn't know this was Paradise Alley, I would never have guessed. The small, white buildings with blue domes are conspicuously absent. The ground is flat—this part of town must be on the steppe behind the tourist town.

"This is it." Vanti stands on the sidewalk, staring up at the Kakuvian Savings Bank. "Why would a kid come here?"

"Maybe he's planning on cashing out his inheritance and running away?" O'Neill's head swivels, checking out the street front. "Why is it so quiet? I know it's Sunday afternoon, but there's no one here."

The street behind them is empty.

"Get out!" I holler, swiping at the controls for the drone. I find the speaker button. "Get out. This isn't right."

O'Neill spins, his eyes searching for the origin of my voice. "Triana?"

"Get out!"

Vanti springs away from the building. She grabs Ty's arm and drags him under the drone and out of sight.

I spin the flying cam. The view swoops sickeningly, then steadies. Vanti's red hair disappears around a corner, with Ty on her heels.

The drone view shakes violently. A roar blasts through the vid, then it goes black.

"What happened?" Elodie shrieks.

"Ty? Are you there?" I swipe away the dead vid and flick my communications icon. My hands sweat, and my heart pounds as I shove contacts away and flick on Ty's image.

Nothing happens.

"You have to click connect." Leo leans over my shoulder to hit the icon.

The call connects. "Ty, are you okay?"

"We're fine. We got out of the blast zone. How did you know?"

I shrug, even though I know he can't see it. "A feeling. These guys are playing for keeps. You don't think Cas was in there, do you?"

Vanti's image appears on my holo, and I bring her into the call. "No. This was a warning to us—or rather to Zhang's rogue agents—to back off. The damage appears to be minimal."

"It would have killed us if Triana hadn't warned us." O'Neill turns on a cam, and the building comes into view. The front windows are blown out, and the façade is blackened, but the building appears stable. Emergency service bubbles hurtle down the street toward us, sirens screaming.

"If they wanted us dead, they would have waited until we went inside to blow it," Vanti says. "This was definitely a warning."

"We'll talk to the first responders, then we're headed back to base." O'Neill's call cuts out.

"That was...terrifying." Leo picks up his frosting bag, but his hands shake, so he sets it aside.

"I could use a drink," Elodie says. "You got any booze?"

"Top left shelf." Leo points toward a cupboard.

"Bar in the family room," I say at the same time.

"AutoKich'n." Kara taps the screen on the front of the device. It lights up, and a holographic menu appears. "You want a straight shot or a fancy drink?"

Elodie gapes at the huge menu for a few moments. "I think I'll just have some tea. Chamomile would be good."

"You got it." Kara swipes and flicks. "Anyone else?"

Leo and I both nod.

We take our tea into the family room and sink into the comfortable couch while Leo puts his creation into the fridge.

"Bring the extra frosting when you come in," I call to him.

"There is no extra," he calls back. "I need it all."

"Now what?" I ask, not really expecting an answer. "How are we going to find him?"

Leo walks in, his flowered apron gone, and a box of chocolates in his hands. He sets his offering on the coffee table and sits beside Elodie. "Maybe I should go to the Leweian Embassy. If the guys who took him are really *Spiitznatz*, they probably took him to the embassy."

TWENTY-SIX

VANTI EYES the slice of cake distrustfully but takes the plate. "Three extra sessions in the gym."

"It'll be worth it." Leo winks. "I promise." Despite his continued positivity, the day has taken a toll on him. His face is tired, and his usual energy is gone. Worry over his brother must be eating at him.

Elodie's eyes open wide. "There's enough caffeine in here to fuel an entire Explorer Corps squadron. Don't ask me how I know."

"Because you helped bake the cake?" Kara suggests.

"No, I mean about the Explorer Corps—never mind." Elodie shoves another forkful of cake into her mouth.

"That was a good call on the embassy." O'Neill takes the plate Leo offers. "We caught sight of him entering at ten twenty-three last night."

Vanti flips a holo-vid onto the table. "Surveillance cam from across the street." She takes another bite and closes her eyes.

On the holo, Cas steps out of the bubble and walks into a building flying the Leweian flag.

"No obvious coercion. He went voluntarily." O'Neill points his fork at the holo. "We've sent a copy to Zijin. Your father did not respond, but it's marked delivered and viewed."

Vanti turns to Leo. "Do you have any idea what he might do with this information?"

Leo holds up both hands. "I haven't seen the man in ten years, so, no. No idea."

"We need Loki," I say. "He's been with Zhang forever. He'll know what to expect." I point at Leo. "Now that he knows Cas went on his own, isn't your dad's response likely to be the same as it was when you left?"

Leo snorts. "Write him out of the succession and pretend he doesn't exist?"

"Except there is no succession anymore. And there's no 'spare' heir," O'Neill says.

"Spare heir?" Elodie repeats.

O'Neill nods. "When Leo left, he already had Cas. And he seemed ready to pass him off as the one and only heir. That's the advantage of no media coverage. Once Cas reached full growth, Zhang could have claimed he was Ervin. Lots of folks wouldn't believe it, but he doesn't care what we think. The Leweians would have believed because they were told to."

Leo sips his coffee. "I'd say that's a pretty accurate assessment."

I flick my holo-ring and tap the contact number Loki gave me. It connects almost immediately.

"Loki."

"Hi, Loki. This is Tri—Annabelle Morgan. We have some additional information about Cas. Could you come over here? We'd like to get some background information." Can I say "information" one more time?

After a few seconds of silence, Loki answers. "Will you let me in through the front gate? I still don't fit through Master Caspian's secret entrance."

I agree and sign off. "He's coming in the front entrance."

"I'm surprised he'd want to be caught on cam entering the estate of a 'capitalist pig.'" Leo starts stacking dishes.

"Ebony Beach is pretty hard on paparazzi, so he's not worried about media coverage." Ty finishes his coffee and stacks his cup on Leo's. "Speaking of which, we haven't detected any mention of political upheaval in Lewei in any of the news sources."

"Which is very strange, if you ask me." Leo stands. "If there was a coup—an apparently successful coup—why aren't the winners bragging about it? I've managed to connect with a couple of expat Leweians, and none of them have mentioned anything. They still have family in the Lewei Empire. They should know."

"Total news blackout?" Elodie suggests.

Vanti finishes her cake and pushes the plate away with a groan. "No. If there was a news blackout, they would have mentioned that, right Leo?"

"Absolutely. There've been several over the last ten years, and my friends have reported on each."

"Do your friends know who you are?" Vanti asks. "Maybe they've been threatened if they pass the information to you?"

He shakes his head. "No one knows who I am. I was very careful."

Vanti snorts. "We figured it out in two days. Anyone actually looking for you could have run a face match years ago."

"I've only been wearing my real face since I moved to Sierra Hotel. I knew I should have used a cover identity when we went to Paradise Alley, but then I would have had to explain to you all why I was doing it…" He picks up the stack of dishes.

"Yeah, I would have started a facial recognition loop before we left the house." I swipe the last bit of frosting off my plate with a finger and pop it into my mouth. "Mmmm."

"I should've stayed here. But after ten years of being careful…besides, Cas didn't recognize me when we were surfing, so I got cocky."

"Why didn't he?" Kara asks. "He's your brother."

"He was only two when I left. And I'm sure *Mr. Zhang* hasn't kept any photos. It was stupid to think just because Cas didn't recognize me, no one would, but we believe what we want to believe. And I really wanted to go out."

My holo-ring pings. "Loki is here. I told the front gate guys to let him onto the estate."

"I'll get the door." Vanti heads for the door with O'Neill on her heels. She pauses on the landing, then turns back to shut the door. "Security first."

The rest of us clear the table, and Leo shoves the dishes into the Auto-Kich'n. He starts some coffee and gets out clean plates for Loki. "He'll probably bring Brunhild or Mos, too."

"Don't they need to stay home and watch your dad?" Elodie asks.

"Don't call him that—he's not my dad. He's barely my father."

The door opens, and O'Neill ushers Loki into the room.

The big man sneers. "Typical capitalist overconsumption," he says in greeting.

"So nice to see you, too," I reply. "And hard to take coming from the guy who lives in a pseudo-Victorian monstrosity full of antiques. That's right, I looked it up. At least we don't have a dungeon."

"We have no dungeon! Our basement is spacious and bright." He stomps to the middle of the room.

"With well-lit cells for dissidents," Leo mutters. He raises his voice. "Would you like some cake, Loki?"

Loki takes the plate and points at the couches in front of the windows. "Please sit down. There, in the middle of the room, where I can see all of you."

O'Neill, still standing by the door, moves his hand toward his pocket. When he's on duty, he keeps a micro-stunner there, but this was a family dinner, not a dangerous situation. Is he armed?

"Why do you need to see all of us?" I take a step toward the kitchen. If he's up to something, spreading out is our best defense. I glance at O'Neill and realize Vanti isn't with him. His lips quirk.

"A simple request. I'm not comfortable in the midst of so many strangers." He gestures with his uneaten cake.

"Oh, for the love of—" Leo strides up to the big man. He grabs the fork and pokes it into the cake, breaking off a chunk. He picks up the piece and sticks it into his mouth. As he chews, he speaks around the food. "See, no poison. Sit down and eat it." He shoves the man toward the couch.

Loki, completely unmoved by Leo's push, bows and strolls to the seats. He surveys the grouping of couches and chairs and selects one near the fireplace. With a push of his foot, he shifts it a few degrees until the stone mantle is directly behind it, then sits. "Occupational hazard. I am not comfortable without a wall to my back." He takes a bite of cake, and his eyebrows go up in surprise. "This is good."

I move closer to Ty and whisper, "Where's Vanti?"

"Doing her job." He gestures. "Shall we?"

We sit on the sofa facing the window. Elodie and Kara sit on the other couch to my right, and Leo takes the last wing chair. He casually rotates it a few degrees to visually align with us, facing Loki straight on. No question who is on which side.

"You said you have information for me." Loki glances at Kara. "Do you have any coffee to go with this?"

Kara's brows wrinkle. "This isn't my house. I'm not sure I'm the one who should—"

Leo glares at Loki. "Kara is a guest, not a servant. If you want coffee, you'll have to ask me."

Loki's eyes dart from face to face. "She's the only one I don't know, so I assumed she was the least important. I've met Sera Annabelle and Sera Elodie. I recognize the man who opened the door as security. This woman is not important enough to be introduced."

"She's too important to be introduced," I tell Loki. "You have no need to know her name. You'll have to make do without the coffee."

"I'll get some." Leo jumps to his feet. He mutters as he returns to the kitchen, "I need to get out—"

I give Loki the evil eye. "Don't upset my friends, Loki. You're here because we invited you, so I expect you to behave yourself."

He holds up a hand. "My apologies. Shall we get on with business?" His eyes dart to the window, then back to me.

What's he looking for? That's the third time he's looked over there. "We need some information about your employer. As you know, Cas went to the embassy. We can't help you unless we know what steps Ser Zhang is likely to take to retrieve him."

"We also want to know why no one knows about this coup," Elodie says.

I shoot her a quelling look.

"Was I supposed to not mention that?" she asks.

Loki sets his empty plate on a side table. He glances at the windows again, then shifts in his chair. Is he nervous about something? Or is he trying to distract us by pretending to be nervous? "The Leweian government believes stability is one of their primary assets. If no one knows there was a coup, there is less possibility of unrest."

Leo returns and sets a cup of coffee on a small table near the kitchen, well out of Loki's reach. He flicks his holo-ring, and the little table slides closer to our guest. After their recent history, it makes sense for him to stay out of arms' reach.

"Are they going to pretend nothing happened?" Elodie asks. "How's that going to work next time Ser Zhang needs to meet with someone off planet?"

"The new premier will be modded to look like Ser Zhang. Just as he was modded to look like his predecessor." Loki spreads his hands as if this is the most natural thing in the world.

"Wait. How long has Ser Zhang—that Ser Zhang—" I point toward Zijin. "How long has he been premier? Who was before him?"

"My father was promoted when I was a kid," Leo says. "The previous premier was my uncle. There was no modding done."

Loki's eyes drop.

"There was?" Leo leans forward. "Did my father look different before? Was that man not my uncle?"

"He was like an uncle."

"What happened to him? I was told he passed away."

"Oh, he did." Loki sounds satisfied rather than sad.

"I see."

"The important thing right now," O'Neill says, "is to know what Ser Zhang's response to the embassy will be."

Vanti's voice echoes through the room. "We got incoming!"

TWENTY-SEVEN

THICK METAL SHIELDS slam down over the windows. The ringing echoes through the house as other bulkheads lock down.

Loki leaps to his feet, his chair slamming into the stone fireplace with a crack of splintering wood. His hand goes to his hip, but his holster is empty. "I need my weapon!"

"Move! Safe room, now." O'Neill hoists me up by my arm and shoves me toward the bedroom hallway.

"Elodie, Kara, Leo, come with us!" I call over my shoulder as he hustles me to the door. "Who's attacking?"

"Not attacking." A smug smile appears on Loki's face. "Infiltrating."

O'Neill pulls out his micro-stunner and fires. The big man's smile disappears, and he collapses to the floor.

"Get going!" O'Neill pushes me toward the door. "They've got people on the grounds. Loki must have hijacked our security."

Boom!

The door to the stairway rattles.

"They're trying to blast their way in."

Hy-Mi appears in an elegant dressing gown, his hair disheveled. "What is happening?"

"Our neighbors are staging a hostile take-over!" I slap my hand on the bedroom wing access panel, and the door opens.

"No." Hy-Mi waves us toward the back hall leading to the security center. "Don't go that way—the safe-room isn't accessible."

"Is it still full of gravel?" Kara waddles after him. "I can't believe it took a year to clean it up."

"No, it's fine, but only Dame Morgan can get in. She wasn't happy with that situation and decided no one else should have access."

"She locked her own daughter out of the safe room?" I put my hand on the panel by the security door, and it pops open. "Should we be going in here? It's a dead end, isn't it?"

O'Neill doesn't answer. He pushes us into the room and pulls the door shut behind Kara. Vanti is already inside, flicking files on a workstation. He slides past me and starts reviewing the screens she's opened. "They've got a big team. Ten came in through the front, another eight coming up the back. I've locked everything down, but they'll get into the family spaces in about twenty minutes. Unless they have a neo-plasma drill. Then it'll be five."

"Let's not wait to find out." Vanti swipes another command, and a screen lights up. The words "Abandon Base?" appear over her hand.

Hy-Mi's face goes slack. "Are you sure it's that desperate?"

"You tell me." She flicks a file, and a series of vids play. Each of them show heavily armed men and women wearing tactical armor. The house is full of them.

O'Neill steps into the next workstation and logs in. "Triana, the system knows you're here, so you'll need to approve." He swipes through several screens with various warnings emblazoned in huge letters.

"What are you doing?" I move closer, trying to read the words flashing by. The only thing I can make out is the last question. "Are you really, really sure?"

"Hit it." He waves at a flat panel on the console.

"But I'm not really, really sure—what am I supposed to be sure about?"

"Do you trust me?"

That I'm sure about. "Yes."

"Then hit it."

I slap my hand on the panel. The DNA sampler pokes my finger for a blood sample, and the retina scanner flashes my eyes.

A pleasant androgynous voice says, "Code zero zero zero. Destruct. Zero activated."

Zark.

The door to the break room pops open.

"That was underwhelming." I shake my hand, even though the scanner applied an analgesic sealant after the blood draw.

"Everyone out." Vanti swipes through some screens and locks down her console.

O'Neill moves to the entrance and engages the hand-cranked dead bolts.

"Where are we going?" I ask as he ushers me into what looks like a closet. Although it's called a break room, it only holds an AutoKich'n and a sink. With all seven of us inside, it's cramped.

"Down to the garage." Ty shuts the door, and he presses the access panel. The floor vibrates and starts to drop.

"Is this some kind of weird float tube?" Kara asks.

"It's an old-style elevator. They're still used in some places." Vanti hands Kara a grav belt. "Put that on—we don't want you slowing us down. When the door opens, wait for me and Griz to clear the way. They have two people in the garage."

While Kara fastens the belt under her bulging belly, the vibration stops. Vanti opens what I had assumed was a closet. She leans around the door jamb and fires off two shots. A thud follows each shot. "Clear." She darts out.

"Hold." O'Neill leans around the door and holds up one hand. "Let her check." He waits a few seconds, then waves us forward. "Go."

I help Kara set her belt to twenty centimeters and grab her wrist. We run across the dark room, jumping over the two downed *Spiitznatz* agents. Kara floats in my wake like a pregnant balloon.

Vanti crouches by the open door of a supply van. "In!"

We scramble in. O'Neill jumps into the driver's seat.

"Sit on the floor," Vanti calls over her shoulder from the doorway. "Griz, get her rolling!"

The vehicle lifts off the ground. At the last second, Vanti dives in and the van rotates. The movement slams the door closed. We take off.

"WHAT *IS* code zero zero zero destruct zero?" I ask.

We're sitting in a ground floor apartment not far from the bank that exploded when Vanti and O'Neill visited. It's one of SK'Corp's safe houses—apparently there are several in Paradise Alley, but none of them are in the fashionable part of town. This apartment is nicer than the compartment Kara and I had on SK2, but it's a big step down from Sierra Hotel.

Vanti's lower lip sticks out—as close to a pout as I've ever seen from her. "I thought you'd recognize the code from your *Ancient TēVē*."

"I recognized it, but since the whole hillside didn't explode and crumble into the sea, I have to assume you didn't blow up a starship."

She grins. "No, but Dame Morgan is not going to be happy. I don't think your wedding is going to be quite what she imagined." She flicks her holo-ring and throws a vid onto the cheap coffee table.

The table may look cheap, but the holo projection system is top of the line. It's almost as if we're there, in the formal "gathering room" on the top level of the house. Three armed *Spiitznatz* agents run through the room. Thick armored plates slam down over doors and windows. More plates drop over the expensive portraits hanging on the walls. Then sticky purple goo shoots out of the walls.

"It hardens up almost immediately. Not completely solid." She increases the speed on the vid. The men attempt to get away, but each movement seems to wrap more sticky stuff around their arms and legs.

"That's going to be hard to get out of the carpet," Leo says. "Why purple?"

"It's supposed to be stainless, but the sample we tested was not as easily eradicated as we'd hoped." Hy-Mi twitches the cuffs of a borrowed shirt. "I need to speak with Dame Morgan. I assume the smaller bedroom contains secure communications?" O'Neill nods, and Hy-Mi disappears, closing the door behind him.

Kara stares out the window. "Are we going to spend the whole afternoon hiding in this apartment? I may as well go home."

"I wouldn't advise that," O'Neill says. "Loki saw you, and he knows your first name. It wouldn't take them long to track down your current apartment. I've instructed Erco to stay in headquarters tonight."

"You spoke to him? I need to call him!" She turns away from the window.

Vanti grabs her arm. "You'll have to wait and use the secure equipment when Hy-Mi is done. Erco knows you're safe. Why don't you rest?"

Kara starts to disagree but lets Vanti lead her to the master bedroom. The door shuts.

"Are we sure this was Loki's guys?" Leo asks. "And not actual Spiitznatz?"

"Loki looked awfully smug. I vote it was him." Elodie drops onto the sofa next to Leo. "I can't believe Dame Morgan had all those sticky guns in her house! I'd be worried they'd misfire during a party or something."

"Since the system requires a family member's DNA to arm, it's relatively safe." Vanti flicks the vids away and pulls up another. "The family areas have a different deterrent."

Thick smoke appears. Air handlers shift it, and we catch glimpses of the family room décor.

"Knock-out gas," Vanti says.

"What if the bad guys have gas masks or air filters?" Leo asks.

"We have other responses for that, but I'm not going to tell you what they are." She flicks the hologram away.

"We're no closer to saving Cas than we were before." I jump up and prowl around the edges of the room. "He's still in the embassy."

"How do you know?" Elodie asks.

"I set some surveillance alerts on the building." I shrug. "If they have a secret exit, he could have been moved, but he hasn't been in any of the bubbles that have departed since he arrived."

"It's an embassy. I'm betting they have a secret exit." O'Neill flicks his holo-ring and moves down the short hallway to the second bedroom. "I'm going to contact a friend in the government."

"Maybe we should just leave Cas where he is," Elodie says. "Is the Leweian government likely to be any worse than his own father? The man who replaced, then imprisoned, then attacked his own son?" She waves at Leo.

"We need to get him out." Leo's hands ball into fists. "He doesn't deserve any of this. He can live with me. We'll go someplace *Ser Zhang* and the *Spiitznatz* can't find us."

"Where would that be?" Vanti asks. Her voice is soft, almost sympathetic.

Leo shrugs. "I don't know. But maybe we can find it."

"Did we ever figure out why Cas went to the bank before the embassy?" Elodie asks.

"Maybe he was trying to cash in those diamonds," I say.

Vanti starts. "What made you say that?"

I shrug. "Just a joke. But that diamond that stuck to my pants was dropped near his secret exit. It makes sense that he dropped it. If he grabbed a handful of them, he wouldn't notice losing one. But anyone tasked with carrying them for Ser Zhang would take better care."

"Good point." Vanti flicks her holo-ring. "I'm going to have a look at the Kakuvian Savings Bank security system. You wanna help me hack in, Triana?"

I yawn. "Sure. It's better than just sitting here."

"I'm going to see what's in the kitchen." Leo jumps up and stalks across the room. "I need to bake."

Two hours later, we've learned that Cas entered the bank and went to a private office. I haven't been able to crack the security for that room.

Twenty-three minutes after that, he left through a back door, and took another Lyfter bubble to the Leweian Embassy. He hasn't been seen since.

"Can you break into the embassy security?" Vanti asks.

"I've never tried. But since you're asking, I'd guess you have and were unsuccessful?"

"Got it in one." She sticks her fingers into her shiny copper hair and massages her scalp. "I need some coffee. You want some?"

"Chocolate would be better." I leave some worm loops running and shut down connection to the secret in-house net hub. As I massage my neck, I look around the apartment.

Kara must still be snoozing in the master bedroom. Leo and Elodie are working in the kitchen. The occasional clatter and laugh filters through the closed door. O'Neill and Hy-Mi are still in the communications center. Or maybe they've come out and gone back in—I was focused on my work.

Vanti pauses by the kitchen door. "Do you think it's safe to go in?"

"Hey, I've been meaning to ask you—what's up with you and Ro?"

"Ro?" She goes still, her eyes still focused on the door. "What about him?"

Ro is Ty's younger brother. At their sister's wedding on Grissom, Ro and Vanti seemed to be getting cozy. "Are you seeing him?"

She turns, her face bland. "How would that work? He's on Grissom, I'm on Kaku." She opens the kitchen door.

Warm, sweet-scented air wafts out. Metal clinks against plastek. Elodie giggles. "Hey, Vanti, taste this and tell me what you think."

Vanti dodges the spoon and my question.

"You try it, too, Triana." Leo thrusts a huge spoon at me as I step through the door.

The white fluff on the end of the spoon has darker specks mixed in. I swipe a fingerful off the spoon. "What is it?"

"Frosting for the cinnamon rolls. The first pan just came out of the oven." Leo sweeps an arm toward the countertop behind him. Two huge trays packed with puffy, beige spirals sit under clear lids. Elodie holds another pan in gloved hands.

I stick my finger in my mouth and the sweet, creamy blob melts on my tongue. "Is that piferroy spice?"

Leo grins. "Not even close. For a foodie, you're terrible at guessing ingredients."

I shrug. "I know if I like something, but I don't really care what's in it. Within reason."

"For future reference, those specks are ground citromon."

"If this is what you do when you're stressed, Leo, we are all going to get so fat." Vanti reaches toward the frosting bowl.

Leo holds out a small blob on the big spoon. "Don't even try to touch the bowl. You might be a secret agent with super speed, but you're no match for a chef defending his unfinished creation." He grabs the bowl. "Have you figured out how we're going to get Cas?"

She shakes her head. "We need to get eyes inside the embassy. We've got our best hackers back at HQ working on it, but if Triana couldn't hack their system, I don't hold out much hope for the corporate drones."

"Aw, that's the nicest thing you've ever said to me." I smirk.

"I could get in," Leo says slowly.

"No good," Vanti replies. "Then we'd have to rescue two of you. We need someone else—someone who has a reason to visit but is untouchable."

"Unfortunately, Hy-Mi may have an answer." O'Neill stands in the doorway, Hy-Mi hovering right behind him.

"That's great!" Leo beams.

Vanti's eyes narrow. "No, it isn't—what's the catch?"

O'Neill steps aside and holds out a hand. Hy-Mi hands him a large, ivory card. "Annabelle Morgan has been invited to the Leweian Embassy to meet the new ambassador."

TWENTY-EIGHT

"Where'd you get that?" I point at the card.

O'Neill hands it to me. "It came in the mail."

"Here?" The card is thick and smooth, with delicate rough bits to imitate high-end handmade paper. The rough bits are too symmetrically laid out to be real imperfections. The Leweian Embassy seal is embossed on one side in lurid color. The reverse gives the date and time, with a chip encoded to provide directions, dress code, and a list of which media reporters have been invited.

At least I assume there's a chip embedded. The paper is too thick to be sure, but that's standard procedure in those circles. "I get mail at your safe house?"

"No," Hy-Mi says. "It was waiting when I returned to Sierra Hotel today. I had just opened it when the attack occurred, so I put it into my dressing gown pocket."

"This thing is tomorrow." I tap the card. "They left the invite kinda late, didn't they? Doesn't that strike you as suspicious? I break into their premier's private estate on Friday, and they invite me to a party on Monday?"

"Former premier," Hy-Mi says. "And that invitation has probably been sitting in the mail since I left on Friday."

"We got a pile of stuff on Friday afternoon," Leo says. "Right after you left. And before Triana broke in to Zijin."

"This reception has been on the books for months," Hy-Mi says. "Dame Morgan declined ages ago. When we arrived on Kaku, I told my contact that Sera Annabelle might attend in her stead, and they promised to send another invitation."

"That explains the package from Garabana's," Leo says.

"Garabana's?" Vanti's head pops up. She turns to me. "You got a dress from Garabana's and didn't show it to me?"

"I have no idea what you're talking about. I assume Garabana is a designer? You know I'd rather wear this." I dust some flour off my stretchy sweater and leggings.

"It doesn't matter if the dress is at Sierra Hotel." Elodie spreads frosting on the warm rolls.

My mouth waters.

"We can retrieve it," Leo says. "I put the package in Hy-Mi's office. We can use a drone to bring it out—unless they've blocked the drones."

I stare at him. "You can do that?"

"Is it still in the box?" Leo turns to Hy-Mi.

"Indeed."

Leo snaps his fingers and flicks his holo-ring. "Easy."

"Wait, won't they trace it to us?" Elodie asks.

"Send it to this address." O'Neill flicks a file to Leo. "The rest of us will need new clothes, too."

LEO WASN'T KIDDING about baking when he's stressed.

The next morning, stuffed with cinnamon rolls, flaky pastries, and two types of coffee cake, we roll out of the safe house and into a waiting bubble. I can barely fasten the seat belt around my bulging stomach. Trying on evening gowns is going to be torture.

The bubble pulls up to a small white house perched at the top of Paradise Alley. A row of similar houses stretches along the narrow street, each sporting a different colored dome. There are no houses on the downhill side

—the tops of buildings on the next terrace barely protrude above street level. An invisible barrier keeps pedestrians from stumbling over the edge into the neighbors' back yards. Those yards are screened by a one-way force shield.

The view of the water and Diamond Beach across the bay is magnificent. I squint into the distance, but nothing appears to be amiss at Sierra Hotel. Maybe later I'll find one of those tourist telescopes that lets you stare at the homes of the rich and famous up close.

Hy-Mi leads us to the front door. A tiny blue plaque displays only the house number—no name. He waves his holo-ring at the plaque, and it lights up.

A female voice speaks. "Please enter, valued clients." The door slides open.

We step into a dimly lit hall. Four plush chairs stand on either side of the room, and huge pots stand between the chairs. The leafy plants screen each chair from the next. The tinkling of water surrounds us, and a faint cloud of lilac and verbenian fills the air.

Kara and Elodie wander around the small room, fingering the fabric and oohing over the plants. Leo slouches in a chair. Vanti and O'Neill stand by the two doors, alert and lethal. I peer out the window.

A bubble is parked behind ours. Two people dressed in plain dark clothes step out. They look familiar, but I can't place them. "Should we have someone following us?" I ask.

O'Neill turns and looks through the small window in the top of the door. "That's Yellin and Limberghetti. They're on duty today."

"They could be a little less conspicuous." I drop the curtain and move away from the window.

"No, they're supposed to be obvious." He flicks his holo-ring to check something. "Top-levs come here all the time. Having security outside is completely normal. If anyone were watching and we arrived without an obvious detail, they'd get suspicious."

"I'm glad you get to worry about this stuff instead of me." I lean in and kiss his cheek. I shouldn't do that when he's on duty, but he's so kissable.

His lips twitch and he winks.

The inner door opens. Vanti spins and drops to a crouch, one hand in a pocket—probably holding a weapon—and the other waving her holo-ring to scan the newcomer. Her ring pings, and she nods.

A tall person wearing long burgundy robes of crushed velvet sweeps through the door. "Sera Morgan, I am so sorry to keep you waiting! You may call me Garabana. Will your entourage accompany us to the fitting gallery?"

I cringe. Entourage? When did I become the kind of person who has an entourage? "Yes, please."

Garabana sweeps around. The long robes swing wide, slapping against the door jamb. Vanti pokes her head through the dark doorway, then follows Garabana.

"It's clear," O'Neill reports. "Follow the leader."

I step into the inky darkness, and it disappears like a curtain of smoke. A large room stands before me, with thick cream carpet, tufted brocade armchairs and a small stage lined by mirrors. It looks almost identical to the bridal salon we visited on Grissom—and like every other designer's studio I've ever seen.

Garabana throws off the top cloak, and it lands on the floor in a puddle. A woman dressed in a flowing white pantsuit swoops out of nowhere. Her hair is done in an elegant chignon. She scoops up the cloak and disappears. Another woman wearing an identical outfit and hairdo appears and hands Garabana a crystal flute.

Garabana blows into the flute, and it whistles shrilly. He plays an awkward little tune, then hands the flute back to the minion.

Kara and I exchange a glance. I try not to smile.

"Come, be seated." Garabana gestures with both arms.

I take a seat in the middle of the room. The others sit around me. The first minion returns with a tray of flutes—the drinking kind this time—and serves us sparkling water with fruit.

"If I'd known you would be coming in person, Sera, I wouldn't have risked my creation by sending it to your home. These delivery services—so unpredictable."

"The package came in a Garabana branded drone," Leo says dryly.

Garabana shrugs, the movement convulsing his whole body. "Anything could happen."

"Sorry about that," I say. "We had an unexpected incident at the house. Don't worry, I'm sure the dress is fine."

Garabana lets out a dramatic sigh. "It is. Thank the crystal stars of Monoceros!"

"Uh, sure. Can I try it on? And do you have anything my, er, entourage could wear?"

Garabana throws both arms into the air. I almost expect them to detach from his shoulders and fly away. "It is impossible! I do not deal in…" his lip curls "…off the rack."

"I know!" I jump up and step a little closer, lowering my voice. "I just hoped, as a favor to my mother—maybe you could wield your influence in Paradise Alley to help us find something for them? I couldn't think of anyone else up to the challenge."

"I am not surprised." Garabana snaps his fingers. Another white-clad woman emerges from the shadows and slides an embroidered blue cloak over his flowing white tunic and pants. "As a symbol of my admiration and dedication to your mother, I shall achieve the impossible."

Two exhausting hours later, everyone has clothing for the reception. The two women assisting Garabana cheerfully escort us to the front door, their good moods no doubt lifted by a massive and subtly delivered tip from Hy-Mi.

I collapse into the bubble. Hy-Mi has arranged for us to return at five to dress—we'll travel directly to the reception from Garabana's private exit.

"Where do they keep all those clothes?" Elodie stares at the tiny house as we drive away. "It looks bigger on the inside."

"There are several levels below ground," Vanti replies. "All of the manufacturing and storage are buried underneath."

"How do you know?" Elodie asks.

"I've worked security for Dame Morgan for a long time. I've had a full walk-through of the facility and do a pre-check any time she's dirtside—in case she wants to visit. Usually Garabana sends clothes to Sierra Hotel, though." She frowns as if my mother does this just to ruin her fun.

"Are we going back to the safe house?" Kara asks. "'Cause I could use some lunch."

O'Neill checks in with the security team in the rear car. "We're safe enough in the Alley. We can hit Manchegos for lunch—it's been swept."

Kara's eyes grow wide. "Manchegos? I've heard of them but never thought I'd get to eat there."

"Let's do it, then." I grin at Kara. "This will be better than our last visit to the Ebony Coast."

She knocks her knuckles against mine. "Much better."

TWENTY-NINE

AFTER A LONG, expensive lunch and an even longer, more expensive visit to a spa, the bubble takes the six of us back to Garabana's.

Vanti had excused herself during the meal, and not returned. Since O'Neill didn't comment on her absence, it must have been part of their plan. She hates spas, so I'm not surprised.

We drive through the most crowded part of town, our two bubbles drawing some stares and complaints from the pedestrians swarming through the streets. At the far end, beyond the exclusive shops and swanky boutique hotels, we turn a tight corner around a building and slide inside.

The heavy doors shut behind us, leaving our support team outside, guarding our backs. Our bubble trundles between two rows of private vehicles, each suspended from its charging cable like a giant melon. At the end of the row, a section of wall slides away, and we enter.

"Why are we sneaking in through the secret passageway?" I ask.

O'Neill says, "Our team noticed some *CelebVid* drones near the house. Better to avoid them."

"Are you telling me they don't know about this entrance?"

"No, but vid of a bubble with dark windows won't go viral. And they can't send the drone inside the building unless they're willing to risk a lawsuit."

Our lights come on, and the bubble picks up speed down a long, sloping tunnel. The walls speed by, covered in tasteful advertisements—the kind that make it almost impossible to guess what they're marketing but no doubt leaving indelible imprints on our subconsciouses.

"If I start booking a ski vacation in New Lucerne, someone poke me," I say as a picturesque villa on a pristine, snowy mountain drifts past.

"If you book it, I want to come with," Elodie says. "I've never been to New Lucerne."

The bubble slows, and a light appears in the distance—a narrow cone shining on a round carpet in front of a plain green door. The bubble stops and we climb out.

"Wow, the drama continues." Leo chuckles. "Garabana must have a background in theater."

O'Neill steps onto the carpet, and the door opens. One of the white-clad women stands there, her hair loose around her shoulders this time. She's traded the white pantsuit for a white dress with a fitted bodice and a wide skirt. She smiles and gestures for us to follow her.

"You weren't kidding," Elodie mutters to Leo. "I keep expecting music." As the words leave her mouth, a violin concerto begins. Elodie and Leo smother their laughter.

I bite my lip to keep from laughing and follow the minion through the dark hallway. At the far end, a door opens, and light spills in, revealing a room almost identical to the one we used this morning. The woman directs each of us to a private changing room. Mine has a pitcher of Teresh-tinis, some small sandwiches, and an InstaFabPro, along with a full bathroom and a chaise lounge, in case all this fabulousness is too exhausting.

I ignore the food—we had snacks at the spa, and besides, there's no chocolate. After a shower, I wrap a huge towel around my body, pull the InstaFabPro pod over my head, and close my eyes.

A ding startles me. I open my eyes as the pod retracts into the ceiling. Vanti sits on the chaise lounge, wolfing down one of the sandwiches. She's wearing her usual fitted black outfit.

"We could have brought you a to-go bag from Manchegos." I step behind a tall wooden screen and pull on the undergarments waiting there. "Aren't you going to change?"

"It only takes me a few minutes. I wanted to check in with you first. I wasn't able to get anything on the embassy. Nothing. Zero. Nada. Are you sure you want to go in?"

"It'll be fine. It's a party. If we get a bad feeling once we're inside, we can skip the snooping and leave early. But I don't want to leave Cas in there alone." I cross to the dress hanging from a hook in the ceiling.

As I approach, the device lifts the dress over my head. I step underneath and hold up my hands. The dress lowers over me, giving me time to put my arms in the right place.

In theory.

In reality, I get an arm through the neck hole and the other one through the open back. "Vanti, help me!"

She looks up from her fourth—or fifth—sandwich and snickers.

My face heats. "Can you just help?"

She flicks her holo-ring and connects to the in-room system. The dress lifts slowly, and I pull my arms out.

"What would you do without me?" She starts the dress down again.

"I'd hold it by the shoulders and step into it like a normal person!" The dress pauses in its downward motion, and I get my arms into the right places.

This sounds like it should be easy, but this is not a normal dress. Gauzy bits wrap around me at weird angles like a mummy bridal gown. The wide skirt is tattered, but my legs are constricted by the sheath underneath.

Vanti finishes rearranging the confusing wraps and fastens the neck. "This is a really odd design and not particularly flattering."

I stare in the mirror and heave a sigh. "I know. But it's a Garabana. And apparently, that's what everyone wants but can't get. Or Mother has a stake in the company and wants to promote it. What are you wearing?"

She flicks her hand at a bag hanging on a hook by the door. "It's an El Satore. Garabana has some clout—he got some amazing second tier designer clothes for the rest of us."

"I hope it's more comfortable than this thing." I totter toward the door, unable to move my legs above the knee.

"Let me fix that." Vanti digs through the vast layers of skirt to the under-sheath. Then she pulls out a knife. A quick slice cuts the constricting material up my thigh. "You should be able to walk now. And it looks exactly the same."

I take a big step. "That's better. But I think the slit ripped a bit."

"Don't take such big steps. Unless you need to run, in which case, who cares? Do you have a knife?" She holds hers out to me.

"Why would I need a knife?"

"If you have to run, you'll want to cut all that extra fluff out of the way." She gestures at the meters of white chiffon floating around me.

"I doubt the embassy will let us bring weaponry inside."

"Good point. Besides, this stuff looks like it will rip easily. Let's go." She opens the door for me.

The others have gathered in the outer room. O'Neill looks amazing in a distinguished yet understated suit. Hy-Mi wears a formal tunic over black pants. Elodie looks fantastic in a slinky, deep red gown with a plunging neckline and a slit skirt. Kara's tailored peach suit shows off her matching hair and her pregnant belly.

"Is that what you're wearing?" Leo juts his chin at Vanti. He's wearing another caftan, this one a deep purple-blue with gold embroidery. His beard has grown in enough to cover his face, and long dreadlocks flow from his golden turban. Kara said she could fix his hair, but I had no idea she could regrow dreads. Or maybe they're glued to the headdress.

Vanti glances down at herself. "Oops. Back in a flash." She disappears into my dressing room.

O'Neill takes my hands. "You look," he glances around, checking for Garabana, no doubt. "Interesting."

"Terrific is the word I've decided to use," I say. "Since the root word is 'terrifying,' it seems appropriate."

He leans in to kiss me. "You certainly look terrific."

Our lips touch for an electrifying moment.

Then Vanti clears her throat. "Are we ready?" Her gold gown matches Leo's turban and fits her like a second skin. The short skirt stretches but magically doesn't roll up her thighs as she throws a couple of side kicks. She nods in approval. "It'll work. Leo, you're on." She tosses something at him.

Leo catches the tiny capsule and tucks it into an inner pocket. As he does, his face changes shape, and his caftan seems to get brighter.

"That's amazing!" Elodie says. "I need some of those—then I can wear sweats and still look great."

Vanti chuckles. "The tech uses your clothes to create the appearance. If you used one with sweats, you'd have a baggy, pant-shaped outfit. Shall we go?"

"Where's Garabana?" I ask. "Shouldn't we say thank you?"

Hy-Mi flicks his ring. "I've sent a gratuity—that should be sufficient. Garabana knows his clients—most of them prefer not to be disturbed at this point." He gestures to the door.

I look back as we exit. "Thanks for the help!" I call over my shoulder.

"You're welcome," Garabana's voice whispers.

THIRTY

THE LEWEIAN EMBASSY occupies a narrow property on the far edge of Paradise Alley, at the end of the bay. The cliff falls away on three sides, offering fantastic views of the sea. The fourth side is bounded by a ten-meter wall, separating the Leweian property from the foul capitalists of Kaku. I've heard the property on the other side is notoriously hard to keep rented.

"What is that stench?" Kara asks as we step from the bubble.

Leo sucks in a deep breath. "That is the notorious *terkfiske*—a delicacy of Lewei. I've missed that smell. It's one of the reasons I took the job at Sierra Hotel."

My eyes water. "Is that what we were smelling at Sierra Hotel last week?" I rearrange my ridiculous dress, snatching a trailing end out of the bubble door as it closes.

"Kind of." Leo offers his arm to Elodie. "Ser Zhang's chef doesn't have a clue how to prepare it. Sad for a Leweian chef to be so poorly trained."

"Please don't ever make that at our place." I kick the streamers of gauze out of my way as I turn toward the building.

The embassy is built in a style similar to Zijin, with the steep roofs, elaborate trims, and many colors of pain, but here the building appears to be a single well-planned structure. It's both more attractive and less charming than the hodgepodge of structures strung together near Sierra Hotel.

Tall poles topped with flickering globes stand on either side of the walkway. Between each pair of lights, a man or woman dressed in Leweian military regalia stands at attention. The salt breeze brings the scent of the ocean —and the *terkfiske*. I cough.

O'Neill crooks an elbow at me, and I put my hand on it like a debutante. I skipped my upper-lev coming out by running away to the Techno-Inst, but the years of deportment classes have stuck with me. To some extent. There were some things that never took.

We parade up the wide, red-carpeted steps, with me and O'Neill in the lead, my "entourage" following, and Vanti bringing up the rear. I glance back —she struts up the stairs as if she owns them, and even though I know she's on high alert, she appears carefree.

The double front doors are thrown wide, and light streams out onto the deep porch. Two men dressed in white caftans—very similar to the ones Leo wears at Sierra Hotel—bow. A blue shimmer fills the doorway—the visible indication of the weapon scan. We step through, and a low chime sounds—all clear. A woman in a severe black suit steps forward, her hand outstretched. O'Neill gives her the invitation. She scans it with her holo-ring, then bows and melts into the shadows.

"I can't believe Mother passed on this—it seems right up her alley," I whisper to O'Neill.

"She gets invitations to things like this every other month. Maybe she's getting tired of them." He guides me into an enormous room. Stairs lead down to a crowded ballroom. Musicians play in one corner, and a few hardy souls dance nearby. Most of the guests stand at tall tables, whispering and pointing at each other.

"More likely R'ger is tired of them." We turn to the right and take a side stair to a higher level. An open balcony runs around the room, with a receiving line on the far end. A mass of people moves slowly forward, with human wait staff offering drinks and food to those in line.

"Vanti is on the move," O'Neill mutters.

I resist the urge to look back—we don't want to draw attention to her disappearance. She'll attempt to infiltrate the private sections of the embassy while we provide cover. The rest of my entourage chatters loudly as they head down the stairs to the main ballroom.

"Are you sure bringing Leo was a good idea?" I whisper and wave off an enthusiastic server. "Won't they have DNA scanners?"

"Highly likely, but that data takes time to crunch. They won't realize he was here until later this week. He's safe enough—unless someone recognizes him. And with Vanti's techno-mods, that's not a concern."

The line moves quickly, and soon we reach the far end of the room. As we round the corner, I catch sight of the official party. A tall woman with a bald head and a body-hugging dress stands between two military men. She's thin—her rib cage clearly visible through the green fabric. Two more robust women and three men—all bald as well—stand behind her. They are armed.

We move closer. Another white-clothed minion steps forward and announces, "Sera Annabelle Morgan, Prime Intern to the Chair, SK'Corp, and her fiancé, Tiberius O'Neill y Mendoza bin Tariq e Reynolds."

I step forward, and my dress pulls savagely. Something tears. "Zark." I lift my foot and kick the streamer out of the way, my face heating.

O'Neill pauses long enough for me to regain my balance, then urges me forward. He bows to the ambassador.

I hold out my fist and bump it against her bony knuckles. "Thank you for your kind invitation, Ambassador. I'm so pleased to meet you."

"My pleasure." Her voice is deep with a rough edge, as if she's screamed a lot in the past.

A vision of her yelling her way into office dances across my mind, and I bite back a smirk. "Is this your first visit to Kaku?"

"It is."

"How are things back home?" I ask. Did her eyes flicker, or was that my imagination? "On Lewei?"

"You only live once, but if you do it right, once is enough."

"Uh, sure. Is that a quote?" I smile my formal smile.

"From one of the great prophets of Lewei, Mae West." She turns away.

I hike up my stupid dress and steer O'Neill to the steps. "What was that about?"

He gives a tiny shrug as he scans the people on the steps. "I don't try to understand top-levs—that's your job. Down the steps and to the left."

We descend to the main ballroom and weave through the guests to join the rest of our group.

Something jerks the back of my dress, stopping me cold, and my hand is yanked away from O'Neill's arm. I turn and see one of my streamers trapped beneath another guest's shoe. More guests close around me, and another streamer pulls tight.

I tap the first man on the shoulder. "Hi. Sorry to bother you. Could you…"

He stares at me blankly, then speaks in broken phrases. "Sera? What is? My pardon?"

I point at his feet. "You're on my dress."

He glances down, then looks up with horror in his eyes. "Mille pardons, Sera! Does I—how this?"

"It's not your fault." I smile and shake my head. I don't want to start an interstellar incident over this stupid dress. "Not a problem. Could you just lift your foot?"

"So sorry. So sorry!" He keeps muttering as he takes an exaggerated step back, bumping into another guest.

"No, it's my fault." I lean down and scoop up the trailing fabric. "Thanks. Sorry." I bow a little and step back, bumping into someone else.

Something wet splashes on my bare back. "Ah!" I spin around.

A large woman stares at me, one hand over her mouth, the other holding an empty glass. "I'm so sorry!" She reaches out with a napkin and tries to swipe at my back.

I jump back, dropping the trailing streamers. "No, I'm good."

O'Neill appears over the woman's shoulder. "Let me get Kara. There must be a restroom…" He disappears into the crowd.

"There is a lounge over there, behind that stand of *sterk* trees." The large woman points to a planter filled with tall blue fronds. "I was headed that direction myself. Let me show you."

"My friend is coming—"

She cuts me off, sweeping me in front of her, like the space trash ships around SK2. "We should get the stain out before it sets."

"What were you drinking? I didn't see any stain." I pause and twist around to peer at my backside, but she grabs my arm and keeps moving. The woman is inescapable.

"Right back here." She pushes me behind the sterk trees, toward an unmarked door. It slides open as we approach, and she hustles me inside.

I stumble into a room with peach walls, pale wooden floors, and two heavy couches. Another door opens, and two more women come out. They're dressed in dark clothing, like Vanti usually wears. One pushes past my benefactor toward the outer door. The other circles around the room.

We face off. She looks me up and down, her eyes flickering over the ridiculous dress, my sleek updo, my professionally applied makeup, and down to my feet.

The woman who brought me in jerks to a stop. "I—excuse me!" Her face goes pale. She turns. The woman by the door steps aside, allowing her to escape, then moves toward me.

I lift my chin. I am in a busy embassy—they can't possibly do anything to me here. And I have mad self-defense skills. Or at least slightly-pissed-off self-defense skills. Plus, a security team. I flick my holo-ring to call O'Neill and Vanti.

The woman in front of me lifts a small, cylindrical device.

Behind me, the door opens, and O'Neill bursts in, with Elodie and Kara right behind him.

"Sera Morgan, can I have your autograph?" The girl barely notices my friends' precipitous entrance.

"What?" I fling up a hand. "It's okay. They're fans, I guess." It's weird, but I've gotten used to it in the last year. They don't usually box me in like prey, though. I turn back to the girl. "What are you doing here? You're not exactly dressed for the occasion."

"We're part of the catering staff." The girl giggles and holds out the pen again. She yanks up her black sleeve and offers her arm. "Right here?"

"On your arm?" I give the others a puzzled look over my shoulder, then scrawl "Annabelle Morgan" on her arm.

The second girl steps forward and flutters her eyelashes. "How about here?" She pulls the neck of her shirt wide, exposing the top of her large breasts.

"How about here?" I scribble my name on a piece of my skirt and rip the streamer free. "Bonus, you get a piece of my Garabana dress."

"I want a piece of your Garabana!" The first girl grabs at the fabric, but her friend pulls it away. She spins and her hand flashes out to grab my skirt.

O'Neill's fingers clamp around her wrist. "You got your autograph. Time to go. Or I'll have a word with your employer."

The girl yanks her arm away. Then her eyes travel up O'Neill's torso to his face. Her lips pucker in an exaggerated "ooh" and she shimmies a shoulder. "I'll have a word with your employer."

Her friend giggles. "That made no sense. She's his employer. You already had a word with her."

O'Neill stares her down. "Time to go, ladies." He points to the door.

Elodie waves her hand over the sensor, and the door slides open. Kara gives the girls a little finger wave as they hurry away.

"I'll speak to the caterer." O'Neill trails a finger along my arm as he turns away.

"Don't do that—they'll get fired." I grab his arm and pull him close for a fast kiss.

"They shouldn't accost guests at an event like this—it's a nightmare for security." He kisses me back. "But I won't say anything if you don't want me to." He nods at Elodie and Kara and disappears.

Kara drops onto the couch with a groan. "I don't know why I thought an embassy party would be a good idea. My feet are killing me."

"You can stay here for a while. They have a MassageBot4000." I flick the holo-ad that popped up when I walked in and push it to Kara.

"Ooh, it's complimentary! Yes, please." She waves her hand through the green icon, and a little bot hums out of a corner. It unfolds by her feet, and she puts them inside. A second later, she moans. "I need one of these."

Elodie returns from the inner room with a wet cloth in her hand. "Let me wipe that sticky stuff off your back. Do you think she spilled it on purpose?"

"Why would she do that?" Kara asks without opening her eyes.

"Kidnapping?" Elodie sponges my sticky back. "She managed to miss the dress completely."

"I thought I felt some trickle down my butt." I cringe. "And I was hoping I could justify ditching this dress."

"Ditch my dress?" a deep voice asks. "Your fiancé said you needed help with a spill. Now I find out you don't like my fabulous creation?"

I spin to confront Garabana, standing just inside the doorway. "It's not your fault—I'm too clumsy to wear a dress with trailing bits." I wave at the dirty streamers around my feet. "And a woman spilled something on me."

"The drink is no problem." Garabana sweeps into the room, waving a hand. One of his minions—now clad in head-to-toe olive green—follows behind. "The dress is treated to repel liquids." He snaps his fingers, and the woman hands him a glass of red wine.

Where was she hiding that?

He lifts a fold of the skirt, bunching it to form a bowl, and pours the liquid into it. "See, it doesn't soak in at all." His helper hands him a white napkin and he soaks up the wine, staining the napkin, but not the dress. "I don't know how you managed to get the train dirty."

"It's dragging on the floor. People are stepping on it!" I swish the skirt around, demonstrating.

Garabana flings a hand to his forehead. "A failure! I am crushed! I should have anticipated—the client is—" He breaks off to pat at imaginary tears. When the wet napkin hits his cheek, he starts and tosses it at the minion. She catches it, and it disappears.

"Look, I think your creation would be lovely for someone else— someone who doesn't trip over her own feet. But it's just not working for me."

"That's because you desecrated the underskirt!" He points at my legs. "If you'd left it intact, you would have been required to take small steps, and that prevents you from tripping over the train."

"Oops." I grimace at my feet. "Sorry."

He spins to face his minion. "I must create. Go out. Do not let anyone else in."

Without a word, she sets a large green duffle bag on the floor and disappears out the door.

Garabana turns back to me. "Okay, let's go find your friend, shall we?" His voice has lost the flamboyant accent, and his words come out precise and clipped.

I stare at him. "What?"

"Vanti isn't getting anywhere on her own, and she wants us to see what we can find. There's a service exit through there." He points to the inner door. "But first, let me fix your dress."

As I gape at him, he opens the bag and pulls out a huge pair of scissors. He snips at the skirt, bits of gauze flying through the air.

"Are you—"

He flings up a hand. "Quiet!" Then he goes back to cutting.

When he's done, my skirt has been cut to knee length, with some longer bits hanging down to my ankles. "This preserves the general appearance but allows greater freedom of movement. I should have realized you'd need more give."

"Who are you?" Elodie, Kara, and I all ask at once.

"I am Garabana. But you can call me Gary."

THIRTY-ONE

Kara volunteers to stay behind and guard our backs. And keep the MassageBot4000 company. Elodie and I follow Gary into the inner room.

"Do you work for SK'Corp security?" Elodie asks.

Gary laughs. "Not quite. Kaku Department of Defense."

"Military?" Her eyes grow big.

"More para-military. Although my current position involves listening and reporting rather than doing anything heroic." He flicks his holo-ring and waves a code slip at the wall. A section slides away, revealing a well-lit corridor. "After you."

"Wait a minute." I cross my arms. "How do we know you're on our side? I want to see some ID."

"Do you think Vanti and Griz would have let me anywhere near you if I wasn't legit?" He flicks his holo-ring and swipes a file at me.

"Griz? Either you're who you say you are, or you've really done your homework." I run his file through a couple of filter apps I keep handy for this kind of situation, then nod at Elodie. "If this is a fake, it's the best I've ever seen. He's the real deal."

Elodie's eyes narrow. "What kind of KDD agent pretends to be a high-end designer? How did you pull that off?"

"You were very convincing." I agree.

He shrugs. "I've always liked fashion, and I studied acting at the Grissom

Sorbonne. Employment was tight when I graduated, and the KDD offered me a job. We don't have all day, so let's get moving, shall we?"

This corridor reminds me of the bot ducts on SK2—blank white walls with scuff marks near the floor from lower-end cleaning bots. The ceiling panels glow as we approach and dim after we've passed. It's narrow—less than an arm-span. Just enough space for the bots and human servants to pass, unseen by those of higher social status.

We pass doors marked in Leweian script. I trail my fingers over one of the plates. "Can you read this?"

Gary pauses to look. "Storage." He moves on to the next. "Break room."

"What are we looking for?" Elodie asks.

"We're looking for Cas." I heroically refrain from adding, "Duh."

"We're looking for evidence of the alleged coup O'Neill reported." Gary moves to the next door. "If we find your friend, that's a bonus."

I turn to Elodie, and she raises an eyebrow. "Does it seem reasonable that Ty would send *you* to help *him*?" she whispers.

She's right. O'Neill would never send me to do an agent's job. Obviously, he doesn't know Gary is taking us back here. What's his game?

"We're here now, and he doesn't care about Cas, so I'm going to keep looking." I tap softly on the door Gary said was storage. "Cas, are you in there?"

No response.

My audio implant pings. "They wouldn't keep him here," Gary says. He's well ahead of us, but his voice comes through soft and clear. "He'll be upstairs or in the basement. I'd vote basement."

I mute the implant and lean close to Elodie. "See if you can reach Vanti."

As we catch up to Gary, Elodie shakes her head. "Not connecting," she mouths.

"This door leads to the upper floors. Why don't you girls go up, and I'll go down. If anyone asks, one of you has a headache and you're looking for a place to lie down."

"This isn't my first recon," I say. If he's letting us go alone, he isn't planning to do anything to us. The little voice in my head suggests he might have partners waiting upstairs.

Thanks, little voice.

"It's my first official recon, but I've snuck into lots of places." Elodie puts a hand to her temple and leans against the wall as if she's spent. "The key is to look like you belong there."

Gary winks and opens the door for us. "I'll meet you back in the ball-room in twenty."

Elodie straightens and darts into the stairway. I pause to look back at Gary. He stops at the next door and grins before opening it and stepping through.

Elodie waits for me at the top of the first flight. "I think we should keep going. They aren't going to risk keeping him anywhere near the guests."

I nod. "Sounds good. We should probably talk through the audio."

"I never learned to do that quietly." Elodie snickers as she rounds the corner and skips up the steep steps.

I tromp up behind. "Me, neither. Vanti and O'Neill are amazing. They can be standing right next to you and have a whole conversation, and you'll never hear a thing."

"That kind of proficiency makes me nervous. You'd never know if they're paying attention to you." She runs up another flight.

"I hadn't thought of it that way." She's as helpful as the little voice in my head.

"Wanna try this floor?" Without waiting for a reply, she opens the door.

This hallway is obviously part of the embassy living quarters. Thick carpet covers the floors, with dark wood paneling on the lower half of the walls, warm beige above. Dark pictures in ornate frames hang between heavy wood doors.

"Is that—music?" I ask.

"I'm not sure I'd call it music, but it's something a kid might play." She cocks her head and tiptoes down the hall.

As we get closer, the music gets louder. And louder. This hallway must have sound-buffering built in, but the noise is overwhelming the sensors. We stop by a door that's rattling in its frame.

I flick the noise cancelling app on my ring, and the music decreases to a reasonable level. Elodie peers over my shoulder, then does the same. I call her on the audio.

"This is my kind of stealth," she says before I can get a word in. "Doesn't matter how loud I talk."

"It matters a little," I say. "Try to whisper."

"Okay. Ready?" She taps gently on the door—as if anyone would hear that—and without waiting for a reply, opens it.

This is clearly the room of a teen. Clothing covers the heavy furniture, socks lay abandoned on the floor, and several mostly empty dishes sit on every horizontal surface. Thick curtains hang from the canopied bed and a pair of feet stick out.

"This can't be Cas—the door wasn't locked." I turn the knob again. "See?"

"Try the inside."

"This side is unlocked too." I turn.

Elodie is already across the room reaching for the curtains. She pushes one aside a fraction and peeks in. Then she wrenches it open. "Cas! We've been worried sick about you!"

The music drops to a murmur. The boy sits up, staring at Elodie. "What do you want?"

At least I think that's what he says. I hurriedly turn off my noise cancelling app.

"I'm Elodie, but Triana is here, too." She points at me.

"Who are you?" the boy and I say together.

THIRTY-TWO

"THIS ISN'T CAS?" Elodie stares at the boy sitting on the bed. He's wearing a red T-shirt and pants with monsters or dinosaurs on them. "He looks like Leo."

I shake my head. "There's a resemblance—he looks like both of them. But this boy is younger."

"Who are you, and why are you talking about me as if I'm not here? I shall call security!"

"No, please don't do that." I put out my hand. "I'm Triana. We're looking for Cas. He's—a friend told us he might be up here."

"I am Tarkhan, the heir to the Leweian premier. Why are you in my bedroom?"

"You're—wait. What?" Elodie sinks onto the edge of the bed. "How can you be the heir? What about Cas?"

"Cas? You mean Caspian?" The boy laughs. "Has he been telling you he's the heir?"

"Is he here?" I ask.

"Yeah, Cas is here. He's in detention." The boy laughs again, but his eyes look worried.

"Can you tell us what's going on?" I point at a clothing-draped chair. "Do you mind if I sit down?"

He gives Elodie a dirty look. "You may both sit. Over there." He thrusts his chin at me.

Elodie stares at Tarkhan, and he stares back, belligerent. Then his eyes waver. Elodie rises slowly and moves to a different chair. With another look over her shoulder, she picks up the discarded clothing and sets it on the bed by Tarkhan's feet. Then she sits.

"Sorry," the boy mutters.

Elodie's definitely got the mom mojo.

I scoot more clothes aside and perch on a chair. "Where is Cas, and why is he here?"

"Cas is my cousin. His father is my uncle."

"And who is your father?" I ask when he doesn't offer anything more.

"My father is the premier of Lewei."

"The new premier, or the old one?" I ask.

"Is he here?" Elodie says over me.

"The premier? Of course not. He's on Lewei."

"How long has your father been premier?" I ask.

"Some time." The boy bites his lip.

"Does that mean weeks or years?" I ask.

He ignores me. "Why do you want Cas?"

"He was living next door to us, then he disappeared," Elodie says as if this were the most normal thing in the world. "We thought we'd check on him when we came to the party."

"Look, we'd love to stay and chat, but we need to get back. Can you tell us where we might find Cas? I, uh, have something that belongs to him."

"Cas owns nothing," Tarkhan says.

"What do you mean?" Elodie asks.

"The state owns everything on Lewei. If you have something that Cas was using, it belongs to the state. And therefore, you should give it to me." He holds out a hand. "Since I'm the heir."

"I'm not sure that's how it works." I stand. "Maybe I'll give it to the embassy steward instead."

"No, don't!" The words burst from the boy in alarm.

"Why not?" Elodie asks.

"They'll punish him. He's not supposed to talk to outsiders." He bites his lip again.

"Are you supposed to talk to outsiders?" I ask.

His head shakes.

"So, maybe you can tell me where to find Cas, and I can give it to him myself. Then nobody will get in trouble."

He points to the ceiling, his lips pressed together.

"He's in the attic?" I ask

"Servants' quarters. Or he might be in the basement."

Elodie holds something out to the boy.

"What's this?" He takes the foil wrapped cube.

"I filched some chocolate from the party. Thought you might like a piece."

He unwraps the candy and shoves it into his mouth. "They don't let me have chocolate. It's good enough for the capitalist pig guests but not the true children of Lewei." He gives Elodie a sideways glance. "Not that you're a capitalist pig."

"Oh, no, I totally am." She pulls a handful of the wrapped chocolates from her tiny purse and drops them in Tarkhan's lap. "Sometimes that's a good thing. We gotta go. Thanks for your help."

"I did not help you." He scoops up the chocolate and hides it under his pillow. "I would not help the enemy!"

Elodie winks. "And I didn't give you any chocolate."

The music cranks back up before we get the door closed.

"That was...interesting." Elodie cocks her head. "Next floor?"

"Next floor."

We find the service stairs and hurry up the steps. This hallway looks much like the last one, but there's no music blasting.

"Let's keep going up. Tarkhan said the servants' quarters. I know everyone is supposedly equal on Lewei, but they wouldn't waste this on servants, would they?" I glance up the steps.

"Probably not. We can always come back here if we don't find him up there. We'd better hurry, though. We've been gone a long time." She takes the steps two at a time.

I puff after her to the top floor.

This corridor is stark, like the stairwell. Patched white and gray tiles cover the floor, and the walls are a dirty ivory. Plastek doors with numbers line the walls—much closer together than the wood doors below.

"Servants' quarters," I whisper. "You go that way; I'll take this end."

I tiptoe along the hallway, stopping to listen at each door. No one appears to be home. They're probably all working the party.

"Cas?" I call softly through each door but get no answer. At the end, a high, tiny window looks out over the grounds. If I stand on tiptoe, I can see the tops of the cliffs overlooking the ocean. The full moon shines on the water, like a silver carpet. It's a beautiful view, but apparently not to be wasted on the lower classes.

"I thought everyone was equal on Lewei," I mutter.

"Some are more equal than others," Elodie says through the audio. "Find anything?"

"Nothing."

I turn back and smack into a broad black-clothed chest. "May I help you?"

THIRTY-THREE

"I, uh, was looking for someplace to lie down." I put my hand to my temple like Elodie did and sag against the wall. "I'm not feeling well. I may be delusional. Are you real?" I poke a finger into the rock-solid chest. "Run, Elodie!" I whisper.

"Runel odie?" The man grabs both my arms and spins me around. He scans me with his holo-ring. "What is that? Some obscene capitalist expression?"

"I—yeah, sure. It means, boy, you're buff for a hallucination."

He twists me around again, facing me down the hall. Elodie is gone. "Move. Back to the ballroom." He pushes me toward the stairs.

I stagger from side to side, bouncing off the wall, to give her more time to get away.

The man grabs my arm. "You need to sleep it off."

"Eggs-ack-ly. Tha's why I came up here. Lookin' for a place to nap."

"No napping for you. I'll call your vehicle and send you home."

"Oh, don' do that! I don' wanna miss the whole party!" I stop suddenly, and he slams into me. "Ow! That hurt, you big oaf!" I slap his bicep, which is like slapping steel. I shake my stinging fingers.

He grabs my hand and scans my holo-ring. A file pops open on his ring, and my name is highlighted on the guest list. "Sera Morgan?" His eyes narrow. "What are you doing up here? Where are your security?"

"I left 'em downstairs. D'you know how hard it's to sneak away? Like, so hard. They watch me. All. The. Time."

"It's their job."

Is that empathy for my security detail? I'll have to tell O'Neill and Vanti. Which reminds me, I don't know where Vanti is, and O'Neill is probably panicking if he's discovered I'm gone. "I prolly shouldn't do that, huh?" I let him steer me down the steps.

When we reach the next floor, he guides me out of the service stairwell and down the thickly carpeted hall. I trip along, knocking into doors as we go. If he's going to get rid of me, I want to make sure someone knows I've been here. "Where're you takin' me?" I say loudly.

"Back to the party." He pushes me through a door at the end of the hall onto the top landing of a grand staircase. "We'll use the float tube—I'm not sure you'd make it down the stairs." He guides me across the landing to the float tube, and we drop to the main floor.

The float tube terminates near the lounge. As we step out, Elodie hurries through the door with Kara on her heels. Both women look terrified. They see me and do a double take.

"Triana! Where have you been? I've been worried sick." Elodie grabs my arm and smiles at the guard. "Thank you for finding her!" She pulls me away.

But the guard doesn't let go. "Triana? I thought this was Sera Morgan." He scans my ring again. His jaw tightens and he mutters something. It sounds like, "Security breach, sector twelve."

Within seconds, three more people dressed in black converge on us. "You will need to come with us—all of you." He catches sight of Kara's huge stomach, and his brow furrows. Then he pushes all three of us toward a curtain. One of the new guards pulls it away to reveal an opening.

O'Neill steps in front of the door, a pleasant smile on his face. He flicks his ID to the guard. "Good evening. I am Sera Morgan's chief of security. Is there a problem?"

"You'll need to come with us, ser." The big man sweeps us all into another white hallway. He steps back, and a female coworker ushers Elodie, Kara, and me into a small room with an even smaller cell in the back. "You'll have to wait here until we decide what to do with you. Ser, there is an irregularity with the woman's identification. I will speak with you outside."

"I can explain! I am Annabelle Morgan. I can show you my SekurID. They just call me Triana. It's been all over the net. I ran away from home and changed my name. But now I'm back and it's all fine."

The man ignores me, and the door shuts. The female guards push Kara and Elodie into the cell.

"Hey—be careful with her! Can't you see she's pregnant?" I grab the woman holding Kara and pull her away.

"Assaulting one of us is not a good way to get out of this trouble!" The other guard squeezes my wrist, and I drop the first woman's shoulder.

"I'm not assaulting her. I'm protecting my friend." I stomp my foot for emphasis.

"Get in there, or I'll use this on you." She holds up a stunner.

"Nope, I'm good." I hurry into the cell and sit next to Kara. "See? No problem."

The cell door clangs shut.

I wake my holo-ring and call Hy-Mi. The call doesn't go through.

"This is a blocked cell," the guard says. "No communications. Even mine doesn't work." She flicks her own holo-ring. It lights up. "Okay, it works, but I can't call out." She activates the communications protocol, but nothing happens.

"There's got to be a way we can use that," I mutter to Kara.

"Don't worry, Ty will get us out. That's his job, isn't it?"

"Technically, no, it's Vanti's job. And Yellin's and al-Karendi's and Limberghetti's." My eyes sting and I sniff. "It takes a lot of people to keep me safe, and I make sure they have the hardest possible time doing it."

Kara pats my arm. "You've been really good this week. And Gary told you to do this—he was a trusted source."

I wipe my eyes. "Listen to you, with your security jargon."

She rolls her eyes. "I've learned a lot in the last year or two."

The guards sit at a small table, with a deck of cards dealt out. The blonde one slaps a card on the table and says, "Four."

Elodie leans against the bars and smiles. "Are you playing Quartile?"

The green-haired woman drops a three on the table. "Hit me." She looks at Elodie. "You play?"

"A bit." She giggles. "I've been on a spectacular losing streak. I'd love to break my luck."

Green glances at Blonde, a smirk playing around the corners of her mouth. "You think it will?"

"It has to eventually, right?" Elodie pulls a credit coin out of her tiny purse and flips it in the air. It sparks purple and gold.

Blonde's eyes follow the coin's arc. "You want us to deal you in?"

Elodie shrugs. "I doubt we'll be here long enough to play a whole hand. I'm sure Ser O'Neill will convince your boss to let us go."

Blonde snorts. "He's not our boss. And they can't let anyone go until morning. Once you're in, the rules say you gotta stay until the prefect reviews your case."

"Where's the prefect?" Elodie tosses the coin again.

Green barks a harsh laugh. "He's back home—on Lewei. Was recalled a week ago."

"Before or after the coup?" I ask.

Green glares at me. "What coup?"

"Never mind." I leave Elodie to her card game and turn to Kara. "I'm betting the previous prefect was recalled after the coup and they're sending a new one. I wonder why they didn't come with the new ambassador?"

"Ty will get us out." Kara pats her belly. "He has to. I have a birthing class tomorrow."

"It doesn't sound promising." I pat her hand, then stand. "My friend can't stay here until your prefect comes back from Lewei. She's pregnant. She could pop at any time."

Blonde stops shuffling the cards and peers through the bars. "She hasn't had any contractions."

"Yet. She's due this week." I cross my fingers behind my back—Kara still has three weeks to go.

Behind me, Kara makes a muffled sound. I turn, and she's sitting with her eyes closed, one hand gripping the edge of the bench so hard her knuckles are white.

"Good effort," I whisper, "but they aren't going to believe it now."

"I'm not faking," she whispers back. "I just have really bad timing."

"Seriously?"

She grabs my wrist and puts my hand against her belly. It's rock hard.

I press gently, but there's no give. "Is it supposed to be like that?"

"It is when you're contracting," she says through gritted teeth. "Time me, will you?"

I stare at her, appalled. She can't go into labor in the Leweian Embassy's dingy cell.

"Time it!" Her voice flicks me like a whip.

"Sorry!" I open my stopwatch app and hit the start button. "Let me get your mom."

Kara shakes her head, then her whole body relaxes. "No, let her chat up the guards. If anyone can talk us out of here, it's *Larin*."

I drop onto the bench next to Kara, then jump up again. "Do you want to lie down?"

"Absolutely not. In fact, I need to stand up. That was probably a false alarm. I've been having them for weeks. But this one hurt." She pushes herself up from the bench and shuffles across the small cell.

I hover beside her as if she'll tip over without my support. The truth is, Kara is one of the strongest people I know. But that doesn't mean she should have to give birth in a cell.

Elodie stands by the bars, holding a handful of cards. As we approach, she drops a couple of them, and they flutter to the floor landing face up. "Don't look at those!" She drops to her knees to scoop up the cards.

The guards laugh. "If you drop the cards, that's your own fault," Green says.

Elodie smiles sheepishly and rearranges her cards. She reaches through the bars to drop one on the table. "Since you already saw that one. Good thing it was a low one. Two."

They play back and forth, cards exchanging hands, money sliding across the table. I keep a sharp eye on Kara, but she doesn't have another contraction. After twelve minutes on the stopwatch, I relax a fraction.

"Tin!" Elodie throws her hand on the table. "I win!" She reaches through the bars.

Blonde raps Elodie's fingers with her stun wand. "Hands off, prisoner. Cheaters don't get the winnings." She shoves half the credit coins across the table to Green and scoops up the rest.

"But I won! Fair and square!" Elodie stamps her foot. "That's my money."

"Such a shame gambling isn't allowed here." Blonde cackles while Green shoves the cards into her belt pouch. "We gotta get back on duty. I'll let Enrique know you're ready for lights out."

"Wait a minute! I want my credit back!" Elodie shakes the bars as the laughing guards shove the table away from the cell and strut out of the room. "You cheated me!"

The door slams shut.

Elodie stops yelling, listening intently. "They're gone." She takes a step away from the bars, revealing a card beneath her left foot. She scoops it off the floor and hurries to the door. "Do you know how to jimmy a lock?"

THIRTY-FOUR

"Do you?" I stare at Elodie.

She slides the playing card between the cell gate and the jamb.

"I learned when I was a kid. It doesn't work on an electronic lock, of course, but they went old school with this one. Probably used to power-outages at home. I've heard Lewei is notorious for them." As she talks, she wiggles the card up and down in the narrow slot.

"You know how to…" Kara stares at her mom, her mouth open.

"If they're watching us, it won't do any good," I say. "We're sure to be under surveillance."

"I don't think so," Elodie says absently as she works the card. "You heard what Blondie said. Gambling isn't allowed. If this room were under surveillance, they wouldn't have been playing in here—and they certainly wouldn't have been playing with an inmate."

"You are diabolical."

"Who are you and what have you done with my mother?" Kara whispers.

The door clicks and Elodie swings it open. "Ta da. Of course, that was the easy part. If that door is locked, we're screwed." She waves the card at the door to the hallway.

"They didn't unlock it when they left." I grab the card just in case. "Green turned the knob. You ready?"

195

The other two nod, and I open the door a fraction. No one yells, so I swing it wide and peek into the hall. Empty. "I wonder where they took Ty?"

Kara whimpers.

I spin around. "Another one? It's been," I swipe open my app, "fifteen minutes and twenty-six seconds."

"Are you having contractions?" Elodie demands. "We need to get you to the birthing center."

"You heard Triana—they're fifteen minutes and I've only had two."

"Sixteen minutes—not that anyone is counting. Except, I guess I am," I blather. Apprehension curls through my chest, squeezing. "We need to go."

I run to the end of the hall and fling open the door. The man standing in front of it spins to confront me. "This woman is in labor! We need an ambulance!" I shout.

Confusion and panic cross his face. Panic kicks confusion's butt. "I don't know what to do."

"You heard me, call an ambulance!" I push him aside and turn back to take Kara's arm.

She grips my hand. "Go find O'Neil and Vanti. And Cas."

"But—"

"*Larin* will stay with me—we have this all planned. I'll see you soon." She squeezes my hand one more time, then lets go and latches onto the guard's arm. "Here's another one. It's a doozy!" She hunches over and winks at me.

Elodie whirls past me, talking up a storm. She somehow manages to close the door with me still inside. I stare at the white surface, bemused.

"Here you are!" Gary appears at my shoulder, his voice chipper. "Griz sent me to get you out of the cell, but you were gone!"

"Elodie broke us out. And Kara's faking labor—kind of. Where's Ty?"

"He's distracting the security detail. Now's our chance to get Vanti out." He turns and lopes down the hall.

I scramble after him, grateful for my shorn dress and flat shoes. "Do you know where she is? Cas is supposed to be upstairs somewhere."

"Nope, Vanti found him in the basement. That place is grim." Gary stops at a door and flicks his holo-ring. A security bypass program pops up, and he flicks a few commands, then swipes a code slip at the door. It slides open. "This way."

I pause in the doorway. "Did Ty tell you to take me with you?"

Gary stops a few steps down. "Of course not. He told me to get you back to Hy-Mi. But Vanti said you're useful on an op, and I figure I can watch you if you're with me. And make use of your crazy programming talents." He wiggles his fingers as if he's manipulating software, then whirls around and clatters down the next flight of stairs.

Should I go with him and help Vanti or get to safety and make O'Neill's job easier? I know which one would be more fun. But leaving this job to the pros would be the responsible thing.

Behind me, a door opens, and an angry voice echoes down the hallway. "Where'd they go?"

Too late—decision made. I jump forward and the door slides shut at my back. I race down the steps, nearly colliding with Gary on the next landing.

"There you are." He hurtles down three more flights before we reach a door. "I was beginning to think you deserted me!"

"This basement is really down there." I lean against the wall, breathing heavily.

"What do you expect of a Leweian dungeon?" Gary plays with his program, and the door opens.

"Do embassies often have dungeons?" As we step through the door, lights flicker on, illuminating a ten-meter long stretch of hallway. We move forward, and the corridor lights up one section at a time.

Gary lifts one shoulder. "Leweian ones do. They don't call it that, of course. I believe this is listed as merchandise storage on the blueprints. It has to be deep to keep the vodka at an even temperature. Or so they claim."

As I follow Gary, I open a message app and ping Vanti. <where are you?>

"Hurry up, Annabelle," Gary calls over his shoulder. "I think I heard a kid crying."

<In the ballroom. Where are you and Griz?>

I stop. If Vanti is in the ballroom, where is Gary taking me?

<Ty is trying to bail me out of embassy jail. I'm with Gary in the basement looking for you.>

<Who's Gary? Nvm. Get out. I'm coming.>

Zark. I should have known anyone working with O'Neill wouldn't have brought me down here. Except Vanti leads me into crazy situations all the time.

"You coming, Annabelle?"

The lights in the hall between me and Gary flicker and go dark—motion activated on a short timer. I glance at the door to the stairs, but it's closed. I'm close enough it should have stayed open—if it uses a motion sensor. But Gary needed a special app to open it. I wave at the door panel.

Nothing happens.

"You can't go that way, Annabelle," Gary says. "It's locked. You need to come with me."

"You don't work with Ty and Vanti." I stay where I am, holding my hand sideways, so I can activate my holo-ring without him being able to read it.

"Took you long enough." He starts down the hall toward me. "No security detail worth their paycheck would bring their principal down here."

"But Vanti might." I bring up a net connection program and worm my way into the embassy's internal system.

He laughs as he strolls forward. "That's what made this so easy. She's a cowboy, and everyone knows it. It was too easy to convince you." The section of lights between us flickers on in response to his movement.

I find the electrical system. If I shut down the whole building, will the doors unlock? According to building codes, they should—for safety. But this is an embassy, and based on reports from Lewei, they care more about keeping prisoners in than human safety. Better to just—

I poke an icon, and the light over my head flickers out.

THIRTY-FIVE

GARY SHAKES HIS HEAD, tsking. "If you don't move, the motion sensors think you're gone, and the lights go out."

"Even if you do move," I mutter under my breath and turn out the light over his head.

Gary curses. "You little *crepiv*. What did you do?"

I set a passcode and firewall around the electrical system, keeping everyone but me out. The light at the far end of the hallway goes out.

He curses again.

I cover my holo-ring with my other hand, but the glow through my fingers will still give me away. Before I shut it down, I flick a command at the door behind me, but it doesn't open. Zark.

"There's nowhere for you to go, Annabelle," Gary says. His voice is nearer.

I slip out of my shoes and pick them up. With my ring off, stygian darkness presses against my open eyes. I step across the hall, close to the wall, and tiptoe toward Gary. The hallway is wide—I should be able to get past him. I duck low in case he's got his arms out.

His holo-ring flares on behind me. Squinting, I increase my speed, padding as quietly as possible. The light from his ring feels bright, but it should blind him to my movement in the darkness.

"Annabelle, turn the lights back on. I will find you."

I trail my fingers along the wall as I move, to keep from blundering into anything else. A whoosh and light blooms behind me. I peek over my shoulder. Gary stands in the doorway, speaking softly. Probably telling his accomplices—whoever they are—to lock down the building.

The wall under my fingers ends. I must have reached a cross corridor. I move to the right and look back. When the corner blocks the light from the open door, I flick my holo-ring.

The glow illuminates a tiny space around me. Darkness wraps around like a cocoon. I'm not in a hall but in an open doorway.

"Who's there?" someone whispers.

I spin. The voice came from my right. I lift my hand, trying to see better. This isn't a hallway but a large room. Things rustle around me. Someone—or something—moving. I turn slowly, scanning the darkness.

"Triana, is that you?" the voice whispers.

My eyes rove over the open room, focusing on a boy standing in a cage. "Cas?" I lurch forward and touch his fingers. They're like ice. "What happened?"

"Sh." He grips my hand tightly. "That guy is still out there. Turn off your light."

I shut down the holo-ring. Black drops like a curtain, then slowly recedes in one corner—the entrance to the room glows. A faint shadow looms and fades. Gary must still be standing in the stairwell door.

"What is this place?" I whisper.

"It's the dungeon, obviously," Cas replies.

"Is there anyone else down here?"

"Not that I've seen. Sometimes I hear sounds over there—"

In the darkness, I can't see where he's pointing.

"I'm going to get you out." I pull Elodie's card from my pocket and feel for the cell door. "Do you know where this opens?"

Cold fingers reach through the bars and tug me to the left. "The lock is here." He guides me to the mechanism.

I slide the card into place. "I don't know how to do this. I saw Elodie—can you try? Just keep pushing and wiggling. I'm going to call Ty and Vanti."

Once I'm sure Cas has the card, I move into the darkest corner of the room. I set my ring to minimum light and send a message to Vanti and Ty.

Vanti's reply comes in immediately. <get out! They are dangerous>

<can't get out. Need distraction>

<working>

"How's it going?" I whisper.

"I have no idea." His breathing gets louder. He swears softly. "Dropped the card. Can you shine your ring over here?"

I tiptoe back to him and hold my ring near the floor. "There. Under the bench."

Cas bends down and retrieves the card. Once he's back at the lock, with the card inserted, I douse the light.

"They shut off the light," Cas whispers.

I turn, but darkness meets my eyes. "Can you hear anything?"

Shuffling reaches us. Lights swing wildly across the entrance to the room. "They have flashlights."

The lock clicks loudly.

"Did you hear that?" Gary says. No one responds—at least not out loud.

"Did you get the lock open?" I whisper to Cas.

"Yeah, but there's nowhere to go."

"Is there room under the bench for me?" I push past him and into the cell.

"I—I think so."

"Give me the card." I wave my arm until it comes in contact with his body. I slide my hand down his arm and take the card. After folding it in half, I risk the light of my holo-ring. I place the card across the lock mechanism, then push the door shut. "Do you have anything to hold the door closed?" I shine the light around the room but there's nothing. "You'll have to stand here. Put your foot against the door." Dousing the light, I scramble across the small cell and fold myself under the bench. "Drape that blanket over the end. Make it look like you just dropped it there."

Cas throws the thin fabric across the end of the bench.

"Stay away from the bench. This white dress is too visible if he looks this way."

Cas moves to the door—a whole two meters away—and leans against the bars.

I curl myself against the end of the bench, getting as much of my body as possible behind the blanket. The stone of the floor and wall leech the heat from my body, chilling me to the bone.

Light brightens, and I curl tighter. If he looks this way, he might see my bare feet and legs, but there's nothing I can do about it. I peek out from behind the blanket, focusing on staying as still as possible.

"Are you going to let me out?" Cas demands when the light shines on him. His face is dirty, with dark circles under the eyes. His curly hair is matted and greasy. "My father will punish you for this!"

"I told you, kid, your dad ain't in charge anymore." It's Gary. "There's a new premier, and the son of the old one ain't worth a credit."

"You said I would be treated well—that my status would protect me!"

"I say a lot of things. Part of them are true. I don't suppose you've seen anyone wandering around the basement, have you? I'll let you out if you help me find her." Gary's voice gets louder.

I hold my breath. He just told Cas he lies all the time—surely the boy won't turn on me?

Cas points at the hallway. "I saw someone—or something—moving. It might have been a ghost. It was pale and kinda shredded-looking."

I smirk. Too bad Garabana is just a character Gary plays—telling him his prize dress looked like a ghost would be a masterful play.

"That dress was worth thousands," Gary mutters, and the light shifts.

"You said you'd let me out." Cas grabs the bars.

He doesn't reply, and the light fades away.

"You can come out now," Cas whispers.

"In a minute." I flick my holo-ring. My little bench and blanket cave lights up and I wince. I send a message:

<where's my distraction? need to get out>

Then I open the power panel again. I shut down lights on the rest of this level and the next one down. Then I try to hack into the doors. "Got it." I roll out from under the bench and sit up.

Cas already has the cell door open. "Which way do we go?"

I pull him back into the cell and swing the door mostly shut. "We wait. Vanti and Ty are going to do something. When that happens, we run for the stairs. That way." As I point, the glow from my ring goes out. "Right now, we need to be really quiet and listen."

His fingers bump into my arm, then slide down. I wrap my hand around his frozen one in an effort to give reassurance. He doesn't pull away.

We wait in the darkness for what feels like forever. The faint glow from the hallway seems to dim, but it never completely goes out. Voices echo from either direction from time to time—they're obviously searching and not finding me.

Finally, a fire alarm blares.

I wince. "That's the best they could come up with?"

Cas drags at my arm, but I hold him back. I put my mouth against his ear, so he can hear me over the wailing alert. "They'll think it's me, so they'll check here again."

Footsteps ring on the stone floor. I let go of Cas's fingers and roll under the bench. My dress has picked up a layer of dust from the filthy floor, so I'm less visible than before.

Light flares and swings across the room, pausing then jerking and pausing again. Feet thunder on the hard floor. Several people—probably Gary's accomplices.

"What's happening?" Cas yells. "Is there a fire? You have to let me out!"

The guards ignore him and the light slides away.

"Now." Cas pulls on my arm. "They're gone."

"Perfect." I follow him out of the cell, then pull it shut behind us. Leave a little mystery. When I reach for Cas's hand, his cold fingers grip tight. "Let's go."

We hurry to the hall and peer both directions. It's dark to the right, but the light from the stairway shines on the left like a beacon. "This way." I pull him along. As we get closer, the door slams shut. The alarm cuts out, leaving my ears ringing.

"No!" Even in his frustration, Cas keeps his voice low.

"It's okay—I finally hacked the lock." We reach the door, and I fire up my holo-ring. I wish I had time to get into their vid system, so I can see if anyone is on the other side, but it's too late now. I flick the unlock icon, and the door slides aside.

Light blinds us. Hands grab. I gasp.

THIRTY-SIX

I THROW my weight to the left and twist, trying to break the hold. The grip shifts, getting an arm around my neck. Beside me, I hear Cas grunting and thrashing.

A voice tickles my ear. "Triana, it's me, Vanti. Stop fighting!"

"What the fork! Why did you attack us?" I relax and the hands fall away. I open my eyes and stare at her.

"Have you looked at yourself? I wasn't sure it was you. And your friend attacked Griz. We thought it might be Garabana. He's a Leweian spy."

"Yeah, I know." I grab Cas's arm. "It's okay—they're with us."

Cas deflates, sagging in O'Neill's grip.

Ty loosens his grip, then wraps both of us in a hug. "Thank God. Let's go." His arms drop away.

Now that they're here, my adrenaline fizzles. My knees sag, and my eyes start to sting. I grit my teeth and follow O'Neill up the steps, keeping my eyes on his amazing backside for courage.

"Leo has the bubble waiting at the back door." Vanti's voice comes through the audio implant. I didn't realize how alone I felt until they found us.

As we climb the endless stairs, the warbling of the fire alarm returns, assaulting our ears. At the top, we take a service hall to a massive kitchen. Trays of food and drinks lay abandoned on all the surfaces. A man in a white hat and smeared apron glares at us as he stirs something bubbling on the stove, but he doesn't say anything.

"Where are Kara and Elodie?" I gasp as O'Neill urges me across the room.

"They're fine—took a Lyfter to the Paradise Alley medical center." He opens the door, and warm, salt-scented air rushes in.

"Close that door—you'll ruin my sauce!" the chef yells over the wailing alarm.

"You should leave—the building is on fire," O'Neill calls.

"No, it isn't," Vanti says through the implant.

Cas yanks my hand. "We need to get Tarkhan!"

I pull him over the threshold onto a narrow porch. Moonlight illuminates a huge vegetable garden surrounded by a tall hedge. "He'll be fine. The building isn't burning."

Cas scowls. "I know that. But you see what happens to us." He gestures to his creased clothing. "We need to get him out of the embassy."

I heave a sigh. "Come on." I force my shaking legs down the three steps to O'Neill. "We need to rescue another kid."

His eyes travel over me, to Cas, then to Vanti. "Who?"

"His name is Tarkhan. He says he's the new premier's son. Looks like he might be related to Cas." I gesture to the boy. "He's little—like seven or eight."

"He's six and he's my cousin." Cas drops my hand. "I understand if you must get Triana to safety, but I can't leave him here."

"Taking a child from their legal guardian is a crime on Kaku." Vanti points across the garden. "Gate is over there."

"I will talk to him." He darts away.

I grab his wrist. "He'll be outside. Probably in front and under heavy guard."

O'Neill shoves his hands through his hair. "Fine, we'll go around to the front and talk to him. You two will go out the back to Leo."

"He won't talk to you. I need to go with you." Cas crosses his arms over his chest.

"And I'm not going tamely out the back if you're all still inside."

O'Neill's teeth grind. "Fine. Leo, bring the bubble around front. We'll meet you on the main drive in five minutes. If we aren't there—" he narrows his eyes at me "—call in the cavalry. No, Kaku doesn't have a real cavalry. I mean the Peacekeepers. Never mind. Just meet us out front."

We skirt around the huge house, ducking through a narrow side yard strung with row after row of clothesline. The wind blows, casting wiggly stripes on the gravel.

"Are those for drying clothes?" Vanti asks.

"Fish," Cas replies. "*Terkfiske.*"

On the far side, an unlocked gate lets us into another garden—this one smells of rosemary, mint, and basil. Then a small lawn with a couple of benches, followed by an ornamental garden with a tinkling fountain and glass doors leading to a conservatory. Sirens howl, approaching from Paradise Alley.

A tall wooden fence with an ornate arched gate leads to the front yard. On the far side, the party guests mingle on the wide gravel drive. Servers move through the crowd, still offering food and drinks. A few of them stand off to one side, their empty trays under their arms.

One of the servers spots me and nudges her companion. The other girl looks up and waves. My admirers from the restroom.

I raise a hand to acknowledge her, then an idea sparks. I make a "come here" gesture.

The girl's eyebrows draw down, and she looks around as if to see who I'm beckoning. She points at herself, her eyebrows going up and her eyes widening.

I nod and do the "come on" thing again.

The two girls rabbit across the gravel, drawing the attention of nearby guests. I step behind O'Neill and glare at the girls. They drop to a saunter, looking around in an exaggerated manner. One of them even starts whistling.

"They need some training." Vanti materializes beside me. "What's your plan?"

"Just going to—" The girls stop a few meters away. "Come here."

They scurry closer. I can feel Vanti roll her eyes. O'Neill moves onto the brilliantly lit driveway and asks the assembled guests if anyone is hurt. They gather around him, leaving us in the shadows.

"Have you seen a boy? About six years old, looks kinda like him?" I point at Cas.

The sirens change tone, and the rumble of the firebots covers the voices of the mingling guests.

"There's a kid over there." The first girl points toward the front entrance. "Bunch of big burly dudes around him. I tried to give the kid a dessert, but they pushed me away."

Her friend leans in close. "They had guns. Big, ugly ones."

"Can you take us closer? Without drawing attention." Vanti gives the girls a glare. "No whistling, no looking around. Just move like you've been called back to work. And give me your jacket."

The girl hesitates.

"I'll pay for it." I flick my holo-ring. "How about ninety credits?"

The first girl gapes. "That's twice what—"

Her friend cuts her off. "A hundred."

"Here's a hundred, and another fifty if we get to talk to the kid." I flick the payout button.

"Deal." She strips off her black jacket and hands it to me.

I slide the coat over my dirty white dress. Despite the caterer logo on the chest, I'm obviously not an employee, but no one will look that closely. I slide my sandals, which I've been carrying all this time, onto my dirty feet and follow the girls into the crowd.

We stop near the front door, in the shadow of the wide porch. A low hedge and a flower bed separate us from a group of huge men in tactical gear. In the center, the boy Tarkhan shivers in a thin T-shirt and pajama pants.

I turn to the second girl. "I'll give you two hundred credits if you give your jacket to the boy. He looks cold."

"I'll give him *my* jacket!" The first girl yanks on my sleeve.

"You already sold it to me. I'm asking her." I point at the other girl. "And she has to talk to the goons, so it's worth more."

The second girl grins and slides out of her coat. She unbuttons the top two buttons of her shirt and pulls her collar open to display the breasts I refused to sign—was it just a few hours ago?

She steps out of the shadows and over the hedge. Hips swaying, she approaches the largest of the guards. Behind us, the firebots sweep up the drive, sirens screaming, scattering the guests. The guards turn with military precision, and half of them spread out, moving the crowd away from the entrance.

The girl looks over her shoulder, and I shoo her forward.

She shimmies her shoulders a little and strolls up to one big guy. He flings up a hand, and she stops and flicks a lock of hair over her shoulder. Her hands fly as she speaks, the coat still dangling from one finger. She gestures at Tarkhan. The guard steps sideways, so he can glance at the boy without losing sight of the girl.

She holds out the jacket. Without warning, the sirens cut off, and her voice rings out, "—see he's freezing?"

The guard looks around. Every guest nearby stares at him. He takes the coat and thrusts it at the boy. "Put that on. You're cold."

The server waits for a second, but the guard ignores her. She puts one hand on her hip. "You're welcome." She pivots and sashays across the driveway, hips swiveling. The guard watches her go, appreciation lighting his eyes.

"Don't let her come this way. I'll send your credits." I push the other server toward her friend as Vanti and Cas melt deeper into the shadows. I flick my ring to send credits to both girls as I move behind a small tree near the porch.

The firebots split into search teams and stream between the girls and the guards, swinging wide to avoid bumping into them.

The second girl pauses by the flowerbed, then looks at her ring and whoops. She leaps over the hedge and hugs her friend. The two girls squeal and jump up and down, then hurry back to the other servers. The guard watches them walk away, but they don't spare a glance in his direction.

Or, miraculously, toward us.

"I guess they can be taught," Vanti whispers.

THIRTY-SEVEN

Cas shifts beside me. "Now what?"

"Now we wait to see if he finds the holo-ring I stashed in her pocket." Vanti grins, her teeth glowing white in the darkness.

More firebots surge forward, their white exteriors decorated with slashes of flourescent yellow and flashing red lights. The guards push the crowds away from the front entrance, moving them into a formal garden on the far side. Tarkhan and his security detail back up onto the porch and let the bots zip by.

"How long do we have to wait?" Cas asks. "They'll notice us soon."

Vanti hushes him.

"Leo can't get the bubble to the front," O'Neill says through my audio implant. "The firebots have blocked the driveway. We need to walk out to the road or meet him in back as we originally planned."

"They'll have firebots in the back, too," Vanti says. "Come on Triana, Cas, we need to go."

"What about Tarkhan?" Cas crosses his arms over his chest, leaning against the porch's tall foundation. "I'm not leaving without him."

"Hey, Cas." A whisper drifts on the breeze.

"Tark?" Cas twists around, staring up at the porch.

The younger boy leans over the balustrade and waves.

"You need to come with us," Cas says. "They put me in the dungeon. If your dad gets ousted, you'll go into the dungeon, too. Climb over the railing. I'll catch you." He holds out his arms.

The boy shakes his head. "I can't. My mom and sisters are still in Lewei. You'd better go." He glances over his shoulder.

"Come with us. We can get them out later."

Tarkhan shakes his head. "No, I must do my duty, as you did. But I have this." He holds a holo-ring between his thumb and forefinger. "I'll call you if I need you. Farewell, Cas!" He jams the hand holding the ring into the pocket of his too large coat and disappears into the gloom of the porch.

Cas droops. Vanti grabs his elbow with one hand, and mine with her other. "We need to move. Now." She steers us away from the porch, across the grass. We skirt a pair of ornamental trees, then step over a low hedge onto the verge beside the driveway.

Somehow, Vanti's gold dress blends in with the jungle, and we don't draw any attention as we hurry down the driveway and around the first corner.

Fast footsteps close in behind. Vanti whirls, pushing Cas and me into the thick foliage. I stumble over a root and land on my butt. More firebots whiz by. Beside me, Cas shifts from foot to foot, but says nothing.

"It's Griz," Vanti reports a few seconds later.

Cas reaches out a hand to help me up. My first attempt nearly pulls him down on top of me, but I get to my feet. The four of us jog along the verge beside the drive.

Lungs heaving, I drop to a walk. O'Neill looks back and slows to walk beside me.

"We'll meet you at the bubble," Vanti says as she and Cas disappear into the dark.

"You okay?" O'Neill wraps an arm around my shoulders and pulls me close. The heat of his body comforts me.

"Yeah. I am now." I rub the top of my head against his cheek.

He jerks his head away. "What is in your hair?"

"Whatever you'd find on the floor of a dungeon, I suppose." I put my hand up and pull away a cobwebby mess of *ew*. Shaking my hand doesn't dislodge any of it, so I wipe it on my shaggy dress as I pull away from him. "We should probably stick to holding hands if you don't want to have to go through decontamination procedures when we get home."

He chuckles and squeezes my shoulder.

We wait by the gate at the end of the driveway. It's programmed to open for vehicles but not people. Vanti and Cas must have sneaked through when the last batch of firebots entered, but there haven't been any for twenty minutes.

"The firebots should be leaving soon," O'Neill says. "I'm surprised none of the guests have."

"If their bubbles are parked around back, they probably can't get through." I fasten my borrowed—or rather purchased—jacket against the wind. "This is the most expensive piece of clothing I've ever bought for myself."

"That's only because the company pays for your designer gowns." O'Neill juts his chin at me. "What happened to this one?"

I explain about Gary chopping it up. "How did he know about Griz? That's why I believed he was working with you."

Moonlight shines on O'Neill's tight jaw. "He *was* working with us. Double agent. If he ever leaves this estate, he'll pay."

The gate opens, and a bubble pulls halfway through and stops. The door opens. "Get in and let's go!" Leo calls.

We scramble into the vehicle. Before we've even reached our seats, the door closes. I drop into my chair, and the bubble pulls away from the embassy grounds.

THIRTY-EIGHT

THE NEXT MORNING, I wake late in an unfamiliar room. I find a plush robe beside the bed. It's white with a star and an unidentifiable blob embroidered in red on the chest. As I pull it on, my stomach growls. I can get something from the AutoKich'n, but I need company as much as I need food.

I wander into the hall, trying to remember how to get to the stairs. With Sierra Hotel full of purple goo, we ended up spending the night at the Starfire Estate next door. Fortunately, Hy-Mi has contacts that can work miracles, even at two on a Monday morning.

Ty, Elodie, Kara, and Leo greet me when I enter the gathering room. Leo jumps up from the couch. "I've got French toast!" He disappears into the kitchen.

This room looks a lot like the family floor of Sierra Hotel, but on a larger scale. Four separate seating areas with couches, low tables, and wing chairs fill one end of the room. The other sports dozens of four-person tables with white tablecloths and chairs. Two of them have been pulled together and set for six.

Leo reappears with a mug. "Dark roast with lots of cream and sugar. There's chocolate sauce on the table if you want to make it a mocha."

"If I weren't already engaged, I would marry you." I take the cup, cradling it to my chest.

"It's a good thing you don't mind being replaced by food," Elodie says to Ty.

"I know she doesn't mean it. But it is why I splurged on the best Auto-Kich'n maps." He joins me at the table and leans in for a kiss. "Good morning."

I kiss him back, long and slow.

"Get a room," Kara jeers as we break apart.

I pick up a gravy boat and ladle some chocolate into my coffee. After a stir and a sip, I twist around to look at the others. "Where's Cas?"

"I took him home this morning." Leo steps out of the kitchen wearing a plain white apron and holding a spatula. "He'll be back later today."

"He's back now." Kara stands by the floor-to-ceiling windows, wrapped in a pink dressing gown. "Just came through the wall." There is a big wooden door in the wall between Sierra Hotel and Starfire. It locks with an old-fashioned key that hangs from a hook on the Sierra side.

"I'll let him in. And make sure he didn't bring an army." O'Neill kisses me again, then disappears down the hallway. "Good morning, Hy-Mi."

Mother's second-in-command pauses in the doorway to bow to the room at large. He's wearing his usual attire—a severe tunic over soft pants, and highly polished shoes. "We have a rather busy day today, Sera." He glances at his holo-ring chronometer. "And most of it is already gone."

"It's only ten o'clock." I pour a little more chocolate into my coffee, stir, and sip. Perfect. "Lots of day left. How'd you get clothes?"

"I ordered clothing for everyone when we arrived last night. There is a package on the chaise in your room."

I guess I didn't look very carefully. I glance at the others. Leo is wearing jeans and a comfortable shirt. Elodie has a long tunic with a wide peplum and matching leggings. "Didn't they have anything for Kara?"

"I wasn't ready to get dressed." She turns away from the window and waddles toward me.

I jump up—she was in labor last night! How could I have forgotten? "What about the contractions?"

"False alarm. They say I'm close, though. Hy-Mi suggested we wait here and have the baby in Paradise Alley. They have an amazing medical suite."

"What about Erco?"

"He's on his way. Ty got him paternity leave early." She beams at O'Neill as he returns to the room. Cas and his father follow along.

"Good morning, Ser Zhang." I pull a chair away from the table for him. "Would you like some breakfast?"

He drops heavily into the seat. "I ate breakfast hours ago. However, a mid-morning snack would not go amiss."

Leo bustles out of the kitchen with a tray holding more coffee and a selection of pastries. "Good morning, Ser Zhang." He offers the plate to his father.

Cas sits next to the older man and puts a chocolate topped pastry on his plate. "That looks excellent, Leo. Thanks."

"His name is Ervin." Zhang glares at Cas, then turns his glower on the rest of us. "And my son should not be waiting on capitalists!"

"Your son *is* a capitalist." Leo shrugs. "And he doesn't mind waiting on others as long as they're grateful."

Zhang mutters something under his breath. It almost sounds like, "Thank you."

I return to my seat. O'Neill pulls out a chair for Kara, then drags another one up to the table and sits. Elodie and Hy-Mi take the other two seats. Leo returns to the kitchen.

"Where's Vanti?" I take a cinnamon spiral from the plate.

"She's at headquarters, giving a debriefing." O'Neill smirks. "One of the advantages of outranking her—I get to delegate the boring stuff."

"Besides, you're still guarding me." I give him a sticky kiss.

"No, you are not my professional responsibility. Conflict of interests. That's why we had Vanti. And al-Karendi and Limberghetti. And Yellin—"

"I get it, I'm hard to watch."

"You're easy to watch, just impossible to guard." He chuckles.

"Which reminds me—what happened with Gary?"

Leo delivers a plate of steaming French toast, setting it before me with a flourish. He goes back to the kitchen to get syrup and butter, while his father grinds his teeth.

O'Neill drags another chair to the table, positioning it on the end between Hy-Mi and Zhang. "Why don't you sit down, Leo? We have a lot to discuss."

Leo gives his father a wary look and sits.

I take a bite and moan. "Leo, this is amazing!"

"You're just saying that." His lips quirk, and he darts a look at his father.

"No, this is the best—the best anything I've ever had. I've changed my mind. I'm definitely dumping Ty and marrying you instead."

Leo laughs. "I don't mind cooking for you, but there's no way I would marry you. Besides, Ty would probably sic Vanti on me, and then I'd be dead."

"Who is Vanti? I will not allow anyone to threaten my son!" Zhang pushes his chair back so hard it crashes to the floor.

"It's a joke." I jump out of my seat and right his chair. "Vanti won't touch a hair on his head. And I don't want to marry him anyway, so it's a moot point." I give Leo a quizzical look behind Zhang's back. Leo shrugs.

"Now that my marriage is secure again, may I have the floor?" O'Neill stands and flicks a file from his ring to the tabletop projector. Hy-Mi moves the sweezenberry jam out of the way, and the blob resolves into a hologram of the embassy.

"We've pieced together the story—I hope you fill in any blanks, Ser Zhang. It's the only reason I let you come in." He stares at Zhang until the older man gives a jerky nod. "There was, in fact, an attempted coup on Lewei. Our friends, Ser Zhang and Cas, relocated to Kaku in a successful attempt to stay alive."

The holo changes to the end of the vid posted on *CelebVid*—the part where the scaffolding tumbles around me and the baby.

"The diamonds Triana, er, intercepted, were part of the funds Ser Zhang attempted to export, so he'd have enough credits to survive and perhaps launch his own counter-coup." He looks at Zhang who suddenly finds his coffee mug fascinating. "Since those funds did not reach Ser Zhang, the attempt to counter the coup failed."

The picture changes to a blurry one of a young boy. "Ser Zhang was replaced by his distant cousin, Greshim Jamis. The boy you met in the embassy—Tark?" He raises an eyebrow at me.

"Tarkhan," Cas mumbles around a mouthful of food.

"Tarkhan is Jamis's son. Next in line to the premier—provided his father isn't ousted before he dies a natural death. As you can imagine, that's a long shot in Lewei."

Zhang's eyes narrow, but he doesn't speak.

"We corroborated most of this after discovering who Cas was. What we've learned since last night is there was another attempted coup. Greshim Jamis realized his tenure was tenuous at best. He sent his son to the embassy here on Kaku in an attempt to keep him safe. The embassy staff are loyal to Jamis—more or less."

Garabana appears on the table.

"Gary Banara was an SK'Corp agent. He went through the academy with me and Vanti. After a few years, he left the service and established himself as Garabana. We—Vanti and I—foolishly believed he was a good risk, since we've known him for a long time. We believed his change of career was a sincere desire to go into fashion, and we were happy he'd been so successful. So, when we needed a safe place to go after the attack on Sierra Hotel, his establishment seemed a logical place."

He pauses to sip some water. "We believe he's been selling information on the wealthy of Kaku since he established himself as a premium brand. Several of his former clients have admitted to being blackmailed, although they had no idea Gary was the source of the information. In the meantime, he was apparently approached and turned by Leweian agents. I don't know what his intentions were at the embassy—we think he might have been planning to ransom Sera Morgan on behalf of the Leweians. I'm not sure his handlers were on board for this plan—the embassy threw him out early this morning, and the Kakuvian Peacekeepers picked him up. You can be sure Vanti and I will be asking questions as soon as they let us."

"What about Cas?" I ask. "Why was he there?"

He gives Cas a sympathetic look. "Cas learned his friend was in the embassy and decided to visit him. Did they contact you?"

Cas gives his father a quick look from under lowered lids, then nods. "Tark wanted me to visit. They said I'd need to bring some credits, to bribe the guards, so I went to the bank."

"How would you get credits?" Zhang asks, his voice loud. "You have no bank account." We all glare at him.

Cas lifts his chin and stares at his father. "I found some diamonds in the house. In that old trophy."

Zhang's face goes red. "And you thought you could simply take them?"

"I asked you about the trophy!" Cas jumps to his feet. "You said it was trash—something left by your brother. I thought you didn't want it, so I took it, and there were the diamonds."

Zhang's mouth opens and closes a couple of times. He slumps in his seat. No one moves for a few minutes.

O'Neill clears his throat. "Fortunately, Triana found Cas, and we got him out. We're not one hundred percent sure, but we believe another coup has taken place on Lewei and Tarkhan's father has been removed from power. So Tarkhan may need a safe place to live. We think that might be why they threw Gary out—he tried to cut a deal with the new government."

"What about Greshim?" Zhang asks.

O'Neill shrugs. "No one knows. As I said, we're not sure there was another coup. He may still be running Lewei."

Zhang shakes his head. "He was nothing but a figurehead. They bribed him to betray me and used him to claim legitimacy. He was never very bright, but he's still my brother."

"Uncle Greshim was actually our uncle?" Leo asks.

Zhang nods. "He is." He pats Cas's hand. "That's why I said the trophy was trash—I was angry at Greshim. I didn't realize he was smart enough to hide diamonds, too. We talked about it, years ago—how we needed a cash reserve, just in case. We had them hidden in Lewei. Last year, when I heard rumblings of a coup, I started ferrying some off planet through the topsoil exporter. I guess he brought some here when we visited."

He stands and addresses O'Neill. "I need to find out what happened to him. Can you help me?"

"For what purpose? If you're out for revenge, I won't help you."

"No, he's my brother. And, as I said, I don't believe he planned any of this. I think he was used. I want to get him off Lewei, if I can."

O'Neill nods. "I'll see what I can find out, but I won't promise anything."

"That is all I can ask." Zhang looks at Cas, then at Leo. "I would like both of you to come home, if you will."

"To Lewei?" Leo asks.

"To the house over there—for as long as they'll let us stay. The embassy will probably send someone to take it away soon."

"That won't happen," O'Neill says. "According to Kaku, the house is in your family's name—I checked the records. Your government can't take it without a court battle. And after what happened last night, and the revelation that Garabana was part of a Leweian scheme, the Diamond Beach homeowner's association is increasing security on all our properties. I think you'll be safe enough."

Hy-Mi stands. "I'm glad to have all of that cleared up. Now, Sera Annabelle and I have work to do, so if you'll excuse us, she needs to get dressed. We have several meetings lined up."

I glare at Hy-Mi but get to my feet. Part of my new, reformed image— doing the things that the position requires. I kiss O'Neill. "I'll see you later today. At lunch?" I raise my eyebrows at Hy-Mi.

The old man looks at his chronometer, then at my clean plate. "I think dinner."

THIRTY-NINE

WE STAND on a hovering platform in the gathering room in Sierra Hotel. Purple goo covers the floors, the walls—it even hangs from the chandeliers. A team of cleaning specialists stands behind us, surveying the damage.

"This will take two, maybe three weeks if the whole house is covered in this stuff." The CEO of the cleaning company, a man named Rondelle, stands beside Hy-Mi.

"Three days, tops," someone mutters from behind me.

Rondelle glares over his shoulder. "Not to get the stains out. This stuff is persistent."

"Then perhaps you should not have signed an agreement with the company that installed our security system." Hy-Mi turns to look at the crew. "That contract promises a return to pristine condition within a week."

Rondelle smiles a clenched-tooth smile. "We will do everything in our power to honor that contract."

"I knew you would," Hy-Mi replies. He touches the controls of his grav-belt and lifts off the ground. "Sera Morgan, shall we?"

I lean closer to Rondelle and jerk my head at the bot jockeys behind us. "You might want to rethink the Vacu-bot 4ks. They don't do well with gum."

Rondelle puffs out his chest. "This is hardly gum. And I think I know my equipment, Sera."

"Good luck." I set my belt to one meter and rise, then follow Hy-Mi to the stairs. As the steps descend, our belts keep us exactly one meter above the sticky purple glop.

"I had to reschedule Lilia for next week." Hy-Mi skirts around a goo stalactite hanging from the light fixture on the first landing.

"You can reschedule her for next millennium," I say. "She's not doing my wedding."

"Sera, your mother—"

I speak over him. "My mother can plan any event with Lilia she wants—except my wedding. That is my affair. If she wants to have a massive reception for all her corporate CEO buddies, Ty and I will put in an appearance, but the wedding is off limits. It's ours, not hers, and certainly not a media circus designed for SK'Corp marketing purposes. Depending on how she takes that, I might send her an invitation."

Did Hy-Mi's lips just twitch? He bows his head in his usual regal fashion and continues down to the second floor.

This landing is thick with goo as well, and a single boot remains encased in a hard, purple shell. A sock lies a few steps down. My lips twitch as I imagine the attacking *Spiitznatz* trying to fight free.

Hy-Mi opens the door and drifts inside. I follow him and drop to the carpet. The room looks just as we left it—even the half-eaten cake sits untouched on the table.

"The *destruct zero* code released sleeping gas, which incapacitated our attackers." Hy-Mi lands lightly beside the table. "Loki was removed by our security team before he revived. The cake is still good." He breaks off a chunk and eats it.

"Are you sure you should be eating that? It probably has nerve agents in it!"

Hy-Mi breaks off another chunk. "No, I checked with the chemical team at SK'Corp headquarters. It's perfectly safe." He slumps to the floor.

"Hy-Mi!" I scream.

His eyes pop open. "Just kidding."

I drop to my butt beside him. "That was a joke? You make jokes? I've known you my whole life—I've never seen you do—"

"You don't remember." Hy-Mi jumps up and offers me a hand. "We used to goof off together all the time." His face is sad.

I let him pull me up. Despite his advanced age, he is strong. "I remember playing pretend with you when I was little, but it stopped."

He nods. "When you got older, your mother wished us to have a different relationship. I was to be the impartial guide, not the favored uncle. She insisted. I didn't want to lose my job, so I complied."

"You changed your personality for her?" I break off a chunk of cake and throw it in my mouth. It's still delicious.

"I respect your mother, and I wanted to continue working for her. And I didn't want to leave you. So, I changed our relationship. It's how relationships work—they change as the participants grow and evolve. To be honest, your teen years were exhausting, so it wasn't difficult."

He surveys the room. "The physical damage here is minimal—we can move back in if we don't mind lifting over the goo. Or we can use the emergency garage exit."

"I'll check the bedrooms." I place my hand on the door sensor and wince when the DNA sampler bites my finger. After our emergency evacuation, the security checks require a higher standard of precision that requires living blood checks.

The door slides open, and I walk down the hall. Each door requires both blood samples and cornea scans. I feel like a pincushion by the time I get to the last one. They're all untouched.

I stand in the opening to the last room. This is the one used by my half-sister, Erika, on the rare occasions when she visits us. It looks like an interior design display, with plush chairs, high-end tables, and a cabinet hiding an Autokich'n. The inner room holds a huge bed with a shiny, striped cover and dozens of thick pillows all in shades of gray.

I wander in and pick up a small box laying on the dresser. It's an antique puzzle box, open and empty. Erika probably left it behind last time she was here—years ago. The staff dusts it weekly, awaiting her return. Hy-Mi said she'll be here for the wedding. If I invite her to my scaled down event, will she bother coming?

As I head back to the family room, I think about the differences between my family and O'Neill's. His siblings all live at home or nearby. They've been together their entire lives and wouldn't miss this wedding for anything. Mine barely know me. In fact, they could be here on Kaku right now, and I'd have no idea.

Which reminds me of something, but I'm not sure what. By the time I meet Hy-Mi near the kitchen, it's shaken loose.

"What's the deal with Agent Aretha O'Neill?"

Hy-Mi goes still—it's his tell, and he's usually very good at suppressing it. So, this is big.

"Hy-Mi? I saw her name on the personnel roster for SK'Corp security. Who is she?" O'Neill's sister is a lawyer, not an agent, and she lives on Grissom.

"You'll have to ask her," Hy-Mi finally says. "It's not my secret to share."

"How will I do that?" I chase him down the hall toward the security room. "Ty couldn't get any information about her—in fact, when he went looking, her name was gone. How will I meet her?"

"She'll be here for the wedding." He opens the thick metal door and swings it wide.

"So, it is Ty's sister? Why is she on the payroll?" I trip over the lip of the door, and he catches my hand, so I don't fall on my face.

"I can't answer that question. But she'll be here—no matter when you plan it."

My eyes narrow. It's definitely Ty's sister. But why does she work for SK'Corp? And how? We don't have many interests on Grissom—or didn't until Ty and I got engaged. Now we have a security team stationed there to watch out for my soon-to-be relatives.

This top-lev life is exhausting.

I badger Hy-Mi the whole time we're in Sierra Hotel, but he ignores every question, parrying them with comments on the state of the house and the need for various minor repairs.

Finally, we lift up the steps, my questions unanswered. A squad of technicians scrape goo from the third-floor landing using long-handled paddles with laser edges. A small bot swoops under the paddle and lifts the loosened sheet of goo, breaking it off. Then another hovering bot sucks up the small bits as the other lifts the sheets into a waiting container.

We soar overhead, ducking to avoid the ceiling, and continue up the steps. Another pair of technicians stand on the next landing, working with a tall panel that melts the goo. Scrapers push the stuff down the wall, and it puddles in a bin on the floor.

Hy-Mi detours to speak with Rondelle, but I head out into the fresh air.

Two Vacu-bot 4Ks lie on the paved drive, their covers missing, and their internal bits jammed with purple gunk. I hide a smirk as I swish by.

THAT EVENING, Ty and I sit on a pair of deck chairs by the pool. The sunset paints brilliant colors across the sky beyond Zijin. A light wind pushes the lingering scent of *terkfiske* out to sea. The lights of Paradise Alley sparkle in the distance, getting brighter as the sun fades.

Ty hands me a glass of sparkling wine. "Here's to us—and our wedding." He waves away the holo-files floating over our chairs.

I take the glass and toast him. "It will be beautiful. Just us and the people we really care about, here on the deck. No media, no high-powered CEOs."

"Except your mother." He grins. "And your siblings. And R'ger."

"And your parents—aren't they CEOs of that winery?"

He laughs. "No, that's Angie, but the whole family owns shares."

"Angie is my kind of CEO. Not afraid to get into a little mischief. Speaking of siblings—" I break off. Maybe I should wait until I talk to Aretha.

"What about siblings?"

"I was just wondering if Ro and Vanti are a thing. She side-stepped the discussion. But I'd hate to have both of them here if there was a nasty breakup."

He laughs. "One of the hazards of dating your friend's brother. I'm sure they can behave like civilized people if they aren't."

We sit in silence. The sky darkens, and soon I can barely make out his face.

"What about Loki?" I ask.

"What about him? He's not related to me. Is he part of your family?" A thread of laughter underlies the question.

"No. Maybe. I'll have to ask R'ger. I'm just wondering about the attack on Sierra Hotel. Ser Zhang claimed he didn't authorize it but taking matters into his own hands seems unlikely for Loki. He's fiercely loyal to Zhang."

"And he disappeared from our custody before Lewei could extradite him. I think Zhang *was* behind that attack—he was desperate to get his son back, and we were his best chance. I think the attack was designed to prod us into action rather than hurt us."

"That was a big risk. He could have just asked."

"That's not how their society works."

I hold out my glass for a refill. "I can't believe you let him into Starfire while we were there."

He shrugs, but the wine doesn't spill. "He was alone. We had his three loyal *Spiitznatz* in custody and had returned his son to him. Still, I'm glad he isn't next door anymore."

"Yeah, now Zijin will just sit empty—unless the new premier decides to visit."

"Or Tarkhan's family shows up."

I stand and walk to the invisible wall enclosing Sierra Hotel. Ty follows me off the deck and across the grass. When he reaches my side, I set my glass on the force shield, using it as a ghostly table. I wrap my arms around my fiancé and set my head against his shoulder. His arms close around me, warm and protective.

"I'm glad I found you—my own family."

He leans his cheek against my forehead. "Me, too. This is what family is meant to be."

"And what ours will always be."

As the last sliver of light disappears behind the horizon, a cloud of vira-bats spirals out of the cliff below us, black against black. They follow a twisted route through the narrow fissure left in our security system solely for them and disappear into the darkness. The lights in Paradise Alley glitter in the distance, and the waves crash below us.

And I hold my family tight against my chest.

———

I HOPE you enjoyed Planetary Spin Cycle. If you want to read about the wedding of the galaxy—and find out if Triana really manages to keep her mother out of her business, sign up for my newsletter at juliahuni.com.

ACKNOWLEDGMENTS

May 2021

Thanks for reading *Planetary Spin Cycle*. It was a lot of fun to write—I hope it was as much fun to read. Even my editor enjoyed it. Of course, she has to say nice things after she scribbles red all over my manuscript.

I think my favorite new character is Elodie. What did you think of her? She might be the star of my next series. Since I'm no longer in my twenties (and haven't been for some time) writing an older character would be a nice change. But don't worry, there will be *at least* one more *Former Space Janitor* story. Ty was just telling me the other day about the honeymoon he has planned, and I'm sure there will be all kinds of trouble. They might be on their own this time, though—even Vanti wouldn't have the nerve to crash a honeymoon.

Or would she?

If you haven't yet, go to my website, juliahuni.com, and sign up for my newsletter! I've got some free prequels to send your way, plus I'll let you know when my next book comes out.

I'm currently working on *The Saha Declination*, the third book in my *Colonial Explorer Corps* Series, and a couple of serials for Amazon's new serial platform, Vella. That's going to launch in the US this summer. If you aren't in the US, or you'd rather go direct, I'll be building a Patreon account to share those stories directly with you. More info in my newsletter as it becomes available.

As always, I'd like to thank a few people. Thanks to Paula Lester, my editor, for making me look good. Any mistakes you find I undoubtedly added after she was done. Thanks to Les of German Creative for the stellar cover.

Thanks to my sister, AM Scott, my eternal first reader. Thanks to my sprint team for keeping me at the keyboard: Paula Lester, AM Scott, Kate Pickford, Tony James Slater, Alison Kervin, and Hillary "The Tomato" Avis.

My deep appreciation goes to my beta readers, Barb, Anne, and Jenny for catching the last few typos and to Your Old Pal, Marcus Alexander Hart, for his excellent story suggestions. Thanks to the ARC team and all my readers for spreading the word. And thanks to my husband David who manages the business side of this authoring gig.

And of course, thanks to the Big Guy who makes all things possible.

ALSO BY JULIA HUNI

Reduced World

Krimson Empire (with Craig Martelle):

Krimson Run

Krimson Spark

Krimson Surge

Krimson Flare

Krimson Empire (the complete series)

ROMANTIC COMEDY (AS LIA HUNI)

Stolen Kisses

Stolen Love Song

Stolen Heart Strings

FOR MORE INFORMATION

Use this QR code to stay up-to-date on all my publishing:

Printed in Great Britain
by Amazon

22693977R00138